A Quest for Simbilis

Spatterlight
Amstelveen 2020

A QUEST FOR SIMBILIS

MICHAEL SHEA

A novel set in Jack Vance's Dying Earth

Published by Spatterlight, Amstelveen 2020

Cover art by Dogan Oztel

ISBN 978-1-61947-387-4

www.spatterlight.nl

Introduction

I cradle a small paperback in my hands: *A Quest for Simbilis*, the DAW first edition of 1974. It is in pristine condition, lovingly sheathed in an acid-free polyethylene envelope all these years. On the colophon page, Michael Shea, my late best friend, has ball-penned

> *Dear Dan — A virgin effort — treat it gently.*
>
> *Michael.*

On the flip side of the page the printed dedication stipulates: "Its universe is that invented by Jack Vance, whose incomparable *The Eyes of the Overworld* is the parent of the present work." (Vance didn't like the latter title, and wanted it changed to *Cugel the Clever*; instead he later wrote *Cugel's Saga*.) The cover art by George Barr depicts Cugel and a crony cornered amongst boulders by dinosaurish, green-and-yellow creatures, presumably erbs.

As I skim through the first pages again, a smile steals uncontrollably across my lips. Michael has captured Vance's ineffably droll humor and sense of absurdity. Already in the first chapter the fraught negotiation between Cugel and the skulldugger is reminiscent of Milton Hack's querulous contractual wranglings in Vance's "The Man from Zodiac," or Cugel's legalistic arm-wrestling with Iucounu in *Cugel's Saga*. One half-expects him to innocently roast and eat some gelatinous creature that it has taken a potent wizard five centuries to coax into the open. But at the same time a faint feeling of ominous foreboding is growing at the root of my mind, and this is what distinguishes Shea from Vance, the underworld of Bosch from the carefree dancing peasants of Bruegel.

What inspires the creation of artistic sequels? In Hollywood it is usually driven by profit — *Star Wars, Men in Black, Rocky*. But for true writers it is more often a labor of love. At least seven authors have written authorized sequels to the James Bond novels since Ian Fleming's death in 1964. Isaac Asimov's *Foundation* trilogy was followed posthumously by seven novels written by others. The project may, however, encounter obstacles: J. D. Salinger's executors threw up insurmountable legal barriers to publication of Frederik Colting's sequel to *The Catcher in the Rye*.

Michael's experience was simpler and more amusing. He came across a copy of *Overworld* at a flophouse during a hitchhiking expedition to Alaska when he was eighteen, and wrote to Jack asking for permission to write the sequel, offering a share of the proceeds. Vance returned a scrap of newsprint with the quizzical handwritten comment that he was "a bit flummoxed by your offer," but gave Michael permission to make use of his swashbuckling yet bumbling character Cugel the Clever.

Strictly speaking, Vance himself wrote the sequel in the two stories *The Seventeen Virgins* and *The Bagful of Dreams*: their colophon pages state "This story is a continuation of THE EYES OF THE OVERWORLD." I realize today that Michael's dedication to me, "A virgin effort"— *vide supra* — was an implicit recognition of this fact. For my money, *Simbilis* is more closely attached to *Overworld*.

Michael went on to write four more novels in the Vancian style, the first of which, *Nifft the Lean*, won a World Fantasy Award. In Tim Powers' marvelous introduction, he quotes Algis Budrys as saying that Nifft's descent into the underworld was "The best entry into Hell in all of literature." That implicitly includes Dante; what a compliment!

In his insightful introduction to *Demiurge: The Complete Cthulhu Mythos Tales of Michael Shea*, editor S. T. Joshi points out that the Nifft novels drew on wellsprings including classical and Near Eastern myths, as well as the sword-and-sorcery tales of Fritz Leiber, even as they evolved their own myths. In his other books Michael went well beyond those, greatly influenced by H. P. Lovecraft and Edgar Allen Poe, but his deep grounding in classical literature is also evident throughout.

Michael and I became fast friends in high school, where we were sternly trained in Latin together. Then we descended into the heavens of hippie culture in Berkeley and San Francisco. For a time we shared dismal, poorly heated rooms behind a flower shop. It was the sixties. The Australian Aborigines have a word for it: the Dreamtime.

The power of his intellect was astonishing. He wrote literally every day. If his work didn't satisfy him, he burned it. In later years I came across this nugget in Balzac's *Cousin Bette*, and realized how well Michael embodied it:

> "If the artist does not throw himself into his work like a soldier into the breach, unreflectingly; and if, in that crater, he does not dig like a miner buried under a fall of rock...the work will never be completed; it will perish in the studio, where production becomes impossible, and the artist looks on at the suicide of his own talent...And it is for that reason that the same reward, the same triumph, the same laurels, are accorded to great poets as to great generals."

Hence Michael's World Fantasy Award for *Nifft the Lean,* and for *Growlimb.* He was also repeatedly a finalist for the Hugo and Nebula Awards.

Michael's best known fiction includes *The Color Out of Time, Fat Face, Polyphemus, The Autopsy, The Angel of Death,* and *In Yana, the Touch of Undying.* His stories were collected in *The Best from Fantasy and Science Fiction, A Treasury of American Horror Stories, The Best of Modern Horror* and others. He was translated into French, German, Italian, Japanese, Swedish, Russian and Finnish.

He graduated Magna Cum Laude from UC Berkeley, even as he defiantly protested at demonstrations for the peace and civil rights movements; I went on to medical school. We lost track of each other for more than fifteen years. It was during that time that he wrote *Simbilis,* while I, by miraculous coincidence, was writing *The Jack Vance Lexicon: from Ahulph to Zipangote,* a compendium of his invented words. (It has since been augmented with the neologisms from the three novels that Vance wrote afterwards, and published by Spatterlight Press as *The Jack Vance Lexicon: from Abiloid to Zygage.*) To this moment I cannot recall our ever talking about Vance in those earlier days.

I saved and now savor all our correspondence, a thick sheaf of papers with their envelopes, and later hundreds of pages of emails. As I pored through them, I discovered again what a wonderful and true friend Michael was.

For months we discussed an impending planned visit to his digs in Northern California. In one letter he asserted:

> *Your tongueless correspondent reopens his barbaric yawp. A colorful blur of wall-painting, hedge-uprooting, fencepost-setting, tooth-extraction (suffered, not performed), and poem-collecting, has of late engulfed him, but now he re-emerges, wet and mewling. I herewith send you, in an invisible care-package, all of my own considerable reserves of Heedless Unconcern and Congenital Irresponsibility.*

And in another he prophesied:

> *And to see you will be delight. Recall Falstaff and his crony: 'Oh we have heard the chimes at midnight!' Have we not, old friend? In the grey post LSD dawns, back in the years when we both could sing? How fine it will be to see you again.*
>
> > *M yr faithful scribe*

In one of my replies I mentioned having "...no fewer than four near-fine copies of *Quest*, including the German version you laid on me." But this was long after its production.

Elsewhere he wrote:

> *Here the fog has come in, not on the little cat's feet of poetic fame, but waddling undaintily on the swollen ankles of the morbidly obese. I am marooned.*

He could be poignant:

> *We limp along amidst sputtering lightbulbs and coughing engines, ludicrously grateful for our lives, our freedom, the sky's boundless blue...*

He kindly took the trouble to analyze a little novel I had (over)written, *The Witches' Brew*, with substantial and compelling suggestions on how to improve it. But I shied from the daunting task, recalling the comments in another of his missives:

> *I'm finding that whenever I set out to 'polish' a novel I've written more than a few years past, I end up neck deep in restructuring. I'm really not much of a plot-structurer, I find. All my earlier publications were very simple, comic-bookish stuff, storyline-wise. Am I growing smarter or dumber as I age? A bit of both, I fear.*

Smarter, I would say.

In recalling Michael I often think of Jack London, whose noble character Martin Eden he resembled. London once said:

> "I would rather be a superb meteor, every atom of me in magnificent glow, than a sleepy and permanent planet. The proper function of man is to live, not to exist. I shall not waste my days in trying to prolong them. I shall use my time."

That was Michael all over.

What sequel can there be to the wonder that was my friendship with Michael Shea?

Dan Temianka, Pasadena 2019

Contents

Chapter I

THE COMING OF CUGEL

Cugel the Clever stood on the beach in the sunset, and stared at the sea. Its waters were gray as a skillet, and upon them simmered a streak of the dying sun's blood.

This time, Cugel decided, he would shun the overland route. This time he would cross this Sea of Cutz to its southern shore, and strike out for Almery from there.

And when he reached Almery, by whatever means he could manage, he would kill Iucounu, the Laughing Magician.

The last time Cugel the Clever had made the journey from this place to Almery, it had taken him many months. Perhaps the sea-route would be quicker. It could not possibly be any more perilous.

And now Cugel pondered on his surroundings, remembering the semihuman bandits he had encountered here before. He turned his back on the sun, a senile star that was cooling toward extinction just as surely as it was setting now. Retreating from the beach a short distance inland Cugel found a rocky hollow closely fenced around by thickets of spurge and throttlehemp. Besides concealment the heavy growth would provide an alarm if any creature of the night sought Cugel's bedside, for it would have to be waded through, and was very dry.

Naturally he lit no fire to advertise his position. He lay long awake, shivering on the stony couch, and brooding sourly on the stars that blazed in profusion above. Brief days ago he had lain on Iucounu's opulent bed — had possessed Iucounu's fabulous manse. The contrast of these memories with his present situation was unbearable to Cugel, and momentarily careless of his safety, he snarled aloud a curse on the Laughing Magician.

It in no way abated Cugel's wrath to consider that it was through his own agency, and not the magician's, that he found himself in these barren regions a second time. In fact when Cugel had last seen him, Iucounu had been powerless to transport anyone, and was himself completely at Cugel's mercy.

This was no extenuating circumstance, Cugel reasoned. For, if Iucounu had not banished him here on the *first* occasion, then Cugel, on his hard-won return to Almery, would not have sought to revenge himself on the magician by transporting him to the same spot. And since it was during this attempted revenge that Cugel, through a mis-pronunciation of the spell, suffered his second transportation hither, the fault was clearly Iucounu's. And thus a double revenge was now called for.

Tomorrow, he decided, he would build a raft. If the overseas route proved substantially faster, then Cugel might come upon the magician before the latter looked for his return, if he did so at all. Iucounu was of course no one with whom to trifle, but with this edge of surprise, Cugel might hope to overcome him. Had he not done so once already? After all, he was not called Cugel the Clever for nothing.

This reflection brought some measure of comfort to Cugel's perturbed spirit. At length, he slept.

Mumber Sull was Thane of the fishing village of Icthyll on the southern shore of the Sea of Cutz, as had been his father and forefathers before him. Now, as he climbed the stone staircase up the face of the crags in the early morning, he was doing what his forebears had done every morning of their lives.

He had risen with the dying sun, and breakfasted. Leaving his house, he had descended this same flight of steps, to make his inspection of the harbor. Having ceremoniously pronounced the boats and the gear to be in order, he had taken his leave of the dock-keeper, and was now returning to where the stone buildings of Icthyll stood among the jagged crowns of the cliffs.

As the Thane toiled upward the noise of the surf against the cliffs diminished beneath him, and scavenging gulls coasted near him with increasing frequency, some of them within his arm's reach, had he thought to grab for them.

So frivolous a thought was not likely to occur to Mumber Sull. He was tall and scrawny, his bulkiest part being his head. This was a prognathous object, oblong of crown and thatched with gray hair that grew in jutting shingles. He was saturnine of mien. His mouth was a grave line of dignity beneath his great drooping nose and stubborn gloomy eyes.

Mumber Sull's next official function would be to unlock the town tavern, where he and the council of elders presided daily until sunset, discussing the larger issues of existence and playing skubbage. In anticipation the Thane patted the pouch of skubbage pieces dangling at his belt. These were carved gems of great value, and the set comprised a civic heirloom, given into the Harbor Thane's keeping as a token of his investiture. Sull plotted several opening moves as he trudged upward.

By the time he topped the stairs, the sea below was inaudible, and he stood in an upper ocean of violet atmosphere where the feeble sun struggled to rise and where great shoals of birds dizzyingly swam. Sull mused briefly on this spectacle, and then turned toward the town.

Striding toward the tavern, he saw the usual gaggle of waiting elders before the doors. But this morning their group was augmented by fishermen, women, and children — it was a gathering of the whole village in fact. Moreover, this group did not face the tavern, but rather the opposite direction, toward the square.

The reason was obvious, for there in the square two trolls — white in color and both fifteen feet tall — were piling stones in a heap. The stones were collected by the trolls from the walls of the nearest buildings and from the paving of the square itself.

The townsfolk stared in fascination at the trolls, while an elaborately costumed stranger gazed indifferently at townsfolk and trolls alike, intermittently barking an order at the latter. Mumber Sull advanced, addressing this stranger.

"Here, sir! Who are you? Do you control these vandalous creatures? They must desist at once!"

The stranger arched an eyebrow at the Thane's shock. He fingered one of the tassels that dangled from his flared collar, and drawled,

"Naturally I shall explain. My laborers now stockpile material for the construction of the pharos decreed here by my lord of the House of Slaye, who has recently returned to the overlordship of Cil, and requires a system of beacons to guide his shipping."

"Slaye? Cil? The overlordship?" Sull watched one of the trolls scoop up a double armload of the Guild Hall's western wall and carry it to the heap in the square. He spun back to the stranger. "Are you bereft of your wits? Had you no thought to request approval of these activities from the town's governing official?"

"Governing official?" the stranger languidly inquired.

"Myself!" rasped Sull. The Thane indicated with a knob-knuckled forefinger the lobe of his left ear. This was an appendage of considerable length, and was further remarkable in that it had the shape of the letter S. A small silver earring — a vanity of Sull's — was lodged in the tip of the lobe. "You will notice," said Mumber Sull, "that I bear the token of Simbilis the Sixteenth, which the archwizard made hereditary to my line on the eve of his victory over the subworld league in the eighteenth aeon."

"A pretty bauble," yawned the interloper. "Is it silver?"

"The token," said Sull through clenched teeth, "is the ear-lobe itself, signifying —"

"Come, come. Surely we have dwelt sufficiently on these tiresome particulars. I assure you your consternation is groundless. Any damage my laborers cause will be fully compensated. Scrupulous reparation will be made to Icthyll in the form of tax exemptions dispensed by its colonial government, whose arrival we look for this afternoon."

"Government?"

"They will explain the tax and tithe schedules, and the labor donations required of each citizen for the servicing of the beacon, once it has been built by my laborers."

"Do you still not grasp the situation here? Icthyll possesses a government, whose chief I am, and I speak for all my townsmen in saying that our existing fiscal and political arrangements are perfectly satisfactory. Your intervention here is hotly resented."

"In this last respect it seems you speak for yourself alone," said the stranger, indicating with a nod the crowd of townspeople. These were a mild folk, unapt to fervent displays of energy. Presently they were wholly engrossed by the herculean activities of the trolls. Feats of exceptional strength elicited appreciative murmurs and spatterings of applause. One or two children toddled forth and worshipfully aided the giants by gathering pebbles.

"My fellow townsmen!" called the Thane indignantly. "For shame! Has civic pride fled from you? Can you —"

"One moment." The stranger's manner was suddenly stern. "I must caution you against inflammatory rhetoric. My lord of Slaye is of course benevolence personified, but he shows scant tolerance for opposition."

"Tolerance you say?" blazed Mumber Sull. "It is my own tolerance your master tries. Does he willfully forget the jurisdictions agreed upon between his ancestor — Pandu Slaye — and Simbilis, whose loyal vassal I am? The Slaye dominion is confined to the sea's northern coast, while all this southern coast belongs to Simbilis."

"I see you are a student of historical arcana," the stranger grumbled. "These legends express merely pedantic truth. Naturally my lord of Slaye respects the precedence of Simbilis in these regions. It would be madness in the greatest of wizards to defy that dread name. But the matter of Simbilis' precedence is academic. It is unthinkable that the archwizard still lives. And should he live, where is he to be found? His whereabouts have been for centuries unknown. My lord of Slaye merely revives a vacated empire."

"Unthinkable that Simbilis still lives!" The Thane snorted. "Could such a one have died without report of his passing? Yet the ages have brought not even the rumor of it. To one of Simbilis' power, the aeons are as decades."

"You are welcome to these fantasies," the stranger snapped. "It would certainly require nothing less than the intercession of Simbilis to alter the plans of my own lord. Lacking such, you are well advised to eschew insurrectionary speeches."

A movement of the crowd caught Mumber Sull's eye. The people were giving away before one of the trolls, which was advancing toward the tavern. "Halt!" the Thane bellowed, and leaped forth. The troll wrenched the gable from the tavern roof. The Thane stopped dead in shock, then sprang forward anew. He gave a bound and seized the troll's neck with both arms. The creature plucked him off and, at the stranger's order, brought Sull thither.

"Your open attempts at sabotage compel me to banish you, in the name of Slaye, from these regions," the interloper said. Mumber Sull writhed vainly. The man summoned the second troll. The Thane was borne to the head of the stairs he had just ascended. He hung, spread-eagled and facedown at the brink of the crag, a troll either side gripping him by ankle and wrist. The trolls gave him a few preparatory swings, and the Thane watched the surf mutely exploding against the rocks three hundred feet below.

"They are instructed," the stranger told the Thane, who was describing ever wider swings over the abyss, "to throw you beyond the rocks. Thus you will quite possibly survive the fall, and may in that case spend whatever time remains before the sun goes dark in looking for Simbilis, to substantiate your claims."

Sull was swept back for the final heave. The mighty arms held him aloft for an instant and then swung him forward. The Thane saw the rock pass under him in a blur and then he was launched, weightless, into violet lagoons of air where white gulls cruised.

And while he was still rising, before the long plunge began, the Thane's shock and outrage crystallized into a single thought that had the clarity of a vision: *That is precisely what I will do. I will go find Simbilis.*

In the matter of Simbilis' whereabouts, Mumber Sull had only legend to guide him, a tradition that after the wars with the subworld league the archwizard had retired to the west. Nonetheless, it was Mumber Sull's nature to proceed with perfect assurance as long as there was the slightest possibility he was proceeding correctly. Having only legend to suggest where Simbilis was, the Thane followed legend as a map, and now he manned the tiller of his small sloop with stolid composure, steering west, with the Sea of Cutz's craggy south coast just visible to port.

This was the Thane's fourth day at sea. He had been allowed, un-molested, to commandeer from Icthyll's docks the vessel he presently steered. He had, in fact, been completely ignored. When, several hours after his plunge, he clambered rigid with cold onto the jetty, he had found the docks deserted. Shaking his fist upward toward where the town perched out of sight atop the cliffs, he had pronounced Icthyll and its usurpers under arrest until his or his lord Simbilis' return. Then he had turned to equipping and provisioning a small craft.

Now, noting that it was midday, Mumber Sull lashed the tiller — lightly, for the day was almost windless. He stretched out amidships to take his lunch. Then he spied a sail, quite distant, to starboard.

The Thane stowed his provisions and leaped to the tiller, setting a harpoon close to hand, for the pirates who prowled this drear and little-traveled sea were a particularly lean and bestial breed.

The sail proved quite a small one, and thus much closer than Sull's first guess had made it. His curiosity outgrew his apprehensions and he began to make toward the craft.

When he was nearer Mumber Sull could see through the reddish light of noon that the sail was a tattered quilt of rags and skins, and its mast a broken oar. The vessel this ensemble propelled was a water-logged raft, on which a man lay stretched, apparently unconscious.

This gaunt castaway, transferred to the sloop, responded slowly to the drops of water Mumber Sull applied to his lips. Once conscious, however, he swiftly gained strength, and ate ravenously of the jerky and biscuit offered him.

"You show great recuperative powers," the Thane said after some time.

"A further ministration of this excellent jerky and my restoration will be complete," replied the stranger. Though gaunt, unshaven, and salt-streaked, he was a man of engaging and resourceful appearance. His long-limbed body seemed swift and agile. His dark brows coved sharply above black eyes that sparkled with wit and affability. On the whole his lean, canny face suggested a humorous fox.

Having eaten his fill, he sat back with a sigh. "Your passing was most opportune. When I embarked some time past I was in haste and poorly provisioned. The loss of my steering oar in a struggle with a giant water-insect left me adrift, how long I cannot say. Are you, perhaps, steering a southern course?"

"Indeed not. I am sailing westward."

"Alas. This is extremely inconvenient for myself. My destination lies many months' journey to the south. Perhaps you have heard of Almery?"

"Never. My own destination is the city of Grag on this sea's western coast. I go to seek redress for a gross injustice I have lately suffered at the hands of certain lawless felons."

"But surely this is a great coincidence," the stranger marveled. "You travel in search of vengeance and so do I. Permit me to introduce myself. I am Cugel the Clever."

"I am Mumber Sull, Harbor Thane of Icthyll."

"Excellent Thane — should not the similarity of our aims be read as an omen? Clearly we were meant to further one another's purposes. Come south with me and aid me in reaching Almery and punishing Iucounu, the Laughing Magician. With this accomplished, I shall in my turn accompany you and aid you in securing your revenge."

Mumber Sull shook his head. "I applaud the notion that we should join forces, but it would be ridiculous to seek the lesser before the greater. Whoever this Iucounu may be, his degree can only be less than that of Simbilis, first among sorcerers, and it is Simbilis that we must go now to seek."

"Your outlook seems to be deplorably self-centered. My wish to encounter Iucounu is urgent, and a trek to the west would greatly delay its fulfillment. In these times, an uncertain star hangs over all. It is folly to postpone my enterprise when at any moment the sun may gutter and go out."

"You are impertinent," replied the Thane with a frown. "Further, how can you speak of a journey to Simbilis as a delay, or postponement of your desire's fulfilment? Is there anything which Simbilis cannot perform for those who ask his aid?"

Cugel stroked his chin. "You imply that you have some claim to this wizard's generosity?"

"And how not? Am I not his vassal, bearer of his hereditary token?" Here the Thane indicated his left ear-lobe. "Behold Simbilis' rune. Moreover, am I not embarking on a hazardous voyage in his service? For I go to inform him of encroachments upon his domain. Even to men who lack such claims as I have upon him, Simbilis' open-handedness is legend."

Cugel nodded thoughtfully. "Might his generosity extend to bestowing on his servants certain ... punitive powers?"

"Beyond a doubt. I myself plan a modest request of that nature."

Cugel nodded again, but then made an impatient gesture. "But the whole project is too uncertain! The whims of a wizard are impossible to guess. What do I know of Simbilis?"

Mumber Sull was aghast. "Can you be unfamiliar with the name of Simbilis?"

"Completely. It is not known in Almery."

"Yours must indeed be a far-flung and outlandish region."

"I am eager to repair my ignorance. Describe the man and his deeds."

"To describe Simbilis is to describe an age, not a man," said the Thane. With a sweep of his arm he indicated the sea around them. "Simbilis made this very ocean we sail on. Once this was the great Valley of Cutz. Cities carpeted its floor. But in the eighteenth aeon certain agencies of the subworlds formed a league designing the conquest of the surface world. Simbilis, archmagician of the northern dominions, chanced to be forewarned, and was able to enlist his two greatest peers — Pandu Slaye and Tarlon the Grim — in an alliance to combat the invasion.

"The ensuing war spanned several generations. Its last battle was fought miles beneath us on the valley floor, and the forces of Simbilis prevailed. It was a titanic engagement, and left the valley a chasm of poisonous wreckage. Simbilis compelled the vanquished sublords, as a first act of indemnity, to dam the valley and divert thither various rivers. Hence the present ocean.

"Tarlon died of wounds suffered in the wars, so Slaye and Simbilis divided the sea between them. Simbilis took the southern coast, and there built cities — Icthyll among them — to house the refugees from the devastated cities of Cutz. Slaye settled on the northern coast. It is his descendant who now usurps the cities belonging to Simbilis. As for the archwizard himself, upon completing his labors of restoration he retired to the city of Grag in the west, whence I now travel seeking him."

"Your account raises a question," Cugel said. "I have seen the domain of Slaye at first hand, and know it to be a realm of great antiquity. Thus by your own admission we are seeking a man who, if he still lives, is centuries old. Surely this is a fool's errand."

Mumber Sull scowled. "Could one of Simbilis' stature and renown have died without report of it? Yet the ages have brought not even the rumor of his passing."

Cugel considered. He did not find the Thane's reasoning convincing. On the other hand he was still too weak to resort to force. If he let himself be carried to Grag, the worst that could happen would be that Simbilis would turn out to be dead, and in that event Cugel would at least have the compensation of being in a center of civilization where new means of traveling south could be found. If in fact Simbilis was alive, of course, then Cugel could hope for great benefits at the cost of a slight detour.

"Is it a certainty," he asked Sull, "that Simbilis will reward our services by dispensing punitive powers?"

"Most assuredly."

"And would he also provide those who serve him instantaneous transport to any locale designated?"

"Unquestionably."

"I accept a partnership, then, in your venture, and will help you seek Simbilis, in expectation of the rewards I have stipulated."

At this the Thane shook his head. "The dignity of my rank forbids the informal camaraderie of a partnership. I can only accept you in the capacity of my Esquire. As my vassal, you naturally become Simbilis' as well, and thus gain title to his recompense. No other arrangement can be considered."

The idea was distasteful to Cugel, but it seemed a slight enough inconvenience if it guaranteed him a claim upon Simbilis' favor.

"How distant is Grag?" he asked the Thane.

"I have been sailing some four days. I expect to arrive there in less than a fortnight."

"You are certain that Grag is where the wizard resides?"

Mumber Sull hesitated just perceptibly. "Were this an absolute certainty, I would have scant need of your services as retainer. The overwhelming likelihood is that he is indeed there. In this case, if you become my Esquire, you will have won great advantages at the expense of minimal exertions: the mere accompanying of myself in Grag. Should Simbilis prove to be elsewhere, you would naturally be bound to aid me in a somewhat lengthier trek — the reward remaining considerable, of course. So you see you are faced with something of a gamble. You are at liberty to refuse, in which case I will take you to Grag; but if Simbilis is there, you will have lost all claim to his aid."

Cugel nodded. "I accept your proposition, honored Thane, and here make formal application for the post of Esquire to yourself." Cugel had his own notions about how binding his indenture to the Thane would prove if Simbilis were not in Grag. He kept these to himself, however. At Mumber Sull's direction, he knelt amidships, and the Thane formally invested him with the rank of Esquire. Cugel then manned the tiller. The Thane relaxed in the bow, and narrated for his Esquire's benefit the interminable history of the family of Sull, Harbor Thane of Icthyll.

It was not a fortnight, but an entire month before the pair sighted the city of Grag. A shortage of supplies caused them, in the latter weeks of this journey, to put in at the craggy south coast, but on one of these occasions they were set upon by certain winged creatures which inhabited the cliffs. These beasts, though rabid carnivores, lacked the bulk to carry off the seafarers, and when Sull contrived to kill several with his sword, they retreated to hover overhead. From there, however, they bombarded the pair with excreta so foul, that Thane and Esquire fled in haste, and were discouraged from making further landings. Thus, when their destination hove in sight, both suffered extremely from hunger and thirst.

Seen from offshore, Grag was a spectacle of magnificence. The coast was mountainous, but at one point its wall was sharply indented, and a broad apron of rock sloped gently from the mountains' feet down to the surf. In this natural amphitheater the city stood, gleaming white and gray in the lap of the peaks.

But once Cugel had steered past the wide-flung arm of Grag's breakwater, flaws began to appear in the city's grandeur. The harbor waters were deserted, and only occasional fishing barks, small and dilapidated, steered through the sluggish swell. The docks, stately ranks to the distant eye, resolved on nearer approach into mossy pilings like rows of fractured teeth, surrounded by a flotsam of rotten plank. Warehouses stood empty, doors broken and sagging. The pair moored their sloop at an abandoned float, clambered by rickety wooden stairs up onto the quay, and set out into the city.

They found the pavements, the proud and varied architecture, of a great capital, a crossroads of commerce. But now it stood two-thirds untenanted. Its citizens, rather furtive and sullen folk, seemed conscious of their city's vanished greatness and were curt and unhelpful in their replies to the queries of the strangers.

Nonetheless the pair quickly found an inn, where they ate and drank avidly. After the meal Mumber Sull beckoned the proprietor to their table.

"Tell me, good sir," the Thane said. "Where is Simbilis to be found?"

The innkeeper stared blankly. "Where indeed? Do you ask me this in earnest?"

"You marvel that we are ignorant of a thing so widely known." Mumber Sull smiled. "You see, we are strangers to Grag, and do not know in what district of it the archwizard resides. We have urgent business with him."

The innkeeper regarded Sull and Cugel a moment, and then took a seat at their table. He was a bald man who wore two gold rings in his ears.

"Gentlemen," he said, "surely you have come from afar."

"From Icthyll. It is but a month distant, but news from Grag no longer reaches us there."

"Ah yes. Grag's great days of commerce are long gone. What you do not realize, sirs, is that Simbilis no longer inhabits Grag, having departed it ages past."

"Alas! Do you know of his present whereabouts?"

Here the innkeeper looked carefully around and leaned closer. "As it happens, you have in your great good fortune encountered a man who possesses information about Simbilis' destination when he left Grag. This is a fact little known, for such historical arcana are not widely current. I stumbled upon it by accident while perusing an old scroll at a curio shop. Naturally I would require substantial remuneration for imparting information so difficult to come by."

Mumber Sull nodded stiffly. "I am without gold. At my departure from my home village, where I am a citizen of the highest standing, I was in great haste. However, I believe I have something you will find acceptable."

Sull drew out his pouch of skubbage counters. Raising his eyes to the ceiling he intoned solemnly: "The use to which I now put this civic heirloom is public, not private, inasmuch as it furthers the redress of crimes committed against Icthyll by the myrmidons of Slaye." Then Sull produced one of the gems.

The Thane proved a stubborn and skillful haggler. In the end the innkeeper pocketed the gem, and tendered a pouch of gold coins in change, along with his information.

"What I know is this," he said in a low voice. "Simbilis, before his departure, made a farewell address to Grag. In it he stated his intention of retiring to the west, to the Vale of Zoo, there to build a highway connecting the sub- and surface worlds. Along this highway a peaceful commerce would flow, which would in the end heal relations and avert further strife between the human and demon realms. Simbilis departed after delivering this address, and left the ken of Grag."

"And where is the Vale of Zoo?" Mumber Sull eagerly asked. The innkeeper shrugged.

"Beyond what I have said, that it lies in the west, I know nothing. The mountains to the west of Grag have long been dangerous. No one comes here from the west, and few travel from Grag thither. Those who do never return, and thus the west remains incognito to those of my city."

Mumber Sull expressed great irritation. "Surely more is known than this! Can one of Simbilis' stature have disappeared so utterly from the knowledge of men?"

"I have told you more than is generally known. The event is extremely remote in time. On that score alone, I wonder that you can expect to find Simbilis still living."

When the innkeeper withdrew, Mumber Sull and Cugel retired to bathe and don new clothing. They returned to the public room later in the evening for supper.

As he sat over a platter of leeks and sausages, the Thane's mood became reconciled, indeed almost cheerful. "We face at worst I am sure only a brief delay," he said. "The innkeeper himself admits that Grag receives no travelers from the west. He is ignorant of the region. Doubtless he has exaggerated its dangers."

Cugel's own outlook was much gloomier, but he said nothing. He had already, upon hearing the innkeeper, discounted Simbilis as inaccessible even if still living. He was now considering the best means of acquiring the Thane's gold and gems during the night. Provisioned with these, Cugel was sure he could purchase supplies and transport to the south.

Before the pair's supper was well ended, a group of red-clad men in black boots and capes of black leather entered the inn. This group had a leader, a burly, rubicund man, who went to confer with the innkeeper in a corner. Something passed from the stranger's hand to the innkeeper's. The innkeeper nodded, and the burly man marshaled his group to one end of the public room.

Here they pushed together several tables and sat behind them in the manner of a tribunal, their bullnecked leader in their midst the only one of them standing. He measuringly, impressively swept his eyes over everyone in the room and, when all attention was fixed on him, launched an oration whose subject was a certain stronghold of cannibals located in the mountains behind Grag to the west.

"Hark," said Mumber Sull to Cugel. "He speaks of the way we must travel."

"You have all heard rumors of the cannibals," the burly man was saying. "They are the primary reason why those who venture west of Grag do not return. The total of human flesh these fiends have devoured is matched only by the staggering wealth they have accumulated in the course of their depredations. The gold, gems, and costly stuffs of countless victims lie even now heaped within the cannibals' fetid lairs."

He paused, and a busy murmur strayed through his audience. Dramatically he held aloft a weathered scroll, and cried: "Behold then the means to both punish and despoil the obscene anthropophagi — it is a map, recently discovered by the Brotherhood of Purgers. For you must know that that is who we are. Perhaps our modest fame has not yet reached you here. We are a fraternity devoted to the extermination of the subhuman menaces which plague the dying earth. When we discovered this map, we knew we had come upon a priceless weapon to wield against the man-eaters. And we have brought this map to Grag that her honorable citizens might be the first to have the opportunity of benefiting by it. Our reasoning was thus: the people of Grag have suffered heavily from the cannibals — who has more right than they to vengeance, and a share of the spoils?"

"But what is the nature of the map?" cried a man of the audience.

"An astute question," replied the Purger chief. "The map reveals a secret access to Cannibal Keep. This hidden passage is so fortunately placed, moreover, that it renders invasion of the Keep ridiculously easy, victory absolutely certain, and danger practically nonexistent."

The public response to this was markedly enthusiastic. The burly Purger explained the Brotherhood's enlistment procedure. This involved no more than the payment of a negligible sum, in return for which each recruit received the black leather cape which he was thenceforward to wear as an insignia. Packmounts and provisions for the expedition, as well as weapons, would be provided gratis by the Brotherhood. The party would leave the next day at dawn.

The chief was a rousing speaker. Nearly all those still stout of limb — half the room, in fact — jostled up to the enlistment tables, chattering and jesting. The chief shook hands and bantered heartily, gathering the festive enlistees into the Brotherhood.

Among those unfit for the enticing foray who remained in their seats, one sour and peevish old man scoffed loudly. "It is truly said that cupidity sires folly. The cannibal stronghold is founded firm and will last as long as any on earth — that is to say, the short time left before the sun goes out. Reconsider my friends — surely you are taking a trip to the Vale of Zoo."

At these words Mumber Sull jumped to his feet, thinking that he had missed something. "This expedition involves a journey to the Vale of Zoo?" he loudly asked.

The heckler replied with fresh spleen. "I will not be misquoted. You willfully misinterpret a colloquialism. My meaning was that this profiteering venture pursues a goal beyond the limits of possibility."

"Colloquialism?" The Thane stood at a loss. A slight movement he made caused the two fat pouches at his belt to chink against the table's edge — a sound distinctly audible in the silent room where all sat staring at the perplexed Thane.

This noise seemed to rouse the chief Purger, who said courteously, "You appear a stranger to this region, and perhaps do not know that the Vale of Zoo was the destination of Simbilis — maker of this city and the sea it faces — when he departed Grag to undertake the building of a highway to the subworlds. His farewell address to Grag, wherein he named these intentions, is legend, and his destination's name has become proverbial for whatever is remote and unknowable."

The Thane and his Esquire looked at each other and shared a realization that made Mumber Sull frown. He looked around, but the innkeeper was not in evidence. "No matter," he muttered. Then, conscious of the still staring crowd, he bowed in the chief's direction. "Thank you for your explanation. The Vale of Zoo is our destination, hence my interest in the matter. I am Mumber Sull, Thane of Icthyll, and this is my Esquire. We are traveling in search of Simbilis."

His words were greeted by utter silence. A voice burst out in a moronic laugh, and stopped again instantly. The chief Purger was the first to recover himself. Shouting various jocularities, he turned the attention of the men back to the business of enlistment. His officers — men as jovial and gregarious as himself — divided the volunteers into several groups, and soon a festival hubbub had wholly effaced the startlement induced by Sull's statement. The chief left his officers to handle the recruiting, and asked Sull if he might sit at his table.

He introduced himself as Verdulga. With great deference he expressed his admiration for the intrepidity of the Thane's quest. "It is most fortunate that our paths have crossed, my dear Thane," he said. "Both of us are bound for the west. If you would join forces with us, the Brotherhood would gain the honor and advantage of an important ally, while you yourselves would enjoy greater safety in the company of our noble expedition. Naturally I do not suggest that you come as a lowly enlistee, but rather as one of the officers, to enjoy an officer's share of the spoils when the cannibals have been exterminated."

The Thane assured Verdulga that he and his Esquire would never consider accepting material rewards, both deeming the honor entirely theirs to be fighting on the side of so dedicated a group as the Brotherhood.

The new allies were soon conversing warmly. Cugel, long silent, left the table, and ambled pensively out to the inn's stables, where the pack-animals for the morrow's journey stood in their stalls. One of the red-and-black-clad Purgers was there ministering fodder to the beasts, and Cugel struck up a conversation with him.

At length Cugel confided with a sigh, "Unhappy is the man who serves a mad master, as I do. The worthy Thane pursues a chimera."

"You do not follow him willingly?" the other, a wiry little man named Trogl, asked.

"Our interests lie in different directions. My own goal is in the south. Tempting though the promised spoils of your expedition are, I find myself loath to go farther out of my way than I have already come. I wish to travel directly south from here, and for this I shall require a mount and provisions."

Their conversation waxed franker. Trogl indicated that one or two of the Brotherhood's pack-beasts might be obtainable through himself, in exchange for a certain remuneration. Cugel alluded to the gold and gemstones which he expected would soon pass from the Thane's possession into his own.

"My dear Esquire," Trogl said, "I feel sure that we can be of service to one another. But you must consent to make one alteration in your plans. Abandon all notion of striking south from Grag — there is no road, and the terrain is impassable. However, if you accompany our expedition almost to its goal, our way will cross the Great North-South Road. At this point I will contrive to have your beasts and provisions ready, and you may slip away unnoticed to the south, traveling by a much swifter route than any you could hope to find from Grag."

Cugel approved of the plan. Trogl told him that the intersection of the Great North-South Road was quite near the Keep, and in the excitement of preparation for the attack, Cugel's defection would go entirely unnoticed. The plan had the further advantage of enabling the Esquire to delay purloining Sull's valuables, for he had as yet evolved no satisfactory means of doing so. He bade Trogl good night, and re-entered the inn.

Passing through the public room on his way to bed, Cugel noted that Sull and Verdulga sill sat together. The Thane had taken out his skubbage pieces, and was detailing the set's history to the fascinated and admiring chief.

Chapter II

CANNIBAL KEEP

Verdulga and his twelve lieutenants led some thirty recruits from the inn the next morning. Sull and Cugel accompanied them as allies — for thus Verdulga deferentially termed the pair.

The Brotherhood's expedition maintained a consistently blithe and boisterous spirit as it proceeded across the treeless flanks of the mountains. The chief and his brother Purgers were a mine of ballads and droll anecdotes, and were skilled at generating festivity.

The liquor ration was remarkably ample, the daily march was brief and easy-paced, and the food was excellent. All in all the venture had more the aura of a holiday pilgrimage than of a campaign.

The company's loose and straggling line of march was lent a certain unity by the identical capes of black leather which all the recruits wore. These capes featured a snug hood and, dangling from the back, a complicated system of straps whose purpose was to be explained to the men later. Only Sull and Cugel lacked these articles.

Thane and Esquire were also exceptions with regard to the general drunkenness. Mumber Sull was abstemious by nature and eyed the riotous ranks with disapproval, though Verdulga's flatteries kept him in a generally good temper. As for Cugel, it was something quite different which prevented him from joining the unanimous carouse: a feeling of menace.

At first his uneasiness was vague. He found the party's casual pace odd, since delay could only increase the chance of the enemy's being forewarned. Why this carelessness?

On the fifth day out Cugel's foreboding received a more concrete, while at the same time more mysterious, reinforcement. During a break in the march the Esquire saw one of the lieutenants slip while kneeling to drink from a spring. The man broke his fall, but the hood of his cape fell back from his head. Cugel realized that he had never till this moment seen any of the officers with his hood back. On the head of this man was something that made him seem tonsured. It was a skull-cap of reddish metal clipped to the lieutenant's hair. The little coppery disk seemed to be inscribed.

But it was not the mere discovery of the skullcap that unsettled Cugel. It was the officer's wary crouch and murderous stare when he caught Cugel's eye that caused the latter's misgivings.

On the day following this Cugel made a second discovery. The company was making camp. Cugel, wishing to sharpen his sword, found he had lost his whetstone. No one else was likely to have one, for only he and the Thane were armed of all the party. The weaponry, which was to be donned just before the invasion of the Keep, was in the meantime borne at the rear of the caravan, in ten chests loaded on five beasts.

Deciding that a whetstone, or even a new sword, might be had from this source, Cugel chose a privy moment in the failing light to saunter over and prize open a chest. It was filled with stones. He checked several others. All held stones.

Cugel slept ill that night, and left his bed before dawn, feeling a need to get out of camp and consider his position. He crept downhill till he was out of sight from the road, then proceeded diagonally across the rocky slopes strewn with fragments of color presaging dawn. He gave himself up to his thoughts as he walked.

Clearly, he reasoned, if the weapons were a hoax, then the expedition itself was a hoax too. It remained to guess what its true aim was, and this Cugel could not do. He tried to imagine what the use of the metal skullcaps might be, but beyond the certainty that it was sinister, he arrived at nothing. The sun rose, but he felt no urgency to return. The wine-sodden company always wakened late.

Whatever the expedition's hidden purpose might be, a more urgent question now demanded Cugel's attention. If the Brotherhood as a whole was engaged in fraud, did it follow that Trogl intended to defraud Cugel in their private arrangements as well?

Not necessarily. Though the amassing of captives was clearly the

Brotherhood's business, Trogl was doubtless not averse to private negotiations profitable to himself. What bothered Cugel was the thought that Trogl's course of least risk was treachery. To actually steal animals and provisions for Cugel would put Trogl in danger of discovery. Much easier simply to call the Esquire aside, receive his payment, and…

Cugel halted with a start. He had almost walked off the edge of an overhang. The fall, some fifteen feet to a broad ledge, could have been fatal.

Cugel shrank down suddenly onto the lip of the overhang. Below, a large erb had just erupted into view from under the projecting rock.

The erb, however, was occupied by something else. Growling and feinting from side to side, it menaced a foe still out of sight beneath the overhang on which Cugel crouched.

A second erb scuttled hindfirst into view and joined the first. The as yet unseen quarry inspired fear in the creatures. Both snarled and threatened, momentarily loath to re-approach the prey who had driven back their first assault.

An instant later this prey made a frantic bid to escape his cul-de-sac. He was a rawboned man in tattered leather garments. He seemed aware that the beasts' hesitation would last only seconds, and he came out swinging his sword with desperate energy.

The erbs exhibited the patterns of extreme hunger. Their dangling jowls leaked orange digestive fluid. Their torsos — squamous blocks of reptile muscle — shook with spasms.

Their need had begun to swallow up their fear, and when the man lunged, the erbs counter-lunged. This caused the man a stagger of indecision, and he tripped. Twisting, he managed to slam his back to the rock, thus breaking his fall and keeping his feet.

But his drive had been contained. Now the erbs moved in. Cugel, hiding overhead, began inching up to a sprinter's crouch. When the erbs joined for the kill and were at maximum involvement with their prey, Cugel meant to make his departure.

He put added weight on his right foot, gathering pressure to launch his flight. There was a snap, and Cugel felt the rotten granite collapse under him. He tried to leap off the falling slab back up to firm rock, but this merely plunged the slab downward with greater force, while at the same time failing to regain Cugel his footing. In the instant during which he scrambled for balance, the slab crushed one of the erbs. Then gravity overcame the Esquire and he pitched backward from the ledge, pushing off at the last second to gain momentum for a flip.

He came down feet first on the second erb. Both went down. Cugel sprang up, drew and swung his sword blindly. The stunned erb, rising, received the steel through half the thickness of its neck.

Cugel surveyed the fallen. Of the first erb no more was visible than its skinny black fingers extruding from under the slab. These bony digits wriggled posthumously, like wounded spiders.

"A dazzling offense," cried the stranger, sheathing his sword and advancing. "I am as astounded by its brilliance as I am grateful for its timeliness."

Cugel made a suave gesture of disclaimer, murmuring that no right-thinking person would have done otherwise. The rescued man entreated the Esquire to his dwelling to take some early-morning refreshment. Cugel accepted, and the man conducted him to a sequestered stone hut which was not distant. The hut's structural integration with the native rock was so artful that it was practically undetectable from a distance of more than thirty paces.

After setting forth a breakfast of leeks and cheese, Cugel's host ruefully indicated the contents of the hut. "To offer you your choice of all I own would be a slight expression of my gratitude. Alas, mine is a scavenging profession and my goods are gleanings of the wastes, possessing little intrinsic value."

Cugel peered at the bones, skulls, crystals, and herbs heaped everywhere. He asked the man what his trade was.

"Skulldugger. A respected craft once, though few now practice it. I work minerals and derelict bones into utensils. In Grag there remain folk who still credit such artifacts with a magic efficacy, and they redeem my labors with a pittance sufficing my needs. The particular slopes your caravan has been crossing are rich sources of erb and grue skulls, of which I make goblets. In fact, these predators' seasonal movements have just returned them to the region. Erbs especially appear in daily-increasing numbers. Your festive expedition has been in constant danger from the rear."

Cugel's eyebrows went up. "You know of the expedition? But why then did you not warn us of our peril?"

"I am not meddlesome by nature, and dislike exposing myself to strangers. These are grim times, and this region is particularly hostile to mankind — that is to say, has all too great a liking for it."

Cugel nodded. Presently he sighed. "It is unfortunate you are so destitute. I know how keenly you must feel the lack of some token or tokens of gratitude. Perhaps you can provide me with a sturdy mount and sufficient provision for a journey from here to the Great North-South Road."

"Alas. I can provide none of these things. But what road is this of which you speak?"

"That which intersects the road my company now travels, at a point just east of Cannibal Keep."

"But no such road exists. I know these mountains to the tiniest stream-course; they are my living. I may be believed."

"Then I am indeed betrayed!" Cugel rose and paced the floor, debating his course. The skulldugger, seeing his perplexity, cried warmly:

"I rejoice the opportunity to repay my debt to you, for it is clear that you have been led astray and are ignorant of this area. Among these peaks as nowhere else such ignorance is fatal. Thus, in informing you about your situation, I render you a service no less crucial than that you have lately rendered me."

Cugel observed that this was a rather abstract requital, but in the end, seeing no other advantage to be gained from the skulldugger, he asked for his account of the region.

The skulldugger told him that the westward road out of Grag was the only road crossing these mountains for a hundred leagues in any direction. At its highest point, in Keep Pass, it ran by the very gates of the cannibal stronghold. After, it descended gradually until, many days' march farther west, the mountains ended in great bluffs, and a flinty desert began. Perhaps Cugel could find a southerly route in or beyond this desert — it lay outside the skulldugger's knowledge. All he knew with certainty was that there existed no southerly road between here and there. In order to enter the desert a chasm, called Yawrn's Gape, had to be crossed. A single bridge did in fact span the abyss, but a toll of unknown nature was exacted from all who would go over it.

"Whatever this toll is," concluded the skulldugger, "the likelihood of your ever reaching the chasm to pay it is small. To get there, the Keep must first be passed, and the chances are excellent that in attempting to do so you will lose your life. The Keep's predatory activities have lately shown a drastic increase. I cannot imagine your party's purpose in proceeding thither."

"Nor do most of its members," said Cugel, "though they think otherwise. But no matter. I shall not need to pass the Keep. You have ignored my most obvious course: to return with all speed to Grag, whence doubtless runs a road to the south. To take this route was my original plan. I was dissuaded from it by a party whom I shall visit before turning back."

The skulldugger shook his head. "There is indeed a road leading south from Grag — in fact, a remarkably safe one as roads go. But as I have said, the terrain you have just traversed is subject to its seasonal infestation of predators. A company the size of yours, if armed and resolute, could perhaps push as far as halfway back to Grag before the last survivors were overwhelmed. A lone wayfarer would not last an hour."

At this moment the skulldugger, who had removed his battered leather cap during his explanations, moved his head in such a way that Cugel noted a thin metal skullcap clipped to the scavenger's grizzled hair.

"Can you explain to me," Cugel interjected, "the purpose of the skullcap you wear?"

Somewhat reluctantly, the skulldugger unpinned it and regarded it. "This trinket, you mean? A slight thing. It renders its wearer undetectable to the flesh-sensitive organs by which the cannibals locate their prey. These shields, the issue of a benevolent magician, were once widely available, but are now rare."

"Indeed, I find this matter fascinating! The cap confers on its wearer total invisibility to cannibals?"

"In effect," the skulldugger conceded. "While there are rumored to be more than one breed of cannibal, the majority of them lack true eyes. They seem to possess in vision's stead a highly developed olfactory perception. The shield neutralizes its wearer's olfactory aura."

"This is a happy moment," Cugel declared. "We have discovered the means by which you may requite me for saving your life. In possession of the shield you hold, I would be able to pass the Keep unharmed, and seek farther to the west some southerly route by which to return to Almery."

"By no means. You have been amply requited by the information I have imparted. My work brings me under the Keep's very walls. Both my life and livelihood depend upon this charm."

"Your reply does you little credit. Consider that it was only in great peril to my own life that I rescued yours. The recompense must meet the service."

"Your request cannot be granted. To throw away my own life would be to vitiate the very service of which you claim reward. The shield remains in my hands."

Cugel contemplated the skulldugger briefly. The latter's rangy muscled limbs, and the memory of the ferocious and skillful swordplay with which he had kept the erbs at bay, convinced Cugel that the skullcap could not be had by force.

"Your ingratitude saddens me," the Esquire said, "but many maxims warn the generous man to expect it of mankind. Perhaps you will perform a lesser service. I require an efficient narcotic — enough to produce sleep in some forty men."

"This I will gladly provide. My lore extends to herbalism, and the neighborhood abounds in a highly potent lichen meeting your specifications."

Provided with a quantity of powdered lichen and instructed in its use by the skulldugger, Cugel took his leave and rejoined the company, which was in the midst of its usual prolonged and bibulous breakfast when he arrived. He received from Mumber Sull, who sat lordly and sober at his meal, a brief rebuke for his absence, but no one else noticed he had been gone.

For the next few days the expedition continued its ambling. Though Cugel often now looked fearfully behind for grues and erbs, the Brotherhood seemed to have set a pace that kept the party just ahead of the returning predators.

The company had grown more liquorous than ever. The wine ration was now double its original prodigal amount, and was augmented by brandy thrice daily. However, Cugel noticed that Verdulga and his lieutenants, while always merry and quick to cry a toast, never betrayed the sloppy, staggering gait most of the recruits developed. The Esquire secretly improvised thirteen rude but plausible skullcaps from the bottoms of tin cups. Then he waited his chance.

On the fourth day after Cugel's interview with the skulldugger, Verdulga halted the march early in the afternoon, and called the company about him. The morrow's march, he said, would bring them to their goal, and tomorrow night would see the enemy and its treasure in the expedition's hands.

This news was the signal for a night of feasting and orgiastic carouse wholly eclipsing all that had gone before. The drinking was well under way when Cugel slipped up to the wine jar and, under the pretense of filling his cup, sneaked a handful of powder under the lid. Then he busied himself circulating among the merrymakers and surreptitiously doctoring what cups and flagons he could with pinches of the powder.

The lichen was potent. Men began to fall where they stood mere minutes after Cugel had drugged the jar. Verdulga and his officers, who in reality drank far less than they appeared to, were among the last to topple, marveling blearily as they collapsed at the men sprawled snoring on all sides. In half an hour Cugel alone remained awake.

Cugel and Mumber Sull. The Esquire, just bending above the fallen Verdulga, jumped at the Thane's voice, and cursed himself for forgetting Sull's abstemiousness.

"Is it not astonishing, Esquire? Never have I seen drink so swiftly and utterly overtake the drinker's senses." He stood, arms akimbo, surveying the fallen.

Cugel took rapid counsel with himself. The Thane must be silenced, or included in his scheme. Naturally it was preferable to have an ally on his trek west, if it was west that Cugel had to go. Then too — and this was just a whisper in Cugel's mind — there was a possibility that Simbilis still lived. Both thoughts disposed him to continue the farce of his Esquireship.

"Esteemed Thane," he said hurriedly, "we are in the hands of brigands, or worse. I have even now contrived our escape. I have until now been denied the chance to communicate my discovery to you."

Mumber Sull guffawed incredulously. Cugel launched an edited account of his meeting with the skulldugger, and the scavenger's explanation of the skullcaps. Then he revealed the officers' heads. Most convincing were the weapon chests filled with stones. This clearly demonstrated deception enraged Mumber Sull.

"Consider, Thane," urged Cugel. "To deprive these scoundrels of the protection they think to enjoy would be an excellent way to begin their punishment." He set to work divesting the twelve officers and Verdulga of their skullcaps, and clipping the tin substitutes to their scalps in exchange. As he worked, he framed persuasive arguments, which in the end won the Thane's terse accession to his plan.

Two of the genuine skullcaps Cugel kept, clipping one to his hair and instructing the Thane to do likewise. Both donned caps to conceal them. The remaining eleven of the charms Cugel cast into a fast-rushing gill.

The pair then retired, and the Thane's cracked snore soon joined the orchestra of the drugged company. Cugel neglected to tell him that, while working over Verdulga, he had discovered the entire set of the Thane's skubbage pieces, along with his gold and silver, in two pouches on the chief's belt. The Esquire quietly transferred this property to his own belt, and weighted Verdulga's pouches with stones.

The dying sun had already declined from its zenith, and the red of noon had taken on a purple tinge, when the company awoke, blear-eyed and sour-bellied. Heads ached, hands were clumsy, and tempers short. It was late afternoon when the crusaders set forth. All about them clots of burgundy shadow bloomed like an exotic fungus in the hollows of the mountain slopes.

Cugel hovered near Sull during the march, fearful that the Thane's indignation at Verdulga's duplicity would show. But Sull kept silent, merely greeting with compressed lips the remarks of Verdulga and his officers. These latter did not notice his coldness, for they found it all they could do to whip up the flagging and hungover spirits of their recruits.

Constant ministrations of wine and brandy soon began to show their effect on the men, however. Before dark had well approached the enlistees were roaring out ballad refrains and cheering merrily at Verdulga's shouted witticisms. All at once the chief held up his arms for silence.

"The objective is at hand," he announced. "Our imminent triumph and wealth should now be solemnized." A new jar of especially potent wine was brought out. At that moment Cugel found the wiry form of Trogl at his elbow.

"Come," the latter breathed in Cugel's ear. "Several toasts will follow and your departure will not be noted. Come aside with me to where the crossroads and your mount await, and we can consummate our bargain."

Cugel nodded. Trogl led him a short distance below the trail and then perhaps a quarter-mile across the rocks to a level place surrounded by boulders. Here Trogl turned and said:

"The crossroads are but a step from here. To prevent misunderstanding, give me your payment now." Cugel acceded affably, counting the Thane's coins into Trogl's palm. Clutching the money, Trogl stepped back and blew on a small pipe which he pulled from his belt.

Cugel drew his sword, but made no other move, as a dozen pale figures swarmed from behind the boulders into the clearing. Trogl's exultant expression turned to dismay as the figures, groping in hesitation for a moment, suddenly converged on himself. He cried out, struggled briefly, and was devoured on the spot.

Cugel looked on, and the pale forms seemed utterly unaware of him, submerged in another medium, as if he were on a shore watching sharks feeding down in murky water. The cannibals had great cheesy snouts with huge nostrils, but their eyes were rudimentary — mere opaque tumors growing from shallow, browless sockets. They completed their degustation of Trogl in moments, melted back among the rocks, and were gone. Cugel strolled forward and extracted Trogl's purse from among the cast-aside garments. Then he slipped back to the company.

When he returned, the crusaders had just completed the prolonged toasting in which Verdulga had led them, and many swayed on their feet. The chief was demonstrating the use of the leather capes whose purchase had been mandatory for the enlistees.

"Notice that we have not required of you a pointless expenditure. The secret way we must go is at a certain point very cold and damp. It passes by underground wells. Your capes are provided with a system of straps which converts them into warm protective garments. The officers are passing among you now to demonstrate the buckling procedure."

The lieutenants moved among the troop, interlacing the straps of each cape so that it was tightened into a loose cocoon around the wearer, though still permitting him to extrude his arms from the opening in front. The party set forth once more on the last lap of its march.

They rounded a curve, and the slopes fell away before them in a long saddle, at whose far end the land surged up into peaks again. Wedged among these peaks was the black mass of the Keep. Above it already blazed the fierce white stars. Their shine glazed the road, which appeared a pallid snail's track following the saddle's ridge and then veering upward to pass by the feet of the Keep's walls.

The red-clad Brotherhood led the expedition swaggering with blithe and raucous bravado across the saddle. They came almost up to the fortress itself — it loomed just above them in the crags when Verdulga signaled for a halt.

They were at a place where a ravine branched off from the road and cut back into the native rock on which the Keep was built. The floor of this ravine was smooth as a pathway, and at its far end was a cavemouth. By its situation this cavemouth seemed indeed to offer a way into the fortress via its foundations. Verdulga gathered the men before him and pointed into the ravine.

"There lies the secret entrance. Your officers will distribute among you a final pledge with which we shall seal our union. Then these same officers, scorning to expose their men to risks they have not faced themselves, will precede us within and reconnoiter."

This was applauded. The officers saw that each man received a quart flask of brandy, and then they assembled before the ravine. Trogl's absence was now conspicuous for the first time. Verdulga registered surprise, but quickly recovered himself. He exhorted the eleven remaining officers with stirring phrases. The lieutenants struck stalwart, careless poses, saluted the men humorously, ran down the ravine, and vanished into the cavemouth. The men applauded more wildly.

Verdulga stood on a slight eminence to make an address. Cugel and Sull, as they had arranged, found each other and retreated behind some rocks, from which they watched.

"Fellow warriors," Verdulga boomed, "hear a brief but urgent word. I swear to you that to be just, we must now be merciless. Our foes are pitiful and weak. Vicious degeneracy has vitiated their race and they are helpless. But we must not be tempted to pity! We must think of the butchered generations of blameless girls, whose breasts had only just begun to swell! Yon citadel reeks of such violations."

The men gave passionate shouts and took fierce, reckless pulls on their flasks. Verdulga's voice grew more fervent. "It is true that our foes' females, many of them deliciously sensual, are at our mercy. Our foes' wealth is ours to take. They are indeed an abject spectacle. But quell the promptings of compassion. Remember that these gargoyles jeered at the tears with which tender-bosomed Innocence begged her life! They polluted and gluttonously sucked down her flesh! Are we men?"

The men shouted with rapture and rage. Someone lashed an empty flask with deliberate fury against a rock. Fists shook at the black walls overhead. One of the officers suddenly reappeared in the mouth of the ravine. "The way is open!" he shouted exultantly.

"Forward then!" cried Verdulga, his voice a clarion. "What need we with weapons? Single file! Fortune and Justice!"

Eyes blazing, the recruits charged one behind the other down the ravine and out of sight into the cavemouth, while Verdulga and the officer spurred them with battle cries.

When all had gone in the chief turned to his underling. "Where is Trogl?" The officer shrugged. Verdulga gnawed uneasily at his lips. "Something is afoot. Did you note Sir Scarecrow and his squire among those who entered?"

"I did not, but there was scant light."

"Well. The matter must wait, for we cannot delay delivery. Let us go." The two men disappeared down the ravine.

Thane and Esquire rose from their concealment. "We are free of them," Cugel gloated happily. "Our way to the west lies clear."

"Esquire! Look in that direction." Sull pointed at the road ahead where it rose to pass before the Keep's gates. A dozen creatures with glittering scaly torsos were swarming up from the rocks and onto the highway, and running toward Sull and Cugel.

"Erbs! We are lost!" cried Cugel. "The slopes in all directions teem with such as these. Quickly — the ravine."

With only a narrow lead on the erbs, the pair entered the ravine. On reaching the cavemouth they turned with drawn blades, for the aperture would just accommodate them and could be held indefinitely.

But the erbs did not attack. They seemed to fear penetrating the ravine more than halfway. At this point they wavered.

"It seems they recognize and dread the cannibals' domain," Cugel said cheerlessly.

"Nonetheless," replied Sull, "they remain sufficiently optimistic to keep vigil, and thus block our return to the road." And in fact the creatures, now increased in number, had sat down, brooding on the two humans just out of reach.

After some reflection, Cugel offered the Thane his counsel. "We enjoy complete immunity to cannibal attack, though we must be silent, for I believe they possess a sense of hearing. Perhaps if we enter here, we may find a passage through the Keep and an exit at some other point, thus eluding our pursuers."

The Thane nodded. The pair turned and darted into the tunnel where the company and officers had disappeared moments before. They went cautiously for perhaps a hundred strides through winding darkness. Then they abruptly crouched down in the shadow. They had nearly burst into a great torchlit chamber. In this chamber a chaotic scene transpired.

The recruits, dazed and torpid with drink, milled confusedly, fleeing from their own officers, who worked among them with swift purpose. One recruit frantically stumbled toward the tunnel-mouth where Sull and Cugel crouched. He was pursued by two officers. One of these drew up to either side of the recruit. They seized his cape-straps and pulled simultaneously. The loose cocoon which the cape had formed was pulled into a tight pod which imprisoned the man's arms like a straight-jacket and sealed the hood shut before his face, blinding him.

The officers then linked the straps behind, stunned their bound and blind prey with a truncheon-blow, and delivered him to the heap of similarly trussed and anesthetized recruits which filled one corner of the chamber. The whole capture had been accomplished in seconds, and the five other pairs working in a similar manner had already accounted for the majority of the thirty men.

The last of the sottish victims were quickly rounded up. "It is finished," said Verdulga at length. "The two foreigners are not accounted for, but no matter. Perhaps they strayed from the road and were taken by erbs. The absence of Trogl is somewhat stranger, but for this we have the consolation of larger shares of the profits. Are all shields in place?"

Each man felt perfunctorily under his hood, and nodded. "Then let our clients be admitted," Verdulga said. One of the officers walked to a wide double door in the wall opposite the tunnel-mouth. He plied a massive knocker thrice, paused, then struck once more. The door swung open.

Cannibals swarmed into the chamber. The more inert of the recruits they hoisted on their shoulders and carted through the double doors. Those of the captives who struggled and resisted were dismembered.

Notable among this second group were Verdulga and his officers, who flailed with amazed horror to find themselves seized. They were armed, and those of them who put up the strongest resistance were eaten on the spot. The others, the red-faced Verdulga among them, were dismembered and carried away piecemeal. Within minutes the ensanguined chamber stood empty. The Thane and Esquire rose and rushed after, fearful that the great double doors would be closed on them.

After climbing several flights of stairs, Sull and Cugel emerged on a vast sublevel, a forest of massive pillars supporting the fortress above. Scattered, murky lights revealed the great extent of these catacombs.

The pair, for want of a better plan, followed a cart which the cannibals had laden with dismembered prey. This creaking vehicle was made of bones, and was drawn by certain cannibals whose more massive stature suggested that they were bred for dray-beasts.

The cart wobbled and rattled a winding way with its ghastly load;

Thane and Esquire were led a mazy path among the pillars and the gloomy sulfurous lights of cannibal smithies and workshops.

They passed groups of cannibals stoking furnaces or stirring great vats where a yellow tissue simmered. In other places, bones were being lathed and bored, and fashioned into tools, while nearby jewelers worked highly polished molars and incisors into rings, bracelets, and necklaces.

As they walked, Sull and Cugel enjoyed an eerie invisibility. The cannibals toiled with energy and dexterity — they showed a lively awareness of their surroundings, despite their opaque rudimentary eyes. But they were utterly insensitive to the Thane's and Esquire's passage. The big-nostriled snouts scanned the air without ever detecting the pair's doubtless savory aura.

At length the cart approached a spiral ramp which rose up through the ceiling and seemed to be bathed in star-shine. "Yonder way promises to lead us aboveground," Cugel muttered to Sull. "From thence, egress from the Keep might be most easily found." Sull nodded and the two continued to follow the cart, which had begun to ascend the ramp-way.

It did in fact bring the pair aboveground. They emerged upon a broad plaza under the stars. The plaza was bounded on all sides by the Keep walls. At the center of one of these walls towered a many-storied building — the Keep's headquarters, by the look of it.

As for the great plaza itself, the starlight revealed that it was filled with what seemed to be garden plots, literally thousands of them. But as Sull and Cugel approached the nearest of these plots (among which the cart had begun to wind its way) they found that the gardener had planted them with strange fruit indeed.

Each plot was a garden of human members, a rectangular bed of the same yellow tissue they had seen cooking below, from which sprouted a gesticulating, disorganized crop of legs, arms, and torsos. No plot, however, featured more than one head, and this, as alive as the other organs, was invariably planted at one end of the tissue bed.

As the Thane and Esquire passed among the plots in the cart's wake, the planted heads, from all sides, set up a hissing and cursing of great savagery. While the cannibals attending the cart heard the noise, they did not seem to attribute meaning to it.

"Mercenary devils!" shrieked one head right at Cugel's foot. "Inhuman traitors to your species — do you go now to collect your foully-earned gold? Where is the infamous Verdulga, your leader? Where is the arch-victualler of Cannibal Keep?"

"Do these creatures understand the import of our speech?" Cugel asked in a nervous undertone. The head snorted as at a flimsy subterfuge.

"What matter that they do not? Those who pay you do."

"Then if we speak safely," Cugel said aloud, "know that we ourselves were nearly victims of the very fate you suffer. A stroke of fortune delivered us and undid Verdulga. We, guiltless, now seek our escape from his hellish fortress. Can you aid us with information?"

The head tilted skeptically. "The human turncoats in the Keep's pay are many. Still, if you are such, I cannot see what need you could have to deceive me. Your tale nonetheless is hard to credit."

"There!" broke out Mumber Sull suddenly. "The proof of our tale lies to one side of you." There, at a vacant neighboring plot of tissue, the bone cart had made its first stop, and the head which the cannibals planted at the end of it was the head of Verdulga. The first head cried out this information exultantly, and a great cheering spread over the plaza as the news moved from plot to plot.

When the gardener had completed the graft and packed the seam with yellow plasm, Verdulga's eyes opened and his head looked about. He understood his whereabouts and emitted a dismal groan. The first head laughed aloud at this. It called out a cheery greeting to the chief, and all of the hands variously located in its plot waved a warm hello.

Verdulga answered with a curse, and turned sourly to watch the gardener plant the rest of his limbs.

"Be fruitful and multiply," the first head taunted him. "You shall nourish many generations of cannibals with your flesh before you senesce and are uprooted. Ah, this spectacle warms my hearts, of which I have produced five to date," the head added, turning cordially back to Cugel and Sull. "I would gladly furnish you any information you require. You have rendered my obscene bondage here bearable by bringing to pass my most fervent dream: to see Verdulga suffer the fate to which he brought me. As to an exit from the Keep other than the way you have just come, I know only that it lies through yonder building. Verdulga was wont to repair thither after completing a delivery, and was never seen returning, so it can be assumed that he left directly from thence. Perhaps Verdulga himself would vouchsafe the data you require."

The head turned jocularly in the fallen chief's direction. Verdulga's head glared and was silent. "You might at least," reproved Mumber Sull, "advise us now in atonement for your gross deception of myself and my Esquire. Your fate is sealed and you have nothing to gain from thwarting us."

Verdulga growled and spat. Imperturbably, the cannibal finished grafting one of his legs to the tissue-bed.

"Be of good cheer," the first head chuckled to the chief. "Your constitution is strong, your limbs will duplicate rapidly. The harvests are only moderately excruciating." It faced Sull and Cugel again. "A parting word. Whoever Verdulga dealt with in yonder building, he must possess human perceptions. Beware."

The Thane wished to speak at greater length with their truncated informant, whose condition excited his curiosity. But Cugel's urgent persuasion prevailed. Taking their leave, they made for the distant building.

The pair passed among beds of limbs, whose heads greeted them cheerfully. In moments they stood before the structure's facade. It featured several doorways.

They entered by the least imposing of these portals, hoping to find an unobtrusive route through the structure and outside.

Once inside, they quickly learned the futility of seeking a straight passage. The very first corridor they followed curved radically to one side, rising at the same time. It was immediately intersected by other corridors of differing curve and slope.

Before they realized it, the pair had gone too far to retrace their steps through the aimlessly arcing passages, and they blundered forward, unable even to guess whether their goal was above or below, to the right or to the left of them.

When their exasperation had reached its limits, Sull and Cugel came upon a hallway much more spacious than any they had yet seen. This brought them to a large and magnificently carved door.

"Surely this is the main door," Mumber Sull cried with relief, "and the road lies without!"

Before Cugel could forestall him with cautionary words, the Thane grasped the latch and opened wide the door. A susurrous voice, soft and unsurprised, spoke from within:

"Enter. You are late. Why did you not take your usual route?"

With their hands to their sword-hilts, Sull and Cugel passed cautiously inside. They entered a dining hall paneled in onyx-wood. Chandeliers of black glass diffused pomegranate light upon elegant diners seated at a long table. The light caused the gold service to shine ruddily, and made the contents of the crystal goblets seem too red to be wine.

The diners were a cadaverous assembly. Their sleeves disgorged skeletal hands knobbed with blue gems. Profusions of yellowed lace sprouted from the collars at their bony throats. Weighty coiffures adorned their skullish brows. He who had bid the pair enter, a figure seated at the head of this table, rose upon the Thane's and Esquire's uncertain approach.

"Ah," he cried with a smile that revealed the black stumps still serving him for teeth, "your lateness is explained — you are strangers to the premises. The excellent Verdulga would never delegate the business of collection, so I assume you to be usurpers."

Cugel tried to speak, but his gaunt interlocutor held up a preventing palm. "We admire ambition. The dying sun mocks all nicety of scruple, and you have our complete sympathy. Kindly follow me to the counting room."

"Sympathy? Counting room?" the Thane asked, but the cannibal lord had already turned and gone to a door in the dining hall's farthest corner. Cugel, in whose eye a light had kindled, ignored the perplexed Thane and followed the cannibal.

Sull stared about him, and a dame seated near where he stood nodded graciously. "You are most welcome here," she said in a voice as dry as a lizard's. "We all applaud your heroic exertions on our behalf." She displayed a mossy ruin of a smile. Sull, having braced himself to meet foes, was perplexed by these civilities.

"You speak of our late exploits?" he asked.

"Indeed, we cannot speak highly enough of them," affirmed a spectral gentleman seated on the dame's left. Sull acknowledged this with a bow and a hesitant smile. He went in pursuit of Cugel, who had followed the lord into the counting room.

This latter was not large, but Cugel, entering it some moments in advance of Mumber Sull, found its furnishings breathtaking. On one wall, covering all the wall's width and half its height, were bins variously filled with coins and categorized gems. Taking up a small scoop, the cannibal lord advanced to a bin and began to dump gems into a leather saddlebag.

"You admire our treasury, I see," he said to Cugel, who stood rapt. "At one time a great traffic crossed the mountains to and from Grag. In those days our own race was more vigorous and numerous than now. We enjoyed frequent contacts with the merchants' caravans, and hence our present…collection."

"Fascinating. As to the delivery, it totaled —"

"Forty-two," the cannibal broke in firmly.

It was at this point that Mumber Sull entered the counting room. Perceiving the lord, who was now scooping rings into the saddlebag, Sull looked with perplexed inquiry at Cugel. "Our host graciously insists on repairing the deficiencies of our purses," Cugel told the Thane in a jocular tone.

"Indeed you are most thoughtful, sir," Sull said to the cannibal. "You have the word of Mumber Sull, Thane of Icthyll, that every cent shall be remitted you tenfold by Simbilis. Of course, we do not make our journey utterly without means. Lest you think us paupers."

The Thane had opened his pouch to display the skubbage pieces, and discovered only pebbles in it — indicating that Verdulga had used the same trick on the Thane which was later used on himself by Cugel. Sull looked for his coins and found more pebbles. An anguished cry burst from him.

Sull's outrage was only with difficulty soothed by Cugel who, speaking in urgent low tones, reminded the Thane that the lord stood on hand to console them generously for their losses. Sull expressed anew his appreciation of this courtesy. The cannibal's eyebrows raised and Cugel cut in hastily:

"We are unfamiliar with the exit procedures. When we have been paid we shall require guidance hence."

The cannibal nodded. "I shall see to it. Indeed, you will have many new things to learn in mastering Verdulga's trade. But your reward will be great. We ourselves are few —" and he indicated the door to the dining hall where his compeers sat around the red-lit service "—but we have many primitives to feed."

During this speech, Mumber Sull's jaw had dropped. His eyes became fires of indignation. "Is this then the meaning of these saddlebags of wealth? How dare you insult us with this foul reward! We affirm proudly that we are your minions' destroyers, not their replacements!"

The cannibal lord rose bolt upright from the bins. "*All,* did you say? His officers too? Alas. Such wanton destructiveness threatens our very lives. The primitives increase hourly. If not fed they will turn on us…and you have annihilated our most effective team? What of their shields, their skullcaps? Were these at least saved, that we might re-issue them to a new crew?" The cannibal's stance showed a dangerous tension as he urged this question. Mumber Sull waved a boastful hand.

"All save two we cast in a rushing torrent."

The cannibal emitted a rasping hiss. "You have destroyed us!" With a shout to summon his fellows from the dining hall, he charged upon the Thane and Esquire.

Sull and Cugel both drew their blades. Cugel swung a warding blow which clipped the cannibal's arm neatly from the shoulder.

The lord faltered under the impact, but he bled minimally, a weak brownish fluid. He stooped down, picked up his arm and gripped it by the stump with his remaining hand. The amputated arm made a fist, its muscles stiffened. The cannibal brandished it like a club, and renewed his charge. A dozen more of the cannibal nobility were crowding through the doorway.

Whirling around to seek escape, Cugel spied a door in the wall behind him. Flinging this open, he plunged through. His feet tripped against a sill and he was thrown forward to slide down a long, smooth tube. He landed with a jolt upon soft matting of some kind, under the stars behind a natural screen of rocks. He heard a hiss and turned, too late, as the bony form of Mumber Sull came hurtling down on top of him from the exit-tube. The two of them leaped to their feet and sprang away into the night.

Chapter III

THE GAMBLE-TOLL

A t last the mountains ended. They fell in a cascade of rock-shoulders — jutting out and plunging, jutting and plunging, surging to the desert floor a mile below. Actually the rocks did not reach the desert's edge, for the great chasm Yawrn separated them from the wastes of flinty sand as a moat would separate a castle wall from the surrounding terrain. Seen from the top of the rock cascade, the chasm was a black sickle which hugged to the contour of the mountains' skirts. On its other side the desert stretched beyond vision.

Thane and Esquire could see no terminus to Yawrn's sickle, which simply passed from sight at either end. Cugel pointed to a pale filament which crossed the chasm, seeming from this height little more than a cobweb strand over the huge blackness. "Doubtless the span of ill-report. Yet the dismal gulf affords no discernible alternative, and our way lies thither."

Replying only with a long-suffering sigh, Mumber Sull set off down the rock-shoulder, disregarding his gloomy and immobile Esquire, who remained for a moment above.

"Obscene obstacle," Cugel muttered, brooding on Yawrn. "A lunatic wizard's work. Or perhaps the gratuitous malice of the earth itself." Then he watched the Thane's spiky gray head dwindling below in a magenta gloom trimmed with scarlet. The weak sun westered, an eerie purple fruit cold and overripe. "In all likelihood the senile star will die before our trek's end," Cugel muttered. "Then I must hear this intransigent half-wit's droning summatory remarks regarding existence. A pleasant addition to the miseries of freezing death." The Esquire followed the Thane down into the gloom.

When they stood atop the last shoulder less than half an hour of daylight remained. At the rock's feet twenty yards below was the slate roof of a stone hut built upon the end of the span, and thus affording the only possible access to it.

The span, seen closer at hand and stained a dusky blue by the failing light, conveyed an irresistible thrill of motion to the beholder. It had no rails. It was a simple marble path a yard wide. The chasm's gape was dreadful. Even at the height of noon it still appeared bottomless, much more so now, and it was a quarter-mile across. Yet fearlessly the slim path sprang over it in a low, unerring parabola, a sublime defiance of the abyss.

"Surely such a thing must be of sorcerer's manufacture," growled Cugel in self-corroboration.

The hut's door was iron, and it boomed with Cugel's knock. The door was drawn ponderously inward, and a bent old man in a dirty homespun smock stepped into view and surveyed them blankly.

"Who will execute his toll first?" he asked without apparent interest. "The second must wait his turn outside."

Two weeks of perilous and exhausting flight from Cannibal Keep had greatly indisposed the Thane to compliance. At this he bridled, crying, "Most emphatically not! Thane and Esquire are rank-united! Though one is vassal, each completes the other's dignity. We will most certainly not separate, whatever other grotesqueries you may compel us to as toll."

The old man studied Sull dispassionately, gauging the fiber of his intransigence. Then he said, "Mark me. Your obstinacy can be acceded to, but to the increase of your risk alone. The protocol insures an even justice, but once the protocol is forgone all guarantee of justice is voided. Be taken singly and be awarded what you merit. Be taken together and risk sharing a reward which only one has earned."

Mumber Sull gave his head a mulish shake. The old man shrugged and admitted them both. Once inside he touched a rune carved in the door's iron, and the portal crashed resoundingly shut. The old man informed the pair:

"This door is now sealed by a compulsion impervious to every known assault. That door —" he pointed across the room to the chasm-ward wall and indicated another door of iron, this one squat, cross-braced, and studded with rivets "— opens on the span. I control it at a distance through my person. Now to our business. The toll, without whose payment no one has ever crossed this span, is a game of cards."

In saying this the old man indicated one of the two salient features of the large, square and otherwise empty room: a massive card-table and benches, made of iron and wood.

The room's second and only other feature was a chaotic dump of gear heaped roof-high at the other side of the floor. While the elements of this swag-heap were wildly heterogeneous, and included many poor and ragged things like cloaks, staves, worn footwear and battered hats, it nevertheless featured many tantalizing things as well. Fat pouches disgorging coins and trinkets peeped from amid the tangle, while costly stuffs and vials of essences were also evident. Gazing on this, Cugel's eyes swam with confused avidity.

"As your associate has already noted," the old man went on, addressing the Thane. "I possess a considerable accumulation of articles. All of them were won in play by me from tollpayers such as yourselves. From this you will correctly infer that I am a master card-strew, and am nearly undefeatable. But play me you must."

"I take it that we must stake some of our possessions on whatever absurd game of chance it is that you compel us to?"

"The game is glifrig, the northern variation also called classic glifrig. The deck is that standardized by Bantrub the Cuckold, last autarch of the dynasty of the Falling Wall. As for your possessions, you are required to play them to the last one."

At this Cugel added his voice to the Thane's indignant remonstrations. The old man silenced both with a preventing palm. "These are the stipulations," he said. "You are required to play me, separately of course, and to stake as your units of wager the articles in your possession, down to the last particular. As for what I shall stake in the game — it is this amulet."

The toll-taker drew from his tunic a chain which circled his neck, and from which dangled a jewel, a pendant drop of yellow fire. It was exquisitely faceted, and it was set in a crenellated collar of massive gold that was engraved with glyphs.

At the sight of this brilliant, Cugel's manner grew thoughtful, and even the Thane abated somewhat his outrage. Distrustfully he asked the old man:

"You claim that this gem may be won by us should the cards decree it?"

The tolltaker shook his head. "On the contrary, I believe it is extremely unlikely that you will win the pendant. I am a player of phenomenal skill. Still, the possibility must be acknowledged."

"Perhaps equally to the point," Cugel now interjected, "is the question whether the jewel, if it should somehow be won by one of us, will be allowed to pass with us from this...toll-room."

"All victories are honored according to the protocol. Be you winner or loser, the span door will be opened to you," the toll-taker gravely affirmed. "Which of you will play first?"

"I shall," said the Thane, "and I cannot help but feel that whatever be your boasts, the cards will favor blameless merit over crass extortion." With a certain scornful bravado the Thane, who considered himself something of a threat at glifrig, sat down to the table. The old man seated himself opposite and dealt out the numerous glifrig deck on the tabletop of polished beams hasped and studded with black iron.

The game-rule stipulated that while the toll-taker risked losing both gem and game in an opening-hand defeat, he was to have this compensation: in the event of a long and vicissitudinous game he had the right to force his opponents to win back their own lost bets before they got another chance at the gem.

In fact, these niceties proved wholly superfluous in the game which ensued between Mumber Sull and the toll-taker. The old man won every hand, and moreover he accomplished this with a brisk efficiency which the Thane found intensely annoying.

As his nakedness increased and spread, Mumber Sull's body and face stiffened in a posture of frigid dignity. He glared at his cards with a smoldering bale which was nonetheless not hot enough to rouse them from their persistent futility. Finally, with the loss of his short-breech, he slammed his cards face-down on the table, with a snarl cursing them and their ilk, then and forever, so long as the sun should linger.

"You are surely aware," interposed the toll-taker with disinterest, "that your abjurations are premature."

"No more remains to me that you might plunder," Sull growled.

"And yet I notice a silver ring in your left ear, the one which is deformed."

Sull's jaw clenched. "Here your slavering concupiscence must be denied," he said. "The ring is a token of rank and family, hence hereditary and commingled essentially with my blood, hence integral to my corporal part. You might with equal justice demand that I wager my liver on your luckless cards."

The toll-taker replied coolly. "You are free, of course, to quit the game and return by the route that brought you, but without wagering your earring, you will never cross the span."

Sull answered him with an obstinate glare. The old man shuffled the cards idly. Cugel was anxious at the approach of night, and convinced of the futility of violence against the old man inasmuch as it would leave them imprisoned. The Esquire murmured to Sull:

"Surely, renowned Thane, a trifle is in question. Simbilis' heirloom is the earlobe itself, whose dread significance no mere gaud could augment or diminish."

"I will not submit to this crass despoliation of my badge of office."

"Judicious Thane," said Cugel, near exasperation, "this attitude is ill-advised. Consider the imminence of night. Consider the creatures we know to inhabit those passes we have so nearly left behind us now — creatures whom your obduracy will compel us to rejoin."

"The ring becomes me."

"Weigh priorities!" Cugel hissed. With a snarl Mumber Sull anted the earring. It was played and lost.

Cugel now took the seat opposite the old man. The latter, eyeing Cugel appraisingly, turned and said to Mumber Sull:

"The articles of my post oblige me to make clear that you are at this juncture free to leave. Thus the two of you would run no risk of sharing a reward which only one of you has earned."

The Thane replied coldly, "I will await my Esquire's divestiture."

With haughty care he lowered his skinny shivering body to a seat on the swag-heap.

The toll-taker made a movement Cugel was too late to catch, and the squat span door swung open. Without, a fraction of the pale shaft could be seen springing out into the gathering night. "Do you finally and absolutely refuse to accept the passage offered you?" asked the old man of the Thane. Mumber Sull ignored him.

The toll-taker shrugged. "Then the chance is gone."

Again Cugel missed the movement causing the door to shut. He asked the toll-taker: "What is this confusion of rewards which you mention now for the second time? If I lose, the Thane and I share nakedness, which is to say, nothing. If I win, how can the Thane be said to share in a reward which would clearly belong to myself alone?" Mumber Sull winced at this, but did not break his contemptuous silence.

The toll-taker replied to Cugel: "The pendant, in addition to its physical perfections, has a certain thaumaturgic potency. In the event of your winning it, the nature of its working will be taught you. The Thane, of course, must necessarily learn the secret too."

Cugel glanced hopefully at the Thane. "Perhaps lord Sull would, in that event, consent to seal his eyes and ears." Mumber Sull did not respond. Cugel expressed resignation. "In any case, let us now play, since play we must."

The toll-taker and Esquire addressed themselves to the game, at which Cugel proved considerably more adept than Mumber Sull. Once again the old man won consistently, but with somewhat less briskness and aplomb than he had shown with the Thane. The hands lasted longer, and the toll-taker had to revise his combinations repeatedly to counter Cugel's own skillfully arranged patterns.

Still, the old man won the Esquire's cloak, doublet, and cap in three successive victories. As the toll-taker shuffled the cards for the fourth hand Cugel, whose losses had not visibly disturbed his equanimity, said casually:

"Our game so far bears out your claim to invincibility. Clearly I shall never possess the jewel. For idle curiosity's sake then could you venture an estimate of its value?"

The toll-taker shrugged and shook his head. Cugel played for some moments in silence. At length, despite the old man's stony manner and unmistakable unwillingness to pursue the topic, the Esquire was moved to speak again:

"A question arises which I cannot forbear seeking to resolve. Is the amulet replaceable? Its excellence argues against its being so, but if it is not I must conclude that you have never lost it to an opponent."

"I have on occasion lost it," the old man replied ungraciously. "The protocol, carefully arranged as it is by another whose servant I am, provides for the amulet's replacement." He fell silent with a scowl that clearly ended the matter, and Cugel, who could not help feeling dissatisfied with this reply, had nonetheless to content himself with it. The intricacies of glifrig soon engrossed his complete attention once more.

The Esquire lost the fourth hand as he had the previous three, but the toll-taker's victory was his hardest-won so far. Cugel played with increasing heat and animation, and the old man's powers of concentration were clearly taxed by the Esquire's strenuous opposition.

During the fifth hand Cugel's animation grew even more marked. He debated points of procedure with great volubility, and squirmed in his seat. He seemed literally to itch with excitement, and scratched repeatedly at the bosom and sleeves of his shirt. This fifth hand marked a turning-point in the game for, amazingly, after lengthy play, Cugel won the hand.

And he proceeded to win every hand thereafter. This was due largely to the surprising occurrence of disaster cards in the toll-taker's hands, which were now dealt by Cugel, to whom the deal had passed in the fifth hand. A veritable rash of these disaster cards broke out in the old man's combinations. Some of them, such as the seven of Were-wurns or the aleph of Tarantulurks, were sufficient in themselves to vitiate the toll-taker's hand, yet he always received several others in addition. It was truly a largess of bad luck.

As for the triumphant Esquire, he was in short order again fully clad, and the amulet itself rode on the issue of the next hand. The Thane, drawn from his brooding by Cugel's victories, now gazed on with astonishment.

"Your good fortune is phenomenal, Esquire," he cried.

"Of course you may be forgiven for a proficiency in gaming which would not be seemly in myself. But now you must scorn this glittering bauble and play to repair the deficiencies in my dress."

"Peace!" snapped the old man, his eyes remaining fixed on Cugel. "This he may not do. The amulet must be played."

Cugel shrugged helplessly to Mumber Sull, and dealt the cards. The toll-taker's hand was a tragedy, perfectly crowded with Disasters and Malignities. Cugel addressed him cordially.

"Be assured that I will cherish the brilliant with an ever lively appreciation that is innocent of crass cupidity." He extended his hand for the pendant. The old man bowed his head.

"A formality," he said. "The protocol requires that your hand divest me of it."

"With your permission then." Cugel lifted it from the toll-taker's shoulders. He dangled the jewel before the lamp and leaned closed to see the flame — myriad, fugitive — within the yellow teardrop.

A violent spasm shook the old man in his chair. The shoulders and bosom of his smock rent loudly. Cugel and Sull gaped. Standing before them in the old man's place was a bull grue, nine feet tall, wearing a grin packed with fangs. The creature addressed Mumber Sull.

"Regrettably, dear Thane, you must now share the reward which only your Esquire's conduct has merited. Having been revealed to you, I cannot let you leave. The most I can do is to delay your fate for as long as it takes me to attend to your Esquire's."

"Surely," cried Cugel, "you will not let resentment of my recent good fortune persuade you to a mean vengefulness?"

"I hardly need to point out," the grue returned, "that your game was a series of flagrant cheats. Repeatedly you augmented the deck to your own advantage."

Cugel displayed injury. "Even if I lacked that probity which makes me incapable of the act you describe, my distinguished rank of Esquire to Thane Sull would remain forever incompatible with such peccancies."

This moved Mumber Sull, who had stared on scowlingly, to announce: "This is my judgment. You, sir, commit a gross presumption in preempting my Esquire, for whatever purposes, omitting even the most perfunctory consultation of my wishes."

The grue disregarded him and said to Cugel, "Friend Esquire, the mere fact of your victory is absolute proof of duplicity. My own game is a perfect web of stratagems, and the deck is rigged. These are obstacles which only further tampering with the deck can overcome. My defeats are infallible indications of trickery in my opponent. It is deceivers of your ilk, detected in this manner, who form my sole diet — with unavoidable exceptions," the creature added, with a bow in the Thane's direction.

Cugel blanched. "This seems an elaborately particular penchant," he croaked.

"My personal tastes are not so fastidious," admitted the grue. "I am bound by the articles of a post to which a wizard, now long-dead, enjoined me. Over the centuries his compulsion, which also secures my vitality, has not diminished. I continue to execute the will of Hawthil and to punish the vice he abhorred."

"I must repeat that any molestation of my Esquire constitutes a direct insult to myself," Mumber Sull warned with increased emphasis.

The grue shrugged.

Cugel burst out: "You assured me that win or lose, the span door would be opened to me."

"Forgive me. I should have said, 'to what remains of you.'"

"But it is madness to serve the gratuitous malice of a will long-dead!"

"Not wholly gratuitous," the grue demurred. "Hawthil was motivated by the death of his youngest son who was despoiled and foully slain in a sharper's den, whither the young profligate habitually repaired to squander the stipend settled on him by his too-fond father. Granted, Hawthil's reaction — the creature of chasm and span, the capture and forcible investiture of myself — might be called extravagant. Despite this, the wizard's arrangements display a rare aptness, and nicety of conception. The honest traveler is encouraged to abhor gaming, which strips him of his substance. The cozener is seduced by greed to self-incrimination, and systematically exterminated. Moreover, the sharper is made to despoil me with his own hand. Thus he releases my pent form, and triggers his doom, with a gesture symbolic of the crime he expiates."

Mumber Sull, considering this, nodded judiciously. "Indeed, the conception is decidedly elegant. Its only flaw would seem to be the protracted periods of hunger to which it condemns yourself."

"On the contrary, for the greater part of my indenture I have known almost unvarying satiety. It is true, however, that of late I have suffered famine due to a freakish increase in the depredations of the mountain cannibals." The grue's gaze, fixed on Cugel, took on a musing look. An unpleasant ripple went through the creature's frame. The muscular concentrations at its shoulders, calves, and great three-toed feet, were like clotted tar and threatened vast strength.

Cugel made a disarming gesture, signifying that he now abandoned pretense. "How rightly it is said, that justice must be as various as men themselves! My own case affords convenient illustration. I have from my cradle detested the greedy subterfuges of sharpers and thimblerigs. While yet a lad I made a vow that I would master these illicit skills myself, and live only to out-dupe and —"

"Your motives, though lofty, are irrelevant. The protocol compels me to an unambiguous course of action." The thought of this course restored the dreamy quality to the grue's gaze. Its tongue, an iridescent blue, slicked across the black lips brimming with fangs. Languidly, the grue took a step toward Cugel.

The Thane blinked at this and scowled. "Is it possible you persist in your designs on my Esquire?" he asked.

The grue, heedless, took another step toward Cugel. Mumber Sull's eyes popped with rage, and Cugel's hindquarters encountered the wall. With a desperate gesture the Esquire drew his sword.

"I cannot overstress," he said, "my unconditional retraction of all claim to the gem. That I surrender it and betake myself from the premises with maximum dispatch seems to me a perfectly reasonable demand."

A second shudder of lustful anticipation went through the grue's coal-black musculature. Mumber Sull in the meantime had reached the limits of self-mastery. He rasped:

"Toll-warden! Imbecile! I demand your attention! You will cease to menace my vassal!"

The Thane was again disregarded by the grue, which advanced another step, pausing just out of sword-thrust from the trapped Esquire. It crouched and tensed for the assault.

At this, Mumber Sull reached furiously to draw his sword. This led him to a rediscovery of his nakedness which brought his wrath to an exquisite pitch. Transported, strangely buoyant, Sull advanced on the grue with spastically clutching hands.

At the same time Cugel, feeling the grue's onslaught at hand, shouted hoarsely, "I reject it utterly!" flinging the amulet from him and grasping his sword-hilt with both hands to meet the impending onslaught.

The amulet, its chain flung out in a perfect ring, spun straight toward the apoplectic face of the advancing Thane, who ducked belatedly. The ring of chain dropped neatly around the Thane's neck, and the jewel raced through one quick orbit and hung at his back. The grue roared, and sprang on Cugel.

Cugel drove his sword-point squarely against the grue's breastbone, which proved impenetrable. The grue ignored the blade and strained to reach Cugel's head with its claws, causing the sword to bend in an ever sharper bow. Cugel, arms aching, felt the sword about to snap in two. Then with a violent jolt it sprang out straight again. Cugel blinked. Uncomprehendingly he stared at the far side of the room where, after a brisk trajectory and a thunderous boom against the wall, the grue was assuming a relaxed supine attitude on the floor.

Almost before the grue's bulk had settled, its assailant was upon it again. This latter, Cugel saw with amazement, was a great banded hoon.

The hoon presented the grue with a series of blows from its huge rat's tail. A glitter caught Cugel's eye: the recently jettisoned amulet was hanging half sunk in the dense striped mane that covered the hoon's skull, shoulders, and spine. Abruptly enlightened, Cugel stood considering frantically.

Darting furtively to the booty-heap, the Esquire scrabbled until he uncovered a long-hafted stave with a metal crook at one end. With this he advanced to hover at the fringe of the combat, alert for his chance.

The combat was one-sided. The hoon lacked the grue's height and mass, but like all of its kind was subject to fits of choler which not even the largest erb would willingly confront. The spleen vented by this particular hoon was spectacular. After exercising its tail as a bludgeon, the hyena-snouted beast threw a bight of it around the grue's head which, thus gripped, the hoon proceeded to hammer against the floor.

Cugel, noting the black giant's baffled but undamaged state, realized that it was too durable to destroy. It would revive when the hoon's fury was spent. The only safety lay in flight. The Esquire scanned the grue's body for a clue to the working of the span door. At length he detected a glitter in one of the black palms. Alerted, he caught its twinkle a second time. It was a small silver stud inset in the flesh. If this was the control for the door, it only remained to wait.

Timing was the ticklish factor. The hoon was now demolishing the massive card-table against the grue's face, but without noticeable detriment to its satanic features. To end the hoon's attack before the larger beast had been at least briefly immobilized would clearly be fatal. To wait till the hoon became bored and its attention wandered could be equally so.

When it seemed that the blinking of the grue's eyes, previously rapid, was growing slower under the constant punishment, the Esquire hefted his crook and gauged distances.

The hoon had just burst the second bench on the grue's cranium when, thrusting out his hook, Cugel snagged the chain of the amulet out of the hoon's mane, and yanked mightily.

Although Cugel had acted with flawless coordination, the hoon's reactions were so hysterically swift that it turned, saw Cugel, and was upon him before the amulet's sundered chain had had time to slip from the creature's shoulders. Borne on one smooth surge of the hoon's superabundant energy, Cugel was lifted and rammed head and shoulders against a ceiling beam.

Through a swarm of blossoming green stars Cugel gaped numbly down into the hyena-snouted face. The face brought him nearer, preparing a second thrust. Suddenly the hoon seemed to diminish, and then it collapsed beneath Cugel's limp weight.

Fighting free of Mumber Sull's tangled limbs, for the transformation had left the Thane dazed, Cugel looked to the grue which, though it answered his gaze, made no move. Seizing the staff, Cugel jammed its butt against the silver stud in the grue's open palm. The span door gaped noiselessly open.

Scanning the floor, Cugel spied the amulet and plunged it in his belt. As to the Thane, it seemed clear to the Esquire that a company of two had more hope of survival in the wastes to the west, and there it was equally clear he must go. Retrieving Sull's gear from the swag-pile, Cugel's eye lingered wistfully on the riot of goods. A glance at the grue, whose eyes followed him more alertly already, ended Cugel's indecision.

The Thane could not be roused, so Cugel hauled the bony form up, dumped it across his shoulder, and fled through the portal out across the slender span.

Yawrn's Gape was a gulf of winds, seething with shrill cold gusts and fierce cold updrafts. Fathomless currents of air raised the Esquire's hair from his scalp, and Yawrn's gigantic blackness surged up beneath him threatening to topple his senses.

Thanks to Mumber Sull's relative lightness, Cugel managed a quick pace. He compelled his feet to move swiftly, for if he lost his momentum the abyss would surely overwhelm him and he would fall. He trained his eyes on a point of the marble path a fixed distance ahead, for to yield to the intense urge to watch his feet could likewise prove fatal.

And as he hastened across the marble beam, it seemed to the Esquire that the stone was luminous. It almost seemed not to be stone at all but a shaft of light on which he ran, light pulsing over the great blackness.

At the span's far end, at the edge of the flinty barrens sprawling to the west, Cugel was confronted by a plaque bearing this inscription:

> *Though now you face a cheerless waste*
> *You are alive to see at least,*
> *Your blood pounds, you can hear, and taste,*
> *You're free to dance till the sun's decease*
> *If dance you will.*
>
> *You've thus won more than one before*
> *Whom cardsharps stabbed in a den of lies*
> *And robbed of what is not restored —*
> *From him they took heart, ears, and eyes.*
> *Thus have I wrought to publicize*
> *That cards work ill.*

Cugel swore, spat, then turned and rushed into the desert, the still inert Thane on his shoulder.

Chapter IV

THE EXORCISM

Ah that night, the next day, and the following night, Thane and Esquire marched, resting only briefly, determined to put the flint wastes behind them. For though the sun was too enfeebled to make this the scorching desert it must once have been, it remained totally waterless. Dehydration was at first slow, but Sull and Cugel soon felt its inexorable acceleration, and they toiled doggedly, hoping to outrun it. The road at least, though it often shrank to less than a path, remained always clear and unmistakable.

At the end of the second night they reached the waste's edge. Before them they saw that the plain ended. Beyond it a purplish full moon, rapidly westering, sketchily lit the peaks and saliences of a wholly different terrain, one whose jagged and crazily upsurging silhouette rose abruptly at the desert's rim. Sull and Cugel pressed toward this sight with a hopeful haste. They stirred their blackened tongues to croak encouraging predictions of water and food, each bracing thus the other's flagging tread.

Another quarter hour's march brought them to the brink of the spectacular rocky badlands. Hesitating before stepping into their darkness, the travelers looked back the way they had come. The sun's rim at that moment inched above the distant mountains, the mountains of Cannibal Keep. Shafts of the old star's smoky copper light thrust searching into the badlands' crazy shadows. The travelers, goaded by their need to find water, resumed their westward road, and entered those shadows themselves.

Under the rising day the new wilderness lost most of its gloom. And yet even in the rosy bronze light of morning the wild rocky landscape awed Thane and Esquire as they walked through it. It was a universe, a tempest of rock — huge fractured slabs of rock all endlessly askew, heaped, tilted, jutting. Certain of the great stones strongly suggested shaggy behemoths, for they were heavily overgrown with what seemed to be a lichen.

This lichen was the only element which softened the harsh predominance of naked stone in the landscape, for indeed soil or earth of any kind were totally absent from the terrain. Water there was, in frequent fast-rushing gills where the travelers drank deep and long, but simple loam there was none. On entering this bizarre region, the road had ceased to be a dirt path and had become an ample thoroughfare made all of masonry.

This highway was truly remarkable for, lacking an earthen bed, even its supports were masonry. A series of pillars, beams, and arches, all skillfully wrought of cut stone, lifted it above the jagged maze. Moreover, while the highway conformed as lithely as a silk ribbon to the region's violent topography, its pavement of unmortared hexagonal flags remained flawlessly smooth through its giddiest sweeps and curves.

"Such a work as this road suggests a flourishing city, one that is perhaps not far distant," Cugel at length observed. He and the Thane proceeded leisurely. They had rested a considerable period at the stream where they had refreshed themselves and, though it was full daylight, they had not progressed far on the new road.

Mumber Sull nodded. "So it would seem. Yet it is hard to imagine how any habitation could be built or any livelihood be won in so forbidding a place."

The jumble of great slabs, jutting like the prows of a cyclopean fleet on turbulent seas, seemed to affirm the Thane's doubts. Yet they had walked less than fifty paces farther when a bend in the road brought an answer, at least to the second of the Thane's perplexities.

For ahead, standing on the steep flank of a slab that thrust itself up beside the road, was a herdsman. This was obvious from the man's staff, leathern pouch and flute, as well as from the flock of small blue creatures grazing on the lichen that grew ankle-deep on the rock.

Sull and Cugel saw as they drew nearer that these blue creatures — about the size of cats — lacked discernible form due to the length of their coats. They appeared as small blue mops which moved frenetically on their dun-colored pasture.

But the herdsman did not passively abide the pair's approach. On first sighting them he had started visibly and then, with apparent agitation, had left his flock, descending the slope and jumping down to the road. Here he stood to confront Sull and Cugel, looking perplexedly from one to the other.

"It is not possible that you come from the trackless north," the man suddenly mused aloud. "Nothing less than an army could cross the spider swamps. Yet it is no more thinkable that you have come from the south, where the vegetation wars still rage."

Cugel smiled. "Then trouble yourself no further, for we present neither paradox. We come from the east, over the cannibals' mountains and across Yawrn's span."

At this the herdsman doffed his cap and performed a meek obeisance. "Even as reason bade me conclude, exalted ones, hard though it was to credit. Please accept my pledge of service and rely on my unflagging devotion."

Mumber Sull, after initial surprise, signified lordly approval of the swain's attitude, and looked on him with a benevolent though still faintly mystified eye. Cugel, for his part, regarded the herdsman with new alertness. A trifle warily, he said:

"You guess our exalted identities, then?"

The herdsman shook his head. "Your identities, no. Only your power. The inference is simple. You, the first in Waddlawg's memory, have come clothed from the span. Therefore, since you have defeated wizardry, you must wield it. That wizardry is practiced by the toll-ward is not doubted by the Major Densities of Waddlawg. Every despoiled victim of the gamble-toll, in his babblings on the gibbet, describes the same uncanny card-play, the same disappearances of companions. These reports are deemed reliable, for in Waddlawg it is said, 'Truth from the gibbet.'"

Mumber Sull stared aghast. "Do you tell us that those who come to your city denuded by the cardsharp's wiles are put on the gibbet?"

"They are because they must be," replied the herdsman with a bow. "You must consider, Revered One, that by entering our city naked, these wayfarers commit carnality, a capital offense than which only one other is more grave. I readily confess that I myself do not view such nudity so sternly. Nor do most of Waddlawg's general citizenry. But it is the Major Densities who wield the law."

Cugel rubbed his hands briskly. "Ah well. Those as far-traveled as ourselves view ethnic peculiarities with detachment. While your governors strike us as overly austere in temperament, we foresee no obstacle to bar us from accepting their hospitality. We feel sure it will be lavish. If you wish to earn our gratitude —"

"Indeed, I would treasure any token of your gratitude, Exalteds," the swain fervently cringed. "Especially if it took the form of a death in agony visited upon a neighbor of mine…To earn this token I yearn to do your bidding."

"Then haste ahead — is Waddlawg far?"

"An hour's walk, Potency."

"Haste on then," Cugel said, "and make our coming known. Inform the Densities of the mighty sorcerers who approach. Convey both our benevolent greetings and our requirements in the way of spacious lodgings and sumptuous refreshments."

In the course of the Esquire's directives, Mumber Sull blinked uncomprehendingly. "What imposture is this?" he berated Cugel. Turning to the swain, he barked, "You shall do none of the things he has ordered you."

"Indeed, under normal conditions, I would certainly not," vowed the herdsman. Sull and Cugel, both startled by this deviation from complete obsequiousness, asked in unison:

"Why not?"

"Because, Potencies, sorcery is the sole crime graver than carnality. Were matters as usual, your august selves, upon entering Waddlawg, would be given one half hour to leave it again. Beyond that period your presence in Waddlawg would be punishable by a venomed gibbet much more elaborate than that allotted to carnals. The Densities abhor magic (another attitude neither I nor my peers share) yet they possess certain paralyzing talismans which have proven most effective in binding delinquent wizards for their execution. But as it happens the feelings of the Densities seem lately to have changed. They actually entertain one sorcerer in the city's first inn; it is rumored they have even contracted his services. They have made public their desire that any other wizards met with should be brought to them. Their motives are much speculated on, but as yet unguessed by the commonalty. Thus, commending myself to your grateful memory, I will run before you and announce you."

With a gesture of his staff the herdsman had called his flock down to the road and set them running before him. The creatures ran at a mincing gallop of great swiftness and the herdsman, jogging behind, was out of hearing in a moment and out of sight in another.

Mumber Sull looked sternly at Cugel. "I take in ill part, Esquire, the false character in which you have presented us. Such masquerading implies a scant esteem for my actual rank and identity."

"Esteemed Thane, be advised to broader views. Your eminence, and renown of peerless Icthyll, may be but scantly known in these uncouth climes. Why should we shun a reputation for power if such is thrown in our way? How much better this than to enter Waddlawg as anonymous vagabonds! It is truly said, 'The stranger is guilty sooner than the citizen,' and also, 'The pilgrim walks in danger's way.' We must not forget that 'He who goes feared goes in honor and safety.'"

"Your abundant maxims do not remove the odium of deception from your actions."

"I protest, worthy lord, that I perpetrated no falsehood. I permitted the churl to persist in his delusion regarding our powers. If the governors of Waddlawg should receive us on similar terms, what harm in permitting their delusion as well? Consider we are penniless." Cugel surreptitiously tested his pouch as he said this. "It means the difference between sleeping in silken sheets and sleeping in an alley."

The Thane shook his head doggedly. "To refrain from correcting a misconception is as much as to lie outright."

Cugel evinced dismay at his lord's intransigence. He replied more fervently. "Consider what must be called the blind arrogance that underlies your scruple. Can anyone presume to rectify the delusions of another? Is this not the acme of futility? In this age of darkness and dying turmoil even the loftiest minds are snarled skeins of dogma, error, and hallucination. Can we have the temerity to pose as error's censors?"

The Thane was silent, his gauntness and haggardness the equal of Cugel's, his hunger as extreme. The Esquire pressed his advantage:

"Further, lofty Thane, it is unthinkable we should omit any measures that would further our quest for Simbilis. As anonymous travelers we would have to rely on wine-shop gossip for our directions, and we would set on our way ill-provisioned for the march. As potent wizards, however, we would have access to official archives, and could expect to continue our trek amply provided with transport, supplies, even armed retainers."

The Thane was sorely moved by the picture his Esquire painted. As they walked on their way Cugel outlined a compromise to which, in the end, Mumber Sull grudgingly assented. The Thane would remain completely silent, adopting a posture of moral abstention. Cugel would be left to manage the town's governors as best he might, provided he spoke nothing but the strict and literal truth. Should he lie or other-wise embroider, the Thane reserved the option of speaking out and exposing the pretense. As for any delusions about the pair themselves found to be current among the Waddlawgians already, Mumber Sull agreed to refrain from correcting them. What was done was done.

With this arrangement made, the pair soon topped a rise — the road's last sharp ascent before it swept down to the valley of Waddlawg. From this eminence they viewed the city itself.

The great depression in which the city was situated was not in truth a valley, but rather a freak in the region's bizarre topography. In the uni-versal maze where slabs lay lawlessly in every possible plane, and where perhaps only the horizontal element was rare — in the midst of this an epidemic of horizontality had broken out. A patch of several hundreds of the great slabs lay in an ill-knit jigsaw that created a huge irregular plaza of crude paving.

The outline of this sunken plaza was teardrop-shaped, and it was clearly marked, for the wild native landscape crowded right to the perimeter of the level area, hemming it all around with a sudden jagged wall as high as fifty feet. The road ahead could be seen to enter the city by a gate in the 'bulge' of the drop, while another road could be made out where it passed from the city, westbound, through the 'point' of the teardrop. This western gate, even though viewed across the entire long axis of the valley, appeared a much more ornate and important one than that by which they were to enter.

From where they stood, Sull and Cugel could see that the great horizontal slabs were more like islands than flagstones. Waterways glittered in the wide irregular interstices between the slabs. Each of these latter was crowned with elaborate stone structures up to eight stories high, but since slabs varied considerably in their individual elevations, the city as a whole had a fluctuating aspect. The panorama of gray slate rooftops peaked and sank, Waddlawg seeming to bob enmeshed in the silver glitter of its tangled canals.

"The city seems indeed to thrive," said Cugel. "Note the gondolas threading the waterways. And the bridges connecting the islands can be seen to throng."

Mumber Sull, already practicing moral abstention, responded with silence, and the pair turned their steps downhill to the city's western gate.

This portal, evidently a minor one and little frequented, was flanked by two stelae, whereon austere glyphs were incised. Standing precisely between these archaeoliths was a committee of Waddlawgians, whose measured nod, as the pair drew near, could be construed as welcoming.

There was, however, nothing welcoming in their faces, which regarded Thane and Esquire with expressions of ill-mastered revulsion. These men were clad in robes of blue clearly woven from the fleece of such animals as the herdsman had had. Their heads were shaven and painted with a pattern of concentric circles, centered on the crown. Their demeanor was stolid and abstemious. Their garb was clearly patrician, readily distinguishable as it was from that of the miscellaneous rabble gathered within the gates. From where he had been relegated in the ranks of these latter, the herdsman could be seen, trying to catch Cugel's attention with mute imploring signals. These Cugel ignored, and confronted the man who seemed the chief of the Waddlawgian delegation.

This was a smallish man whose air of cold rigor surpassed his fellows', and whose skull-target was painted in red pigment rather than the black they used. He spoke.

"Greetings. I am Spurp, head of the Synod of Densities. It is reported that you have defeated the wizardry of the toll-ward of Yawrn. We have come to ascertain if this is so."

Cugel replied with a genial bow. "Most interesting. You have come expressly to ascertain this? Is such a report a matter of importance to you, then? This contradicts what we have heard of your views on necromancy."

Cugel's innocently uttered remark produced a murmur among the populace, and caused Cugel's interlocutor to share a look of apprehension with his fellows.

With a face somewhat reddened, Spurp stiffly replied: "We readily acknowledge a deep repugnance for what we take you to be, that is, sorcerers. Considerations best unspecified at present compel us to entertain relations with you which, if you be in truth magicians, will prove highly profitable to yourselves. But first, is it true you have confounded the sorcery of the toll-ward at Yawrn?"

Cugel glanced at Mumber Sull and replied: "I will be succinct, eschewing vainglorious hyperbole. We encountered the keeper of the span; we unmasked his true nature; we threw him down and passed on in defiance of him. I feel I cannot speak more plainly, and more than this I will not say." Mumber Sull glared and said nothing. Spurp nodded.

"If you will accompany us, you will be lodged and refreshed according to your requirements, and the terms of contract will be laid out more fully."

The Synod of Densities escorted Thane and Esquire into Waddlawg. They came to a halt, however, after only a few steps' progress. The pair confronted a contingent of what were evidently the city's patrician females. Clad in the noble blue, they were women of imposing corpulence. Over their shaven or close-cropped heads they wore tight leather skull-socks. Their gazes were as imperturbable as the men's.

This rank of massive figures, upon confrontation with the Thane and Esquire, gave in unison an acknowledgment, the faintest of nods. Sull and Cugel responded politely, whereon the huge ladies ceased to notice them.

"Thus you have been thanked by the Matron Densities of Waddlawg," Spurp advised them, ushering them once more on their way. "Your action has put an end, we trust, to the flagrant carnalities that have long plagued our eastern gate and rendered their precincts unwholesome for the Matrons."

The procession, viewed by an alert but subdued populace, wound for some time across the stone islands thronged with elaborate multi-storied walls of masonry. Of the many bridges they crossed, no two were of the same style, all were marvelously conceived. At certain crossings the pair glimpsed gondolas in the canals below, and they noted that the primary cargo of these craft consisted of wire baskets filled with some species of large newt. For what purpose these creatures were thus collected was not evident.

The party arrived at a large inn on one of the central islands of the city. The pair were conducted to a private banquet chamber within the building. In one of the walls of this room was set a window which opened on an inner court, revealing the inn's ground plan to be that of a great hollow square. The chamber's only other salient feature was a lone occupant, a portly figure who sat drinking alone in a corner, his back turned to the wall containing the window. This figure perked up at the pair's entry.

Spurp advanced no more than a few steps into the room, his Synod having remained outside. "The best of lodging and refreshment afforded by the inn is at your disposal. Fortunately the wizard Polderbag is on hand —" Spurp indicated the fat solitary drinker, who smiled ingratiatingly at Sull and Cugel. Spurp continued:

"Polderbag can inform you of the circumstances of your employment, whose recapitulation would be a painful matter for us to undertake. You have all the night to consider. Tomorrow morning, your answer will be asked." Bowing briefly, Spurp vanished.

The man introduced as Polderbag, after solicitously commanding a tableful of meats and beverages for the pair, urbanely ushered them to his table in the corner, there to await their repast's coming.

"I myself would prefer a better lighted table, one by that window perhaps," Cugel said. "Why do you seclude yourself in the gloom of this corner?"

"Precisely to avoid the sight of yon window. It affords a view of the inn's central patio, where several of the Synod's gibbets are located." A glance out the window confirmed this. In two of the engines, fragments of recent tenants remained. Sull and Cugel turned away with a shudder and took seats where the fat man bade them.

"A gloomy reminder of the reward that attends failure to satisfy the Major Densities," Polderbag explained darkly. The wizard livened, however, when the innkeeper appeared with wine-pots, cheese, and loaves in a basket. "No such grim thoughts need detain us, however," he boomed, tearing a loaf. He beamed jovially upon Thane and Esquire, who but half heeded him as they bent to their plates with famished attention. Polderbag looked on benevolently until their hunger was somewhat abated and they were readier to heed him.

"I wish to stress at the outset," he began, "that I warmly hope ours will be a collaborative rather than a competitive relationship. Indeed the task at hand favors such an arrangement. I assure you I greet your arrival with unmixed goodwill."

Cugel regarded Polderbag warily, taking him in for the first time. The wizard had a round white face and black hair whose scalpline was serrated, the hair growing in a neat row of pointed shingles on his brow. This latter was often shiny with the sweat of Polderbag's emotion, for he was an easily agitated man. At present he exuded frankness and amiability, and his corpulence trembled slightly within his coarse pilgrim's robe. His midriff was girt with a belt of plaited thongs, from which petty icons and amulets depended, tied on with twine.

"The cooperation you hope for between us," Cugel asked, "what form does it take?"

"Why, the simplest of alliances — increased strength through a pooling of powers. I do not for an instant imply, of course, that your powers are in need of addition. Indeed —" Polderbag crooked his brow "— no more do I denigrate my own competence, which is as thousands can testify. I mean simply to urge that a united front, a sharing of spells for instance, represents our wisest strategy. The forces which oppose us are not inconsiderable."

"And what forces are these?" Cugel interposed. "Perhaps an explanation of our circumstances and projected duties is in order before questions of alliance are taken up."

Polderbag acquiesced with a stiff nod. "Of course. The services presently expected of me — and of yourselves if you undertake the post — are those of exorcist. Certain of the Matron Densities are afflicted with a night spirit of an obscene nature. The estimable women are possessed in their sleep and toss in raving delirium while under the spirit's power. In their desperation for a cure, the Major Densities have overridden their passionate scruples against sorcerers, and engaged my services."

"Since you touch on these odd scruples which the Densities espouse," Cugel put in, "perhaps you might pause a moment to enlarge on them. How is it that nakedness and sorcery are so abhorred?"

"What you broach is no digression. The Densities' religious tenets are highly apposite to an understanding of Waddlawg and our own situation in it." The fat wizard clearly warmed to this subject, and ceased to attend to the sweet aspic the innkeeper had brought as dessert. Sull and Cugel, nearly sated, took desultory mouthfuls and harkened to Polderbag.

"Though so contrary to my own views," the wizard began, "I find the postulates of the Densities' world-view endlessly fascinating. For them the highest virtues are immobility and concentration. The most perfect states of being are solidity and stasis. Their cosmology provides succinct illustration of these principles.

"They hold that in the beginning, in the center of the world, all was chaotic and disordered rock. The great god Inka Slomb viewed this disorder, and wearied of it. He seated himself to take counsel with his thoughts, and to ponder on order, evenness, and permanence. His great bulk caused the rocks to flatten where he sat, and this was the valley of Waddlawg. The labor of Inka Slomb's great meditation caused sweat to flow from all parts of his body, and this became the waters of Waddlawg's canals.

"This sketch of Waddlawg's mythology is doubtless sufficient to make obvious to you the ethical system flowing from it." The wizard paused, hesitant to insult his hearers' intelligence.

"Substantially, yes," Cugel replied. "Still, a brief commentary on the system would not bore us."

"I am glad. As I have said, the Densities' moral solidity is a topic that diverts me. This despite the fact that the art whose acolyte I am is in its very essence the art of mutation, metamorphosis. Is it any wonder that the Densities regard sorcery as chief among capital offenses? And if the Densities, devoted as they are to Moral Gravity, abhor magic as something fanciful, hallucinatory, and fleeting, it is precisely the same qualities they detest in fleshliness — for so much the term 'carnality' be understood, denoting sensuality as a whole, and not nakedness alone. The Densities' thinking has an admirable consistency. They are also —" Polderbag here paused a moment and glanced about "— sensitive to economic convenience. All those gibbeted for sorcery or carnality are automatically consecrated to the Matron Densities. It is held just that offenders should thus make reparation to the ladies whose piety they have, even if only indirectly, offended."

"In what way could gibbeted corpses be consecrated to the estimable Matrons?" Cugel asked.

"By providing fodder for the Matrons' newt farms."

"Are these newts of the species we saw in baskets in the gondolas?"

"The same. Those you saw had been harvested and were doubtless being ferried to the Matrons' Holy Refectory, where the Matrons sit, mornings and afternoons, at their devotions. It is their diet of sacred newts which enables the Matrons to achieve the massive solidity essential to their religious progress. The creatures' farms are located in the deepest sectors of the central canals. They are amply provendered, for in addition to strangers like ourselves — most of whom come from the west near the Vale of Zoo — capital offenders are frequent among the plebeian orders of Waddlawg itself. The ghastly engines visible from our window are by no means the only gibbets in Waddlawg, and all are well used."

Polderbag was cut short by Mumber Sull who, staring fiercely, his vowed silence forgotten, spoke to the fat wizard for the first time.

"Did you not mention the Vale of Zoo? Can it be you know the whereabouts of this place?"

The question curiously affected the wizard. The eagerness of exposition which had marked his account of Waddlawg deserted him. He replied somberly, "Can I not? Respected colleague, I am a native of Millions' Gather."

"And where is this?" the Thane asked.

Polderbag's eyebrows arched. "You are outlanders indeed, I see. Millions' Gather is a great city built in the north end of the Vale of Zoo. It is the last earthly capital of Simbilis the Sixteenth, before his departure for an uncertain destination."

"Aha!" blazed Mumber Sull. "Do you hear, Esquire? Friend Polderbag, we are not, at least, such outlanders that the name of Simbilis is strange to us! Know, estimable Polderbag, that we are Simbilis' very vassals, and journey even now in search of him." The Thane was radiant. He exuded a benevolent glow of triumph and vindication. "We have not lost the path!" he cried.

Polderbag's eyes betrayed dubiety regarding Sull's competence as he replied. "The path you follow is indeed correct. The Vale of Zoo lies west from Waddlawg a month's trek. But ages have passed since the great sorcerer's departure thence. Millions' Gather is an ancient city. Already it senesces. Yet it was young when Simbilis left."

"Nevertheless," replied Sull, undeterred, "further perseverance can only bring further encouragement. I am convinced of it!"

The effect of the meal and the hopeful news was to set the Thane's spirit at rest. He felt a great drowsiness, and shortly afterward retired. Cugel, his weariness dispelled by wine, lingered at the table with Polderbag as the red light of late noon streamed suggestively through the patio window.

"Your friend's mention of Simbilis put me in mind of matters in the west, and thus in gloomy thoughts," Polderbag confided. "For it is there, in my native city, that the evil I am engaged here to correct originates."

"Indeed?" said Cugel. "How so?"

"Perhaps you know that Simbilis' purpose in coming to the Vale of Zoo was the construction of a highway connecting the surface with the subworlds?"

"Yes, there was some report of this in Grag, whence we have come."

Polderbag nodded. "Simbilis' intention was that further cataclysmic wars should be averted by putting commerce in their place. When he arrived in the Vale of Zoo, he decreed a great convocation of the creatures of the northern world. Their delegations gathered in the valley.

The weirdly hybrid descendants of that epic assemblage still inhabit the vale, and are the source of its name.

"Simbilis told them of the highway he planned, and of the city which he intended would stand at the highway's point of entry. This latter was to be a natural fissure in the rock, called Steep's Jaw. Thus around Steep's Jaw the city of Millions' Gather was built, in the north end of the Vale of Zoo. The highway, descending from Steep's Jaw to the subworlds, was likewise built. The thousands convoked by Simbilis joined in the labor, and stayed on to inhabit the city, and the floor of the valley. Commerce flourished between the lower and the upper worlds.

"But when, long after, Simbilis left Millions' Gather, subworld treachery began to put itself increasingly forth. The highway is now used mainly by demon myrmidons issuing out to do ill, or leading back down chained contingents of men whom their wiles have entrapped and brought into bondage below."

Polderbag paused in his narrative to lean closer to Cugel. "There is also an invisible traffic constantly flowing from Steep's Jaw: ectoplasms, entities whose dispositions range from mischievously obscene to broodingly malign. The constant flow of these creatures is perhaps little noticed in Millions' Gather itself, for the folk there are so given over to sorcery and intrigue, that the ectoplasms do not often choose them for prey. You must realize that such things as succubi, incubi — even the small-fry obscenotrobes, one of whom plagues us here — prefer as their hosts psyches which are more or less virgin, innocent of supernatural lore and thus more hysterical in their reactions to being possessed. So these ectoplasms drift out from Millions' Gather, they spread thence, like a vortex in reverse, in widening rings over the land." Polderbag paused gloomily.

"The creature we would be employed to exorcise — it is a part of this general invasion, then?"

"Yes. In itself it is a minor entity. What I would make clear to you is the magnitude of the phenomenon of which the obscenotrobe is a part. You must be made to appreciate the necessity of an alliance, an exchange of spells. Individually, we are potent. In league, we could banish whole flocks of succubi with the merest gesture."

Cugel remained noncommittal, without, however, disclaiming the identity of a sorcerer. In fact he encouraged this idea in Polderbag in terms that the Thane, if present, would have instantly and indignantly repudiated.

The door of the room was thrust open, and Spurp appeared. The Density's manner, while composed, had a steely edge of strain. He addressed himself to Polderbag alone:

"Your services are once more required. This time the afflicted one is my wife. We had hoped ourselves rid of these manifestations."

Polderbag bowed. "I hinted, revered Density, that as there are many of these pestilent creatures, each might have to be banished in its turn. Hence the necessity of a resident sorcerer."

Spurp replied tersely, "We had expected at least a longer abatement. Attend at once!" The Density stalked from the chamber.

Polderbag made further hurried remonstrations with Cugel, exhorting him to alliance. Finding the Esquire still evasive, Polderbag flew after Spurp. He had still not returned when Cugel retired an hour later.

In the morning, after a large breakfast, Polderbag conducted Sull and Cugel on a stroll about the perimeter of the slab on which the inn stood. They wandered no farther because they awaited the arrival of a deputation of Densities to receive Cugel's answer regarding the proffered post.

Before descending to breakfast the Esquire had spoken with the Thane. He had come expecting resistance, but had found the Thane surprisingly amenable to the acceptance of the post. Newly reassured regarding their destination, Mumber Sull felt a contentment which rather disposed him to just such a recuperative layover as this sinecure (such Cugel assured him it was) promised. The inn's board and bed were excellent. The Thane merely renewed his stipulation that Cugel utter no falsehood, and declared himself content to resume his silent moral abstention.

Polderbag was subdued, even gloomy, when he had appeared at the breakfast table. But he brightened markedly when Cugel told him of their acceptance, and now, as he conducted them along the canal side, he was a voluble and informative guide.

Waddlawg, it seemed, flourished by certain native industries whose products attracted a lively trade from the west. The result was a healthy economy, if, incidentally, a great deal of labor as well for the lower orders.

For the Densities' immobile and contemplative ethos prohibited participation in the rude trades of raising and shearing sopkirttles, or farming canal crops. This latter was a thriving pursuit. The sacred newts were only one of many crops raised. The waterways thronged with gondolas bearing harvests of purple watersalad, or baskets of minced sopkirttles with which to mulch the shellfish beds of the shallower canals.

"That the sopkirttles are used thus," said Polderbag, "is an illustration of the Densities' efficiency and thrift. The little blue creatures produce but a single shearing of silky wool, senescing rapidly and dying a few days thereafter."

When the three returned to the inn they found Spurp and two of his peers awaiting them within.

Cugel ceremoniously stepped forth. "I will be brief. I and my lord do unhesitatingly undertake to place whatever sorcery we possess at your service, providing the emoluments be satisfactory."

Spurp bowed and produced two fat pouches of coins. "Such will be your daily stipend. The inn remains at your disposal. I will conclude by reminding you that delinquency of any description is punishable by the venomed gibbet. Now we bid you good day — you are at leisure until notified of a need for your arts." As he turned to go, Spurp fixed Polderbag with a look. "My wife still sleeps," he murmured.

"The exorcism was taxing," replied Polderbag. "She requires recuperative slumber, perhaps for several hours more." Spurp nodded, then turned away without replying. Cugel noted there was sweat on the wizard's brow, saturating his jagged hairline.

Throughout the morning and afternoon, which the trio passed in the indolent degustation of pickled shellfish, cheese, and wine, Polderbag ate less than the other two, and seemed to be wrestling with an inward dilemma. At last, summoning determination, he motioned his companions to a more confidential proximity.

"What boots proud reticence between colleagues?" he began, attempting suavity. "I require aid — minimal aid, to be sure. Why should I not declare it to you? Would I not heartily welcome such a trifling petition from yourselves? I will speak then, and we can solemnize our alliance by a first act of cooperation. I require a banishing formula. The one I have employed shows diminishing effectiveness."

"The obscenotrobes are too numerous?" Cugel inquired noncommittally.

"There is only one such entity. I was forced to offer Spurp a necessary fiction. The creature at first responded to my compulsions only temporarily, returning each time more rapidly than before. Now it will not be banished at all. It made its fourth reappearance last night, unfortunately choosing Waddlawg's Matron of Foremost Gravity, Grimba Salta, for its host. I could not drive it out. To gain time I secured the woman in a strong narcotic trance. Thus, though still possessed, her ravings and writhings are stilled, and Spurp convinced of his wife's cure. The drug will soon fade, however. In the interval it grants me, I ask your assistance."

Cugel did not reply, and the fat spell-peddler urged, "Be persuaded, alliance is imperative. We must present a united front. Consider the over-growing swarms of ectoplasms which issue from Steep's Jaw. I have described their widening menace."

"You yourself admit that your foe is a solitary and minor presence," Cugel said with irritation. "Why do you insist on spirit hordes? I see no evidence of them here."

"That is so only because of Waddlawg's great insensitivity to ectoplasmic events," said Polderbag. "The Densities' age-old and utter renunciation of fantastic thoughts acts as a positive barrier to the prowling presences, and only stray entities find their way hither. The folk of Waddlawg are innocent of the supernatural, but this very quality, which protects them now, will render them especially appealing to the ectoplasms when the latter discover this city."

The fat man paused, and shuddered. "The situation is chilling to conceive. Here sits this stony city, blind to and thus unseen by the presences with which the upper atmosphere teems. Great schools of succubi and incubi patrol the darkening upper air. They glide over Waddlawg, palping for the scent of active human imaginations on which to feed. Thus far the city has been odorless, undetected, and unvisited. Let me assure you, this has not been the case in other regions."

Polderbag looked now from Sull to Cugel. His voice fell lower. "Examples abound. Consider Juggler, a crossroads village three days to the west. Recently, invaders of sleep cuckolded every man in the town. All of these illicit couplings bore fruit on the same day some weeks subsequent. All the births were bizarre. One woman, a cousin of mine in fact, was brought to bed of a keg of nails which her husband, a carpenter, did not scruple to use. Other deliveries were less to the purpose. For example a spinster of mature years dropped a litter of twenty-seven full-grown black rats. She mothers them still, having doted on them strangely from the first."

Cugel nodded, somewhat impressed. "At least these pranks seem relatively harmless," he ventured.

"Others are less so," Polderbag snapped. "The essential point is that Waddlawg's danger is great, and its shield of innocence is not invincible. Yet if we merely pool our skills to purge such minor infestations as are inevitable, who knows how long, with our maintenance, the city's immunity might not last! An island of safety in an increasingly threatening world — this is what I knew Waddlawg to be before I had been in it ten minutes. I rejoiced when my proffered services as sorcerer-errant were, amazingly, accepted. And I rejoiced rightly! A living of safety and luxury *is* to be had here, only we must act in concert!"

Cugel, feeling hard-pressed for a commitment, studied a reply, but before he could frame it, Major Density Spurp was in the room with a crash of the flung-open door.

"Man-witch," he rasped at Polderbag, "this black obscenity has returned. My wife writhes anew. If her cure is not effectuated now and finally, your obese form will expiate your failure on the venomed gibbet."

Polderbag produced a rictus intended as a smile. "Venerable Spurp, these jocular hyperboles are unnecessary to arouse my zeal —"

"Silence!" Spurp looked at Cugel. "Will you accompany this incompetent?"

Cugel demurred. "We do not collaborate as a rule," he said. Polderbag gasped. Spurp nodded. "Very well," he said, "but you have received

from which the gibbets were visible. Then, snarling at Polderbag to
follow without delay, he left.

Polderbag's agitation was wondrous. Indignation at the Esquire's
stand won uppermost. He hissed at Cugel, "So! Your crass egoism
shuns honorable alliance? Very well. I condescended, but now I retract
the offer. We shall see who prospers best without the other's aid." The
fat magician paced, panting fitfully. His thoughts turned to wrath at the
absent Spurp.

"The insolent mannikin!" Polderbag ranted. "Very well. I have
restrained my full potency out of nicety and discretion, but tonight
a massive spell, one designed for ectoplasms of incubus caliber, will
utterly disintegrate this wretched obscenotrobe that mocks my reputation. And then — *then* I shall adduce a compulsion to transmute every
last one of Spurp's bones into erb manure!" Having thus reached a
climactic state of rage the fat man looked wildly about, seized his cloak,
and rushed out after Spurp.

As soon as they were alone, Cugel turned earnestly to Mumber Sull.
"Far-seeing Thane, ah how right your reservations were regarding this
charade! Would I had heeded your wisdom from the first. But there is
time to mend all. While the Densities wait on Polderbag's last doomed
efforts, we may still abandon this city unnoticed. Night is near. I will
ready certain provisions, and we will trust the darkness to cloak our
departure."

Mumber Sull regarded his Esquire with dignified opprobrium. "Is
all chivalry dead in you?" he asked his Esquire. "As I read our position, we have sworn fealty and service to the Matron Densities, who
seem ladies of unexceptionable accomplishment. What can be more
exciting," he went on, "to a man of nobler mold, than the prospects of
striving on so fair a behalf?"

"I have only applause for these views, Thane. But consider that
we are devoid of even the most trifling necromancy." (Cugel had not
deemed it necessary to tell Mumber Sull that he had retained the toll-
ward's amulet.) "You have yourself stressed," urged the Esquire, "that
our position is a false one. We cannot tilt unarmed with dark powers

- 70 -

and expect to survive. Better to remain true to our original quest, and press forth from this pious, bloodthirsty metropolis!"

"In no case could consideration of the odds we face have the slightest effect on our rendering of service," the Thane warned loftily. "But as it happens, I am not devoid of magic."

Cugel looked at Sull in surprise. Sull closed the topic. "Enough. What services are asked, we shall render as best we may. Meanwhile, we may take some supper."

All through the meal Cugel in gloomy silence revolved his options. The danger was manifest, and to remain longer in Waddlawg was to court it. He might flee alone, leaving the Thane to his inexplicable impulse of doomed gallantry, but his prospects alone on the western road were slim — for there lay his only open course. On the other hand if he remained and they were actually brought to cure the patient Polderbag had failed, they would probably be at liberty to contrive a later escape. Perhaps, securing themselves in the patient's room on the pretext of treating her, they could effect a secret exit thither — Thane Sull would doubtless accede to the project once the futility of a cure were clear.

Unwillingly, Cugel determined to wait. He peered sourly at Mumber Sull, who sat imperturbably munching a cheese, his elongated ear waggling contentedly with his chewing. The Esquire reflected on the indignities to which life's necessities might subject even the most resourceful and cleverest of men.

One thing, at any rate, seemed perfectly clear. The Densities' feelings in this matter were capable of becoming quite hysterical. Impregnation among the Densities, Polderbag had said, was an elaborate affair. The husband, having solemnly collected his seed in a receptacle, introduced it into his wife by means of a ceremonial bellows which he plied to the accompaniment of a ritual mumble he and his wife intoned in unison. So austere a people, Cugel reflected, must greet this lustful spirit's infestation with particular loathing, and their reactions could become proportionately severe.

Some two hours after his departure, Polderbag re-entered the room. His face, frozen in a ghastly counterfeit of calm, was dead white. He advanced with mechanically brisk steps.

"Who could have credited it?" he asked with a jaunty croak. "A contretemps. Quite amusing actually. A droll mispronunciation —" With this word the fat wizard's voice cracked. He collapsed tragically to a seat, where he slumped with a vacant stare, sweating prodigiously. A tremor of fear roused him. He looked around and motioned Sull and Cugel closer. "The entire Synod sits in the lower chamber of Spurp's house in commiserative prayer. I am thought to be obtaining a forgotten implement, necessary to the exorcism. I was sent with guards, who attend me without. Meanwhile, upstairs in Spurp's house, Grimba Salta, his wife, lies beneath —"

The miserable warlock clasped his hands imploringly, but for a moment he could not speak. He only recovered his voice by adopting a much lower tone. "Dear colleagues, I have made a dreadful mistake. I stammered the conjuration. The accursed obscenotrobe is gone, but not by the means I intended. It was devoured — nay, swallowed whole with a single gulp by an entity no less lewd and lascivious than itself, but vastly more formidable. My friends — may I say 'allies'? — I have inadvertently summoned an incubus, and it lies now in possession of Grimba Salta."

"Naturally we profoundly deplore your bleak position," Cugel began, but the Thane cut him off.

"We will gladly add our efforts to yours in an attempt to expel this shocking ectoplasm," he said cordially to Polderbag. "You may lead on. Take heart in the knowledge that I have at my disposal a spell of no negligent potency. And yet there is something that perplexes me."

"What can it be, most magnanimous of wizards?" the fat wizard inquired.

"How is it that the uproar which would naturally ensue from such a possession as the Matron has suffered — I mean to say, how is it the lady's screams did not undeceive the Densities, and prevent your own release from the premises?"

The fat man shook his head. "You touch on an awesome matter," he said. "While the obscenotrobe plagued her sleeping mind she raved and squirmed. But the invasion of so powerful a spirit has wakened her fully. Her will has come into play, and she resists the ectoplasm's first exploratory assaults. She had maintained utter immobility and silence up to the moment I left her. Her intransigence is immense. Nonetheless, even she will soon be overpowered by the presence, and then her outcries will surely alert the Densities downstairs from her."

"Then we must waste no further time," Mumber Sull decided. He roused his unwilling Esquire, and the trio presently fared forth into the streets, the guard closing in around them as they emerged from the inn's front door.

The sun had set. In the brief afterglow, Waddlawg's elaborate and graceful masonry thronged the purple air. The bridges were nearly deserted — isolated couples stood by the rails conversing inaudibly. In the canals, infrequent laggard gondolas towed their spectral red stern-lanterns home. The city's bobbing skyline, the uneven thrust of its rooftops and steeples completed an effect of pervasive fantasy and hallucination wholly out of keeping with its rulers' most fundamental tenets.

After a while Cugel noted that the valley's jagged perimeter could be seen to converge from two sides as the party progressed. Polderbag informed him that Spurp's house lay in the patrician faubourg located in the point of the valley's teardrop, just before the city's western and principal gate.

Spurp's house was impressive for massiveness more than height. It was a two-storied affair whose walls were singularly thick, much more so than considerations of stress demanded. Tapers burned gloomily at either side of the wide, low front door. Moreover, the house seemed of a pattern with every other house visible in the area. The trio passed inside.

When the door — a massive stone slab hinged, framed, and hung in iron — swung to behind them, they found themselves in a vast lamp-lit parlor furnished only with benches around the walls. On these benches, forming a continuous row around the room's perimeter, sat all the Major Densities of the city.

While the Matron Densities sat in the simple squat of meditation, the men, similarly squatted, displayed an additional feature, for they sat with stones of meditation balanced on their skull-targets. These were stone blocks of varying weight, supported by a metal leg which terminated in a circular 'foot'. Polderbag had previously alluded to this ceremonial headgear. Neophytes began with light stones supported by a large 'foot' which would fit that area of the cranium delimited, by the skull-target's outermost ring. Religious progress consisted in the gradual increase of stone size and simultaneous reduction of foot size. The highest adepts, of which Spurp was one, sat with a tenth-magnitude stone on a foot the size of the skull-target's bull's-eye. These men were deemed to experience Ultimate Density and Concentration when they meditated.

The only response the Densities made to the entrance of the guarded trio was an opening of eyes. Polderbag made a haughty bow to Spurp, who eyed them keenly from under his brows.

"The miscreant entity is in our power," said Polderbag. "We act in committee now to choose the most final means of destroying it and preventing the future molestation of its ilk. You shall see the lady delivered in the hour."

Spurp's only answer was to close his eyes again, resuming prayer.

The sorcerers passed up an echoing stairway, and down a drafty high-ceilinged hall. After a pause for courage outside a stone door no whit smaller than that downstairs, Polderbag waved back the guards, and ushered Sull and Cugel inside. Entering himself, he closed the door with a boom behind his back.

They were in a room as high-ceilinged as the hall outside, and almost as bare of furniture. In one corner was a wooden cot. In the center of the room was a table, one of the room's few other furnishings, though it seemed now to have usurped the function for which the cot was intended.

For underneath a gray canvas shroud bulked what could only be the prone figure of the afflicted Matron Grimba Salta — though indeed the bulk was great, even for a lady of Matron's proportions.

Polderbag looked in fascination at the veiled mass, whose drape appeared to be a crude conjurer's canopy amateurishly painted with glyphs. "She is astonishing, inhuman! I had expected at least a whimpering, a tremor, however faint. But nothing! She remains imperturbable!"

Cugel had, on entering, experienced an unpleasant shock on finding the room windowless. Its walls and flooring were all of stone, and it seemed in fact a wholly inescapable cul-de-sac. Thus he took Polderbag's words, with their strong implication of the Matron's inevitable surrender, very gravely. He looked expectantly at the Thane, as in fact did Polderbag.

Mumber Sull was aware of his companions' gaze. He moved a few casual steps nearer the draped figure on the table, and cast an unhurried, judicious eye upon it.

"So. Thus it stands," he murmured. "I cannot help remarking that the matron — I trust she cannot hear us?"

Polderbag blinked. "How could she? Her every thought and ounce of will are bent upon resisting the incubus. She is as if in another world."

"Then I am at liberty to remark that she seems an extraordinarily large woman, even by Waddlawg standards."

The fat wizard shuddered. "You fail to understand. Half that bulk, the upper half, is not her own."

Mumber Sull looked with new comprehension at the table, and shuddered in his turn. Then his sense of outrage was awakened, and he drew himself up to his full, gangly height.

"Ectoplasm or no, this creature's gross presumption cannot continue!" The Thane stepped forward.

Cugel had watched Sull intently, resisting a dismal conviction that the Thane in fact possessed no spell that could save them. Now, when Mumber Sull advanced on the table, Cugel was filled with alarm that he *had* a spell, and was about to wield it with his characteristic impetuosity.

"Hold, sire!" he cried, springing forth to detain Sull. "Stay a moment! I must ask what agency it is that you command. We dare not continue the haphazard invocation of ectoplasms."

Sull looked at his Esquire with disapproval, and replied stiffly, "It is a Thane-wield, a hereditary command of a servitor spirit whom I shall order to eject the foul incubus." Sull paused. "Our family has not compelled the spirit for generations. I do not know his semblance. But of course this is a trifle."

Once more Mumber Sull straightened himself and advanced on the table. When but a few steps from it, he took his stance. There he stood, broodingly silent, staring with concentration at the veiled bulk before him.

And yet the Thane seemed not to see it, for as he stood there he gave no sign of noticing a change which at that moment came over the draped figure. Polderbag seized Cugel's arm and hissed, "Look! It begins to move!"

The two stared aghast. A slow roiling movement had begun under the canvas shroud. Slow bulges, as if of a gaseous medium, swelled up at the foot of the hidden figure and rolled lazily over the length of it. "Now it stirs! Now it moves to take full possession. And still she is silent! Ye gods!" the wizard exclaimed. "Such stubbornness of will, such indomitable resistance to eroticism, is *itself* an enormity. Monstrous woman!" he cried, shaking his plump fist at the sluggishly boiling shroud. "Are you made of gallows wood? Do your veins ooze lead, or saltpeter? Cry out, capitulate!"

Polderbag stopped himself, looking fearfully at the door, beyond which the muttering and shuffling of the guard could be heard. In a frantic whisper he addressed the Thane, who stood still silent before the table, oblivious to the movement beneath the sorcerer's canopy.

"Thane Sull! Why do you delay? Why do you not call your servitor spirit?"

"Its name," muttered Sull. "It has eluded my memory. It must be invoked by name."

The reply seemed to paralyze Polderbag, who looked at Sull with a blank face. Mumber Sull gnawed his thumb. "It has a smack of *walk*, or *wall*."

Cugel abandoned all hopes based on his lord's spell. Desperately he cast about for some expedient. He might admit the guards, transform Sull as he had accidentally at Yawrn, and escape in the ensuing uproar. But the chain was still broken. Perhaps if he tied it about his *own* neck, he would be capable of slaying the guard and winning free of the city.

It made his hair stir to consider the total mutation of his own flesh, but already the canvas drape had begun to jerk with a bubbling motion that added itself to the roiling to produce an uncanny agitation up and down the length of the veiled figure. Surely the matron would soon cry out. Cugel extracted the amulet and tied its chain around his neck.

Without result. He stared at his hands, but they remained his through the tense seconds. He pocketed the gem with a curse. Leaping forth, he shook Polderbag, who still looked helplessly at Mumber Sull.

"Polderbag! All now depends on clear thinking. Do you know where you erred in the spell originally? Can you repeat it correctly now?"

"The spell. The spell." Fiercely Polderbag strove to focus his thoughts. "I cannot be sure I mispronounced an element. It is possible I introduced one from a different spell." He wrung his hands. The shroud's movement had grown more rapid.

Mumber Sull cried out suddenly in triumph: "*Prawlk*! Its name is Prawlk!" And in the next instant, all three of the exorcists leaped back as a hairless orange homunculus materialized before them. "It works!" crowed Sull, enraptured.

"Command him, quickly!" exhorted Polderbag and Cugel together. The Thane drew himself up and addressed himself to the orange creature. "Greetings, obedient Prawlk. I am your lord, Mumber Sull, Harbor Thane of—" The creature, having seen nothing of interest in the three exorcists, inserted one of its barbed claws neatly into its single nostril, and turned away idly toward the table, where the canopy's bizarre pulsations had grown more frantic.

Mumber Sull scowled at this disregard, and boomed sternly at the homunculus, "Prawlk! Attend my instructions!" The creature offhandedly produced a loud and acrid flatulence, and jumped up onto the table on the edge of the turbulent shroud.

Prawlk lifted an edge of the shroud and peeked under. The creature stooped there, staring in under the drape for a long time. Then it dropped the canvas and sat down meditatively on the table's edge, dangling its wrinkled orange legs for a moment in thought. It snickered. It got up, raised the edge of the drape again, and crawled inside.

The three exorcists watched fascinated, forgetful that their lives were implicated in the drama, and absorbed in its unfolding. The boiling accelerated. There was a lewd sigh, and then a voice, shrill and unmistakably female, burst out counting, and counted at incredible speed from one to two hundred and thirty-seven before collapsing to breathe.

At the voice's outburst, Polderbag's legs wobbled under him. "That will bring the Synod instantly. We are doomed to the gibbet!" Cugel sprang forward and shook the panicked wizard. "The spell! Nothing can now be lost — attempt it once more, banish the incubus!"

Somewhat rallied, Polderbag grasped his brows with both hands, summoning his will. A violent puffing had begun to shake the shroud, as if jets of air were being squirted off within. The female voice had begun to shout, amid frequent shrieks of laughter, the elements of a recipe for minced sopkirttle. She was accompanied in this recital by an energetic duet for hoot and gurgle, apparently supplied by her shroud-fellows. There was a pounding at the door.

The fat wizard's face became wild and grim. Yanking back his sleeves he brandished his chubby arms at the obscenely bulging canopy, where-under a honking — clearly the Matron's — could be heard to harmonize with the gurgle and the hoot. The guards outside pounded on the door, and the footsteps of the alarmed Densities could be heard ascending the stairway at the end of the hall. Drawing breath, Polderbag bleated out the potent syllables.

The shroud, though still bulging, became perfectly still and silent, as if those under it were listening. Sull, Cugel, and Polderbag all stood frozen with a sense of foreboding. Without, they could hear a file being applied by the guards to the hinges of the door, but they scarcely noticed. Polderbag clasped his hands and whispered in anguish: "I made an error. I am sure of it. But what will happen? Why this horrible delay?"

Then Cugel pointed with a cry to the far wall of the room. There, a blob of shadow was leaking out of the stone to drift shapelessly into the room. "It seems to grope, or sniff," muttered Mumber Sull.

And it seemed to catch a scent, for it rushed toward the draped table. Then Polderbag yelped and pointed to where a smoky tangle of arms was crawling out of the floor, and heading likewise toward the table.

Then a great manta shape of green gelatin peeled off the ceiling and dropped to hover over the shroud, which had begun to move with a kind of festive spasticity. The shadow had already seeped inside, and the thicket of arms was climbing the table leg.

"They are outside as well!" cried Cugel. "Listen!" The filing at the door's hinges had ceased. The hall outside was filled with a stampeding sound which fled and returned crazily, accompanied by an unnatural hubbub.

"A portal has been opened," wailed Polderbag. "Unwittingly I invoked the presences *en masse*. They have found Waddlawg! They will swarm from leagues around to feast on the rich virgin psychoplasms." He covered his face. The shroud had begun to whirl, having absorbed all the strange invaders.

"Come," cried Cugel with sudden hope. "We may yet pass unhindered! The ectoplasms' preference will surely be for the virgin fare. As for the Densities, surely they will be too engaged by the invaders to threaten us."

"Do you consider abandoning the Matron, who is our sworn charge?" the Thane cried ominously.

"Will you persist in this folly?" gasped Cugel. "Behold!" The whirling canvas had just risen from the table, which was bare. With many a cavorting swerve, the spinning gray mantle danced in the air, and then passed through one of the walls.

"Our charge has fled, and so may we," Cugel said. The Thane nodded. Cugel unbarred the door, peered out, then flung it wide. "The way is clear," he crowed.

Hallway, stairwell, and lower parlor were strewn with the routed Synod, all queerly afflicted. The robes of many bulged with a second occupant, foaming lips jabbered witlessly, and a Density smote down a Matron with his prayerstone and leaped upon her. Outside bands of rabid Densities besieged the houses of the citizenry, dragging their daughters and wives into the streets, only to be in their turn assailed by the sons and husbands of the commoners.

"We must fly west," said Polderbag. "East of Waddlawg lies no passage, for Yawrn is a one-way crossing, unless," he said with sudden hope, "the toll-ward is in fact overthrown."

Cugel shook his head. "He lives still, and our way in any case lies still to the west." Sull nodded silently in affirmation of this.

"As does my own, now," said Polderbag. "I find wizard-errantry a profitless enterprise, and Millions' Gather, despite its infestation, is relatively safe for those who know it, and are cautious." The trio hastened toward the western gate of Waddlawg, which was close at hand.

When they were well out of the city, the road topped a rise, much in the manner of the eastern road, from which the whole of Waddlawg was visible. The three paused here to look back.

The city's great teardrop swarmed with torches and the stern-lights of gondolas. Tumultuous processions threaded the complex pattern of her streets, and from every nook of the great stone city a faint sobbing or cheering rose into the night. The three wizards turned west.

CHAPTER V

MILLIONS' GATHER

The westering sun merged spectacularly with the purple and ebony welter of receding storm wrack. Sull, Cugel, and Polderbag, shivering with the recent drenching of the rain, rounded the shoulder of a last great hill, and stood looking over the Vale of Zoo.

At the great valley's farther end lay Millions' Gather, its dusty stone blazing here and there where the sun's horizontal rays flashed on a window. More than half the city rose on the slopes of the valley wall, and the travelers had the vale's whole length to cross to reach it. The road plunged down before them and could be glimpsed afar, a pale filament threading the dark glens of the valley's floor.

The trio sat down exhaustedly by the roadside. Mumber Sull apostrophized the distant city:

"Ah, longed-for sight. Here, I feel with strange certainty, we shall surely find our way to Simbilis. Our labors approach their recompense. Those who have wronged me approach their doom."

"I urge that we do not linger at the threshold of comparative safety," said Polderbag nervously. "The wooded regions below harbor encampments of hybrids, descendants of the great convocation called by Simbilis. Many of these are of an aggressive temperament."

Nonetheless, none of them stirred immediately. They were bone-weary. The way west had been hard.

Though the journey had taken no longer than the month that Polderbag had projected, it was attended by more perils, by his testimony, than had marked it on his eastward journey to Waddlawg. Both highway and town, of course, had their own special types of predator.

But added to this there was a particular hostility toward Polderbag himself, who seemed to have made various enemies on his way east. Though he showed great caution and self-effacement when entering any town, the fat spell-peddler was recognized often, and he and his party were even chased outright from one village by a militia of its menfolk.

"It is imperative we go," Polderbag now said. He heaved himself to his feet. The others followed suit, and they started down to the valley floor.

Cugel found the Thane's enthusiasm for Millions' Gather infectious. His spirits rose to think Simbilis might after all be found. He was not normally optimistic on this point, and had only come this far perforce.

For the party had failed to encounter any southbound highway. Cugel had made inquiries regarding the nature of the roadless terrain to the south, considering a desperate and solitary venture in that direction. But the reports his inquiries elicited were uniformly dreadful. In one city he was told that acid quagmires haunted by sneaks and shrills lay south. In another he learned of vast tracts of smoking rock which burned away the stoutest boots within half a league, after which the barefoot and madly dancing wayfarer was ambushed and pulled down by the giant armored toads of the region.

The trio followed a twisting, downward way, marching at the briskest pace Polderbag's stumpy legs were capable of setting, which was considerable. Nonetheless, despite their haste, dazzling white stars blazed thickly overhead by the time they had reached the great valley's floor.

The road, now more or less level, twisted among low, heavily wooded knolls. Occasionally they crossed a wooden bridge where a loud stream ran invisible in the dark below their feet echoing on the planks. Otherwise they walked through an eerie quiet on all sides where the crunching of their feet in the gravel mingled with the slow erratic dripping of a forest after rain.

"Hark!" hissed Polderbag, when they had gone about a mile. As he spoke he whirled to look behind them, down the road they had come. Alarmed, Sull and Cugel turned with him and listened. A second sound became distinguishable from the dripping of the vegetation. Steadily, if gently, approaching from out of the murk there came a dainty incessant whine. A pale form became visible, distant but clearly advancing.

Polderbag peered anxiously, and then said with great urgency, "It is a witsucker! We must have light without an instant's delay. A torch! There is a resinous vine native to the valley; it will burn even when wet."

"But how are we to find it in the dark?" Cugel whispered.

"Its thorniness will identify it."

The starlight was uncertain. Little more was visible than a few yards of the road, and the shadowy masses of the forest on either side of it. Into this the trio plunged, groping frantically in the black vegetation, thrusting blind hands among hairy creepers and cold slippery blossoms with enormous petals.

Polderbag yelped, not entirely with the excitement of discovery. "I have found some of the cursed plant. Help me break it!" This proved a task which left the hands of all three bloody. This in turn made the flint and steel slippery and hard to manage, but Cugel at last set one end of the rude torch ablaze and thrust it aloft.

He did so just in time to repulse the witsucker, which had advanced to within two yards of them. At the upraising of the fire, the creature recoiled with a shrill of pain. Its hands stretched toward them with a clutching of leprous fingers. The soft, bulbous sac of its head tilted back with eyeless grief, while its black proboscis uncoiled and made mournful kissing sounds in the air.

The trio resumed their way at doubled speed, the brand held high. Polderbag moaned, "I fervently pray our light does not fail before we reach the city. This is the worst form of psychic vampire. Its victims become zombie-like predators who themselves menace other passersby." The witsucker raised its keening whine, and followed them just out of reach of the torch's light.

Perhaps through a combination of that light and the menacing figure that dogged their steps, the trio met no new menace on their way — at least nothing more substantial than certain indeterminate shapes hovering at the dark edges of their vision.

The torch burned out just as the travelers reached the first outlying buildings of the city. Polderbag cried, "Safety now lies in flight!" Cugel flung aside the smoking stump, and the three plunged into a headlong dash, with the pale creature suddenly swift behind them.

The structures they rushed past clearly represented the city's high-water mark. Its population was much shrunk since then, and these taverns, hostels, and villas were now lightless ruins. The three, as they fled, looked in vain for human presences. They saw only collapsed walls in dark robes of grass, and doorjambs standing against the night sky like empty picture frames containing stars.

Their legs toiled and their lungs gasped mightily, while behind them they heard the light, tireless stride of their pursuer. The tenantless sub-urbs seemed unending, and lights promising inhabited districts were not in prospect. In a delirium of flight the trio sped past these starlit skeletons of roofless masonry.

Polderbag's gasps grew harsher. As he and his companions rounded a corner, the ungainly wizard's legs gave way and flung him sprawling to the cobblestones. Thane and Esquire, too close to dodge, tripped on his prostrate bulk and were likewise thrown stunned to the pavement.

For a paralyzed instant all three awaited the onslaught of the wit-sucker. Then they realized that they were unpursued, and lay in a puddle of sulfurous light shed by a streetlamp. Assorted pedestrians regarded them from several sides, apparently startled by their flamboy-ant entrance. The trio had arrived in Millions' Gather.

Somewhat sheepishly, Thane and Esquire rose and hauled the fud-dled Polderbag to his feet. The citizens who had paused to stare were already drifting on. Their manner implied that they were inured to unusual behavior and paid it but scant attention.

Indeed the overall impression the citizenry made on Sull and Cugel was one of guarded neutrality, every man going his way quickly, with-out loitering or even glancing aside. Nor was it perfectly accurate to speak of 'every man', for a substantial portion of those the trio passed were, though heavily cloaked, still clearly too squat or too precariously tall to be human.

Polderbag had in fact to some extent prepared his friends for this situation, saying that such mingling was the result of years of peaceful commerce with the subworlds, though now the commerce was com-pletely one-sided. Yet for all Polderbag's hints, Sull and Cugel watched with a profound unease when a passerby extruded from his cape a bouquet of purple digits, to draw his hood closer, or when another was seen to pass through the smoky lamplight with a mincing, multi-legged gait.

At the end of a half hour's progress Polderbag brought Thane and Esquire to a quiet inn of modest dimensions, whose clientele were all human. It came as something of a surprise to be conducted to the inn, for Polderbag had several times in the weeks prior mentioned a colleague in Millions' Gather with whom they could stay in great luxury. He had for some time, however, not alluded to this colleague, and had clearly had second thoughts on the matter as they had drawn nearer Millions' Gather.

Now he referred once again to the colleague, but only as a person to whom the Thane might repair for counsel on his quest. Polderbag would himself, that night, visit the man, to prepare him for a consultation on the next day. He made no mention of staying in the colleague's house.

Sull accepted this arrangement easily, concerned as he was with immediate needs which could be met as well in the inn as elsewhere. Cugel for his part harbored a certain distrust of Polderbag, whose felonious inclinations were not dissimilar to his own. He was made highly curious by the spell-peddler's tacit shift of position, as well as by a certain nervousness he detected in Polderbag's manner.

The three retired to a bathhouse behind the inn and there bathed and changed into new garments which a stable boy was sent out to purchase. The ample stipend paid the trio by the Densities had stood them well in their trek, but as Polderbag had been longer in their pay, his purse was much fatter than Sull's or Cugel's, whose coins were now few.

Through their copious supper, Cugel noted that Polderbag's air of apprehension grew more marked, and even slowed his appetite. His own hunger satisfied, Cugel felt greatly restored, and at liberty to puzzle over Polderbag's manner. He decided he would follow the fat man when the latter left, allegedly to see his colleague, Warpl the Old.

Soon after the meal Mumber Sull rose and took a chair before the fire in the inn's common room, where shortly he began to nod. At this point Polderbag excused himself. Cugel waited till Polderbag had passed out the front door, then sprang from his chair and rushed after him.

The erstwhile exorcist made portly haste through neighborhoods that grew ever darker. Following him through the cramped alleys overhung by dank propped-apart walls, Cugel realized that Millions' Gather was an old city indeed. And it seemed they were penetrating its older precincts, to judge by the gaunt and rickety structures looming up around them.

At length, turning into a cramped street less illuminated than any previous, Polderbag ducked down the stairs of a sunken doorway. He plied a knocker discreetly, and then entered.

As Cugel came to the head of the stairs, he heard a wail of distress from within. The house was a structure of one story, and its roof rose to little more than a man's height above the street's level. Cugel noted that the neighboring building was much taller, and its second story jutted over the squatter building at its side. About a yard separated the roof of Polderbag's building from the over-jutting second story of its neighbor.

Cugel scrambled up onto the low roof and worked himself under the shadow of the overhang. Sandwiched in this space, he was invisible from the street. He moved upon all fours till he came upon a flaw in the roof's shingling which granted him a view of most of the room beneath.

It was a dim room, paneled and floored in wood. Behind a laboratory desk heaped high with instruments and scrolls, an old man stood. His face was hidden, due to the angle, but voluminous white hair and beard were visible under a peaked cap. His form was skeletal, but at the moment was trembling with power and rage.

The sagging form of Polderbag was on the opposite wall, splayed and pinned to a wheel. At a sign from the bearded figure this wheel began to spin, while the hapless Polderbag emitted piteous yelps. The mechanism spun increasingly fast, until Polderbag's form was no more than a series of blurred concentric circles which the wrathful old man faced, as if facing a target. He extended a bony hand and flung a thorny spasm of green fire at the whirling wheel of punishment.

Polderbag cried out, his voice distorted by the velocity of his spinning. The aged figure flung another smattering of fire at the target, and again the spell-peddler protested. The old man made a disgusted gesture, and the wheel ceased to spin, bringing Polderbag to a dizzied halt, head-down.

"This is useless," the old man growled. "I have no stomach for such chastisements as your folly merits. Be thankful, witless apprentice, that I re-admit you to my service. Are the spells you purloined intact? Or have you sold them to scroll-merchants for a foolish price? No matter, the spells are minor, or I would have apprehended you before now."

"Esteemed master," Polderbag cried woefully, "a malign influence, some subworld worker of ill, clouded my reason with ambitious fantasies and delusion. I have only lately freed myself of its curse, which done I turned with haste back to you!"

"Graceless villain, cease your threadbare prevarications. I know your craven, greedy nature too well to be deceived by your plausible evasions. You have returned — so be it. Return the spells and expect a daily discipline harsher than you have yet known from me."

Polderbag, whom another gesture from the magician freed from the wheel, cringed up to his master.

"Most generous of wizards," he melodiously suspired, "you shall see that despite the evil influences that compelled me, I have been scrupulous in your service, and have brought you two clients. Touching the matter of commission —"

"What? You have the impudence to speak of commissions? Bring them here tomorrow, and see that you impose no fraudulent charges on them. They are to pay no more than my consultation fee. What is it they seek?"

"They seek Simbilis, master," answered Polderbag. The old man registered surprise, then muttered, "I will provide what counsel I can. Such fools as these have need of it. You have leave to retire…"

Polderbag bowed himself through a door in one wall. The wizard himself extinguished his lights a moment later and, with a violent burst of radiance, imploded.

The effect of the wizard's last remark on Cugel's spirits was decidedly negative. The quest on which he had been forced to pin his hopes began to seem more than ever a fool's errand. What added to his dismay was the realization that he had not the slightest notion of the way back to the inn, nor of the inn's name. Even had he anticipated

Polderbag's spending the night at Warpl's, the closest attention to the tortuous route they had followed would not have sufficed to enable him to retrace it now.

So Cugel passed a night of fitful and shivering sleep on the rooftop. In truth, he did more shivering than sleeping. Yet his frequent awakenings had the result of making him a witness of a strange scene. In the small hours, as he moved to adjust his comfortless position for the hundredth time, he spied a troop of men walking silently along the narrow street, their heads but a few feet below him.

They were all chained together at neck and waist, and were conducted on their way by several creatures who were exceedingly tall, with heads obscured by great heaps of matted hair. They had a zombie-like gait, and seemed by their vestigial dugs to be female. Moreover, they exuded a nauseating pungency which hung on the air long after they had ushered their mute charges past, and out of view. In like manner, the doubt and unease which the scene aroused in Cugel lingered in his mind a long time after the procession had passed.

In the morning, stiff of joint and muscle, Cugel followed Polderbag back to the inn, which he himself entered by a rear door. Dashing up the service stairs he came down via the main stairs into the public room, stretching as after deep repose. He found the Thane already at table, and Polderbag seated at his side speaking earnestly.

"My associate, Warpl the Old," he was saying, "is in fact my erst-while mentor, for which reason you will note that I still accord him the courtesies and forms which a servant owes his master. It is a private kindness I do an old man. I am loath to seem boastful in speaking of it, but I wished you prepared."

Sull and Cugel nodded. Polderbag resumed, "Warpl is, however, while perhaps not my equal in thaumaturgy, a great master of lore. In cases like your own, historical questions, I often refer clients to him, for antiquities are his special province. Naturally for such referrals I regularly ask a commission."

Sull greeted this statement with stiff silence. Polderbag said, "You must not think I wish to obtrude crass commercialism on our ami-cable relations. I merely observe the Law of Equivalences, in which I am a great believer. Even as it is I will scant myself, and require of you only half of what remains to you of the Densities' stipend. For I know your funds are low, and you will need the other half to pay Warpl's honorarium."

Mumber Sull nodded stoically and gave Polderbag his purse. Polderbag bowed suave thanks. A few moments later the three set out for Warpl's house.

The wizard greeted them without ceremony and indicated chairs. "I am informed by Polderbag that you seek Simbilis. Can this possibly be true?"

"Your incredulity seems ill warranted," Mumber Sull replied with irritation. "We are Simbilis' vassals and bear news that closely concerns him."

The wizard gave a sardonic grunt. "If Simbilis still lives, it is certain that his concerns lie far beyond your guessing. In any case, you seek information. I will tell you at the outset that I have only conjectures to offer. As to the certainties, they end with his departure from Millions' Gather, and I am sure Polderbag has already acquainted you with them."

"If only conjectures are to be had, we will have them," Mumber Sull replied. "Of the city's building and the highway, Polderbag has told us."

"Has he also told you my consultation fee?"

Here Cugel broke in to reply, "Indeed, your colleague mentioned it." At the word 'colleague', the wizard looked at Polderbag, who quailed. Cugel turned to the fat man and, ignoring his surreptitious signals, continued brightly. "You must know, esteemed Polderbag, the lively appreciation my lord and I feel for your procuring the venerable Warpl's services. I stress again how willingly we supplied the small remuneration you required for this service."

He turned to count out the wizard's fee, the Thane's purse being already gone, while Polderbag read great meaning in his master's look. Then Warpl turned to Mumber Sull.

"Fantastic rumors abound, even at this late date, regarding Simbilis' destination when leaving Millions' Gather, and his present circumstances. Three theories in particular, however, may be said to prevail. The most popular of these legends holds that Simbilis entered the subworlds and built there a haven of retirement, a miraculous garden where he meant to pass his remaining centuries in contemplation.

A line from a fragmentary epic of the tenth era is cited as evidence of this, for it contains an allusion to 'the fabulous glades of Simbilis' deep retreat', but the line is now widely held to be the recent interpolation of a scribe of the last century.

"Somewhat less widely held is the theory that the arch-wizard did in fact enter the subworlds, but with the purpose of quelling an insurrection there. Since he was held to be invincible, his failure to return from this sortie is taken as proof that the struggle still rages, and that Simbilis is locked in eternal stalemate with the demons.

"Lastly, there is the belief that Simbilis departed the moribund earth to seek a new world to which, when found, he will transfer the city and folk of Millions' Gather, there to live in bliss under a new sun. Adherents of this third theory form but a small percentage of the itself exiguous group who still concern themselves with such antiquities as Simbilis and his whereabouts. Though they are but a small part of this scholarly group, they are nonetheless by far the most fervent in conviction."

Mumber Sull shook his head. "Regardless, I must dismiss their hypothesis as inadmissible. It renders our quest impossible. Moreover, what little consensus exists among these opinions indicates the subworlds as our goal. What guidance may be procured thither?"

Warpl stared broodingly at the Thane before he answered. "You are of an abrupt and stubborn temper. Beware the headlong entry of domains outside your experience. The situation here is complex."

"These vague admonitions are futile. Can you not speak more plainly?"

"The subject does not admit of it. News from the sub-regions is scarce and unreliable. The interworld highway is no longer, as it was in the archwizard's day, the joint property of both upper and lower realms. Our city is deep in debt to the subworld merchants, who from the first proved themselves negotiators of superior subtlety. The highway is now their property, and few surface folk have descended it in recent years, other than those debtors led captive below, and these of course do not return to make report of what they see. The demon lords issue a limited number of spice-harvesting permits, but at a fee so exorbitant as to render even this highly lucrative enterprise almost profitless."

"What sort of sum is in question?"

Warpl shrugged. "The payments demanded by the demon merchants are often bizarre. Currency properly so-called is rarely involved. The hooded traders do seem to place consistently high value on periapts, amulets of any description, presumably because these often command forces from their own domain."

"Alas that we permitted the skullcaps to be lost," said the Thane. "These would surely have purchased our entry."

Warpl's manner grew attentive. "You imply that you are now destitute of talismans?"

"Of course. Are we mountebanks, spell-peddlers, to be stocked with charms and wards?"

"And yet I sense that you have a talisman of high potency presently in your possession," said Warpl. Cugel shifted in his seat. The wizard made a gesture and the amulet sprang from Cugel's pouch and hung in the air before him.

"Ah, what a day of fascinating arcana," exclaimed the wizard. He beckoned and the amulet drifted to his fingers.

He studied the glyphs in the setting and looked at Cugel, at whom the Thane was also directing an intent gaze. "How did you come by this?"

"It is a dull tale, long to recount," Cugel demurred. "Indeed I had forgotten that I still carried it."

"It is a curious piece," said the wizard, continuing to examine it. "It is the work of the brilliant Korloo. He sought to demonstrate that the anthrodegenerate races are the psychic shadows of humankind. He devised the amulet as a demonstration of his theory which, briefly, supposes that for every man there exists somewhere an erb, grue, or vampire whose instants of birth and death are the same as his own, and whose soul is perfectly congruent with his own. The periapt superimposes upon its wearer his counterpart's form, an operation damaging to neither party due to this congruence. I do not doubt the subworld merchants would deem such a rarity as this sufficient payment for a harvesting permit."

"Then we shall lose no time in offering it to them," said the Thane. Cugel squirmed, but held his tongue. Warpl repaired the amulet's chain with a spell and handed it to Mumber Sull. He then instructed Polderbag to conduct the pair to the customs house at Steep's Jaw and there assist them as far as he could in their transaction before returning. The wizard stared after Thane and Esquire as they left, neglecting to reply to their farewell.

The way Polderbag led them lay increasingly uphill, for their goal was the prominence halfway up the valley wall where Steep's Jaw stood, and around which the city's most cramped and ancient districts lay. The avenues they followed shrank to little more than brick footpaths meandering through a submarine gloom where the old walls loomed crookedly on all sides. Narrow strips only of the morning sky's violet were visible overhead, heavily crisscrossed by ramps, gangways, arches, and bracing-beams.

Sometimes a particular street they were following would end in a cul-de-sac, whereupon their route entered a subterranean phase, passing through dusty cellars of abandoned taverns, old hallways, and torchlit sewers. At other times their route climbed creaking wooden stairs and proceeded as a pathway of weathered planks across the tiled roofs of the city where all around them sprouted quaint and tilted chimney pots.

After some little time Polderbag proposed a brief refreshment. The trio turned into a tavern which was built on the roof of a long-defunct public bath. The tavern was reached by a ladder from the street, and it had a terrace, whereon the three took their drinks.

The terrace's only other occupant was a dour man wearing a conical hat of white fur. This individual hunched uneasily over his table, and when the trio entered he turned to peer at them with unconcealed suspicion. Cugel was made curious by this evident discompose, and kept the man in view from the corner of his eye.

Meanwhile Polderbag was earnestly broaching a topic whose discussion had evidently been his true motive in stopping here. "I will be direct," he began. "In mulling over your projected journey I have discovered an arrangement whereby we may all reap great advantage. Into the sub-worlds as far as the spice preserves I propose to accompany you."

"But to what end, worthy Polderbag?" asked the Thane, raising his eyebrows.

"To be frank, the rights you are purchasing are greatly coveted. Subworld spices bring a fantastic price on the market due to their special psychic effects. For you the harvesting permit is a mere pretext for entry of the lower realms; for myself it is a matchless opportunity. Permit me to capitalize on it. I in my turn will aid you in eluding our escort, for this you must surely do if you wish to penetrate the region's greater depths. I will create some diversion in the spice groves which will permit you to slip away. My reward will be my harvest."

Mumber Sull, pleased by Polderbag's stratagem, had scarcely finished nodding his regal assent to the plan when a harsh cry erupted from the nervous man at the far table. This individual had just reached out his hand for the flagon before him. Then suddenly the hand with which he grasped the flagon had ceased to be a hand. It had become a large spiked toad which seized the vessel with its forepaws and quaffed the contents with noisy gusto.

For a moment the fur-hatted man merely stared at this creature in which his right arm now terminated. He was brought to himself by a great bray of wheezing laughter that issued from the air behind him. With a cry the man lurched up as if to grapple with the laughter, but meeting no solid resistance he plunged to the floor, at which the laughter burst out with new force.

Not moving from where he lay, the man raised his arm and smote the floor with the spiked toad. There was a detonation and a cloud of fine blue dust boiled up around him. This dust clung to all it touched, including the heretofore invisible form of a man, now clearly perceptible as a skin of blue. Upon this form the fallen man sprang. The two struggled and fell down with a force that broke through the flimsy flooring, plunging the combatants into the deserted baths below.

Rushing to the edge of the hole, Thane and Esquire saw that the fur-hatted man was conjuring up a horde of snakes while his blue assailant was filling a great dried-up cistern with yellow spiders to meet their attack. Polderbag called Sull and Cugel away. "Let us resume our way at once. It is folly to remain in the vicinity of such feuds as this."

When the trio were once again on their way the Thane inquired the meaning of what they had just witnessed. Polderbag sighed. "Occurrences of its kind are common enough in our city. They are evidence of the fatal addiction which has led to its subjection to the lower regions."

"The combatants were agents of the demon worlds?"

"No, merely the victims of their infernal seductions. From the beginning of the interworld commerce the men of this city have prized above all the subworlds' products their sorcery. In the early days traffic in spells and periapts was discouraged. Nowadays it is perfectly blatant and discord prevails. Townsfolk exhaust their fortunes purchasing dark powers with which to carry on their innumerable petty vendettas. Many sink so deep into the debt of the lower powers that they pass into their legal possession, and are led off to the subworlds in nocturnal caravans."

Cugel nodded thoughtfully, recalling what he had seen the previous night. "And yet what leads the demon lords to sell what they seem, by Warpl's account, to covet so?"

Polderbag shrugged. "Since all the spells sold to a man revert to the demons' possession when that man is taken possession of, such spells are not truly lost, but merely form a kind of investment which is recouped in the end. Not only the man himself, but all his worldly goods as well may be ultimately won, merely by allowing that man the temporary ownership of a few talismans and formulas."

The way they followed had been growing increasingly steep. Now it took a last turn between overtowering walls and entered an open space. In the pink light of late morning, they saw the city of Millions' Gather spread around them, its black and purple rooftops falling away in long gradual slopes whose outskirts merged with the dark zone of the great valley's forests.

But this panorama did not long detain the trio's attention, for near the center of the hilltop plaza whence they observed it stood something of much greater import to them: Steep's Jaw. This portal, they could see, was a natural one, a jagged fissure in a great perpendicular outcropping of black rock. Before this fissure had been set two massive stone buttresses which leaned together to form an aperture in the shape of an isosceles triangle. Both of these great stone beams were graven with runes.

"Those glyphs are a prohibition inscribed by Simbilis and still potent, as far as is known," said Polderbag. "It bars the passage of any stolen object over the portal's threshold. But now our business lies there, in the customs building."

He indicated a low, porticoed structure occupying the corner of the square to one side of Steep's Jaw. To this they repaired.

The portico, each of whose arches was triangular like Steep's Jaw itself, was the scene of a furtive but quite brisk activity. A dozen little colloquies of men and subworld agents raised an intense haggling murmur in the shadows. Ignoring these transactions, Polderbag led his friends down the line of triangular doorways which corresponded to the arches of the portico and which entered the building itself. He ushered them through one of the last of these doorways.

They passed into a narrow room, poorly lit. It was bisected by a counter, behind which a figure on a high stool sat facing them. Behind this figure, at the room's farthest end, there sat a group of hooded figures. They were perceptible only in outline, for a gloom surrounded them which was somehow denser and more wavering than the darkness produced by the room's poor lighting.

The small pale figure seated behind the counter addressed the three in what seemed a scratchy, mechanical approximation of a voice: "State your business."

Polderbag bowed. "What we seek of the honored Frontier Authority is a spice-harvester's visa. We propose —" He was cut off by Mumber Sull who, after a moment's disbelief, gripped Polderbag's arm and cried, "What madness is this? This is no living being you speak with, but a wooden doll!"

At this the dummy, for so indeed it was, turned its lacquered white face to Sull and said, "It is clear you have not dealt with us before. Such of us as lack the organs involved in speech employ this intermediate mechanism in deference to human sensibilities. Your species responds negatively to our own means of communication, which is psychoplasm exchange. What payment can you offer for your visa?"

The Thane instinctively addressed his reply to the hooded figures in the gloom back of the counter. "We have this amulet of great age and potency."

"If you please," said the dummy, extending a carved hand with delicately hinged fingers. Mumber Sull tendered it the amulet with a distrustful look at the shadowy synod.

The dummy held the periapt before its face. Its forehead swung open like a trapdoor, and a phosphorescent orange palp extruded to caress the brilliant. An eager nodding and stir passed through the dark group behind. The dummy's forehead closed and it surrendered the talisman to the Thane.

"In view of the remarkable rarity of the charm," the dummy said, "a visa can be arranged for you. As you know we grant them rarely in latter days, for we wish to discourage the gawkers and vagabonds who would, left unhindered, soon overrun our native regions. Payment is to be tendered in the subworld, just prior to entry of the spice preserves. If you will step to the rear of the customs building, you will find a guide awaiting you."

The dummy sagged, abruptly motionless. Mumber Sull attempted to addressed further questions to the hooded figures, but Polderbag dissuaded him and, bowing profoundly, escorted his two companions from the room.

Passing around to the rear of the customs house the trio met a gangly, malodorous creature which Cugel identified with some distress as one of the species of female zombie which had overseen the procession of chained men on the previous night. At this point the Esquire's resolution to pin his hopes on the Thane's quest underwent its severest shaking. If it did not fail outright, it was only because Cugel found so few alternatives open to him. Doubtless, he told himself, these creatures served the sublords in a variety of capacities, not all of which were sinister.

"Spice party?" the she-zombie asked. Polderbag nodded and the creature motioned them to follow it. It led the way to a small booth which stood at the very mouth of Steep's Jaw. To one wall of this booth was affixed an aged parchment written over in arcane script. The zombie began to read aloud from this parchment at great speed — an incomprehensible performance as the language was one that was long dead. The ritual had apparently some legal import, but Mumber Sull, whose thoughts had wandered, suddenly broke in.

"I have been struck by a troublesome consideration. Polderbag has mentioned a prohibition inscribed over the portal which bars the entry of stolen objects. If this is so, how may we pass through with this amulet which, though justifiably wrested from an unscrupulous and felonious party who sought to work our harm with it, must nonetheless be accounted as stolen?"

"No difficulty exists," said the she-zombie. "All periapts control powers which were at some point wrested from the lower worlds. On the instant of the amulet's reentry of those realms, it ceases to be a stolen object. The point was clarified long ago in the course of litigation in Simbilis' commercial courts."

The creature turned back to the parchment and resumed its recitation. During this time Cugel, who had himself grown thoughtful, unobtrusively extracted from his belt the two pouches containing the Thane's gold and his skubbage counters. Just as surreptitiously, he bound the pouches together with a thong, and to the thong affixed a hook he improvised from a pin.

The zombie, having finished reading, turned back to the trio. "The essential provision of the contract I have just read is that you agree to forfeit both your possessions and personal liberty as penalty for any major felony committed by yourselves while in the subworld's domain."

To this Mumber Sull replied loftily, "As it is unthinkable that any of my party should be guilty of criminal activity, we may accede to your insulting stipulation as in the performance of an empty formality."

"The spirit in which you enter the contract is immaterial to my masters," replied the she-zombie. "Each of you must press his palm to the parchment to signify his agreement."

The three did as directed, and each was then presented by the guide with a small fat reptile of lavender hue. These creatures wore tiny collar chains which the travelers were directed to pin to their jerkins so that the lizards were perched on their shoulders. The she-zombie then led the three through the great triangular maw of the subworld portal.

Cugel fell a step or two behind the Thane, and just before they passed under the great pointed arch, he deftly hung his pouches of coin and gems from Mumber Sull's belt by the hook he had made. They passed over the dark threshold, and Cugel retrieved the pouches before the Thane had even noticed their weight.

The little reptiles responded to the gloom within the portal by radiating a dull pink light, giving each of the three a personal ambience sufficient to light his footsteps. A pack-animal laden with stores brought up the rear of the party. The little procession had begun its advance into the subworlds.

"How is it," Cugel asked Polderbag in an undertone when they had gone a considerable way, "that we see no evidence of the great if one-sided traffic you have alluded to? Where are the caravans of attached goods being borne below? Where are the processions of manacled debtors which you have led us to expect, and which indeed I myself have had some glimpse of in Millions' Gather? Instead of the thronging, infernal activity I envisioned, I find unvarying desolation."

It was so. The silence was total. Other wayfarers, of any description, there were none, nor had there been in the several hours they had gone thus far. The glow produced by the lizards bulged out against the darkness before and behind the party. Within this frail bubble of visibility they descended the broad pavement, worn but still firm, as it sank in wide leisurely sweeps into the blackness. At every turn were terraces, where once caravans had broken their march, but where now the crumbling balustrades stood like fractured teeth, and the broken lamps wore jagged crowns of glass empty of fire.

As for the surrounding terrain, it was for the most part unguessable. They could see at least that the region abounded in a certain rock that was veined with dim green phosphorescence, for great masses of this stone would loom in unexpected walls at the sides of the highway, or abruptly swoop down from above in ceiling formations.

But the glittering rock fell away from the highway as unpredictably as it came near, and in these intervals the road might as easily have been flanked by abysses as by towering peaks — the dark gave no glimpse, and the windless air no clue.

"The desertion you note," Polderbag murmured in answer to Cugel, "is due to the policy of the sublords. They do not wish to advertise the extent of their depredations, lest it rouse the surface dwellers to organized resistance. All appropriated parties and properties are brought down by night, many by portals less well-known than Steep's Jaw. Once underground, the trade routes of the subworlds are many, and the men and goods brought below are widely dispersed."

Cugel desired further discourse, but Polderbag lapsed into the blissful calculation of spice profits which had engrossed him for much of the way, while the Thane was likewise mute, weighing the conflicting legends Warpl had imparted concerning Simbilis. Silence prevailed.

Time passed without feature, and the imperturbable she-zombie seemed insensible to fatigue. The party stopped twice to eat, then once to sleep — for how long they could not know, though it seemed to their aching limbs that they were roused all too soon. And then they marched endlessly once more.

At length, when Mumber Sull's patience had been exhausted by the respite-less monotony of their march, he called out to the she-zombie, demanding a halt and some refreshment.

Their malodorous guide had, in the latter stages of the trek, taken to walking rather far in advance of the trio, leading the pack-beast by its bridle. The creature had tersely explained that the condition of the road in these lower reaches demanded this precaution. Mumber Sull called a second time, but no guide emerged from the gloom ahead.

"I thought her to be in the darkness just before us," marveled the Thane.

"Indeed, I am now brought to realize," Cugel put in, "that it has been some time since I have noticed her noxious pungency, something that remained perceptible even when she was shrouded from view."

"The creature has deserted us, and taken with her our pack-beast and provisions."

The initial disquiet this discovery caused gave way, in Polderbag, to near-elation. "Surely we must see that we could hardly have been more fortunate," he cried. "The problem of eluding our escort is removed, our escort having eluded us."

"Yet it is precisely the malfeasance which this desertion indicates that disturbs me," Cugel said. "To what end has this duplicity been worked on us? And assuming we are to deem ourselves lucky in being unwatched, how are we to find our way? How are you to find the spice preserves?"

Mumber Sull, more of Polderbag's opinion, shook his head at these objections. "In all likelihood no duplicity is involved, but merely an individual dereliction of duty on the part of our guide, whose slovenly and sullen disposition were manifest. As for finding our way, what could be easier than to follow this highway which lies so plainly before us? We must eventually meet some of this place's denizens, and these will provide more particular directions."

"We are agreed to fare forth together, then," said Polderbag. Cugel retained his misgivings, but held his tongue, and the trio continued down the broad paved way.

They had not gone far, however, before the road began to level out and, at the same time, to diminish. It lost its curbing, its rails and wayside benches. In a remarkably short time it had dwindled to nothing more than a stone path across a flat, steaming bog.

The reason that this vast level terrain was visible — as the steeper terrain of the descent had not been — was evident when the travelers looked overhead. The green-veined stone which had hitherto been the landscape's only discernible feature had risen to form a gigantic ceiling, while at the same time undergoing a noticeable increase in its luminosity. Thus great sweeps of crazily vaulted rock, encrusted with a pox of limegreen light, shed an eerie sheen upon the glistening dim swamps that now surrounded the road.

But the road underwent even further disintegration. The pavement became intermittent, and the travelers progressed by hopping from island to island of dry stone. Soon even these failed, and the trio had to slosh ankle-deep in viscous mud. Their effort to stay on drier ground led them on a zigzag course among black tarns where floated yellow carpets of bubblefungus.

To keep themselves on a generally straight course they fixed on one of the green constellations in the vast rock ceiling. They had walked a long way before they discovered that the phosphorescence in their stone sky was in a semifluid state, and was constantly changing pattern and position. Their cynosure was proven a will-o'-the-wisp, and they realized that they had wandered far from the line of the highway. It was an inhospitable-seeming region in which to be lost. Endless tracts of muck scattered with sheets of stagnant purple water, foul ponds whose brinks were trimmed with ratslettuce and throttlehemp.

It soon became evident that this waste supported a considerable population. Its denizens were generally of a low-hunching, swift, and stealthy nature, but with practice the travelers could distinguish them with increasing clarity in the uncertain light. A tarnhaunt peered whimpering at them from behind a clump of scab-cactus. A hidling was startled by their passage, and leaped into a pool.

A bat-winged grat was likewise alarmed by their tread, and fled squawking into the air, flinging down at them a clot of its rank, glowing ordure as it ascended. A pack of bandit-rats charged across their path in pursuit of a shrill, which they caught after a moment's chase and devoured, while the hapless beast emitted unearthly shrieks with the frantic rubbing of its chitinous forelegs.

And then, but a moment later, the travelers jumped at another out-burst — less loud perhaps, but more startling because it was articulate, and directed at themselves.

"Felons! Fiends! Halt! I will have justice!" On hearing this, the three turned and confronted a female hidling who was in a transport of rage, and who pointed an accusing central digit (each paw featured three) at them.

It would be more precise to say she pointed at Polderbag, for it was him she now particularly addressed. "You! You are the murderer, obese hulk! You and only you are the murderer who has killed my child, and these beside you are your accomplices." The frantic creature addressed something which she clutched to her breast. "Yes, he it was, my son, whose obscene waddling bulk crushed you! O my priceless Snoddkip, irretrievably lost!" The thing she apostrophized thus appeared, pre-sumably because of its crushing, little more than a rag of nondescript material.

Polderbag, as the more seriously accused, was the first of the three to find his tongue. "Infanticide? Murderer?" he sputtered. "What groundless slanders are these. You utter the grossest perjuries!" The fat spell-peddler looked uneasily around him, for the hidling's outcry had drawn — from precisely where he could not have said — an ominous, large, and steadily increasing crowd of swamp denizens.

The growls, mutterings, and angry spittings of these evermore numerous bystanders indicated a clear and unanimous sympathy with the hysterical hyperboles of the hidling.

The latter, unabated, had resumed her charges. "I am witness to your guilt! It is you who perjures. Do you dare add mendacity to murder, brazen surface-worlder? O my son, my cherished Poddlewort, you shall have justice. I will have a trial, a trial!"

The crowd, quite large now and decidedly hostile, kindled to the hidling's cry and with amazing suddenness were chanting it in thunderous unison: *"A trial, a trial!"* The three travelers shrank together.

The chant was broken by a shrill voice at the crowd's periphery: "Bogwad!" Again with astonishing quickness the crowd took up this cry, and rocked the gloomy air with it: *"Bogwad! Bogwad!"* And then the throng gave way and a vast squat figure waddled into the clearing where the three stood. It raised thin, rubbery arms and the swamp creatures fell silent.

Bogwad's flat, neckless head sat on his body's bulging corpulence like a lid on a kettle. He surveyed the travelers and his mouth, a huge slot, curved in the hugest of smiles.

"How profoundly pleasant it is," Bogwad boomed, "to encounter wayfarers. They bring a breath of change to our somber precincts. Yet I puzzle over what can be the meaning of the great attention you receive from my subjects."

"Puzzle no longer, my lord," screeched the hidling. "These foreigners are guilty of childslaughter and stand accused."

Ignoring the protestations this elicited from the travelers, Bogwad genially inquired of the hidling, "Charges are lodged, then?"

"Charges most emphatic and unequivocal."

"In that case," said Bogwad to the trio with an urbane gesture, "a trial is in order." With an abruptness that forestalled protest, the crowd parted and a jury box sprouted up from the bog. The box was instantly filled by a remarkably carnivorous-looking assortment of swamp creatures. Nearby a commodious chair of state was likewise thrust up as if from underground. Bogwad, after taking a yellow mat of bubblefungus from a nearby pool and ceremoniously donning it in the manner of a judicial peruke, took his seat in the chair of state. "Counsel for the victim may now exhort the jury," he announced, addressing the hidling.

The bereaved mother came forward and faced that eerie tribunal of visages — some gaunt, oddly snouted or tusked, some lacking eyes and one or two others studded with them — and made a genial, helpless gesture. "Dear neighbors and fellow patriots, I will be candid. Though examples and illustrations abound, it seems futile to multiply instances when the essential point is clear. What profit do we derive from life if we are dead? A manifest truth. But did it give the slightest pause to the destroyers of my winsome, irrepeatable infant offspring squashed by them so shockingly flat where he played by a puddle? Alas! Sooner expect scab-cactus to blossom!" The hidling paused, and the jury, the spectators, and Bogwad himself all applauded politely.

Polderbag, unable to restrain himself, burst out, "I must insist on an examination of the corpus delicti." He came forward. "The article you display as the remains of your child appears to be no more than a scrap of refuse or shriveled leaf."

"O ghastly disfigurement, o death made doubly odious," the hidling cried. She handed the remains to the jury for inspection and they vanished among the jurors before Polderbag could lay hold of them. The frustrated spell-peddler was waved back by Bogwad, and the hidling renewed her wail:

"How handsome were my Gloobnag's childish features. How splendid were his prospects! O remorseless mutilation! What remains of him seems little more than a scrap of refuse, a shriveled leaf! Can it be that your indignation still sleeps, beloved neighbors? Can your outrage slumber still, and your wrath be unawakened?"

The hidling's exhortation was greeted by hearty applause, once more from all present save the trio. She received this with a gracious bow, and resumed her seat. Bogwad addressed the travelers. "A stirring peroration, I am sure the Honorable Malefactors will agree. Do the Honorable Malefactors choose to vex the jury with a tedious counter-exhortation?"

Mumber Sull now spoke up with great energy. "Most assuredly we will counter the baseless calumnies which asperse our character! We will eschew the rhetorical excesses of our accuser, and avoid tedium by plain speaking. In the first place, we strenuously and categorically affirm our innocence of the alleged crime."

"But this you may not affirm," interrupted Bogwad in an echoing voice. "It is a clear usurpation of the jury's province. Will you presume to deliver the verdict of your own case? You must be penalized for Inappropriate Utterance. Your penalty will be the forfeiture of your right to testify as character witnesses in your own behalf. But after all, gentlemen —" suddenly confidential, Bogwad leaned forward with a smile hugely suave "— this is hardly a punishment. It greatly abbreviates the tedium of litigation, for which I am sure you share our dislike. We may now proceed directly to the Browbeating of the Honorable Malefactors."

A squadron of bog-giants, each nine feet tall, appeared and surrounded the travelers. These creatures held, bludgeon-wise, jagged stalactites of crude metal graven with symbols. Bogwad spoke again. "Now a final formality will establish your innocence, and we will detain you no longer. Note the ceremonial maces the giants hold. These instruments lie under an injunction, laid by Simbilis upon all the apparatus of ritual in the subworlds: they are powerless to harm a just man. The giants will apply the clubs to your skulls with all their considerable strength. Naturally the maces will be as feathers falling on you, and you will be exonerated, for you will be proven just, and no just man would ever be guilty of child-trampling."

Mumber Sull answered these words with an exultant cry. "Ha! By your own words you acknowledge Simbilis as your lord. He still lives and reigns over you! Know then that we, whom you slander and prosecute so offhandedly, are the liegemen and appointed agents of Simbilis the Sixteenth. Your wisest course is to abandon these futilities and conduct us to your lord."

At the Thane's outburst Bogwad arched a ragged brow and the blubbery expanse of his smile developed a wry contortion. "Your zeal exaggerates your master's dominion in the subworlds. While we may assume that he still lives, for he continues to resist those who besiege him, his domain is greatly dwindled — a small and embattled fief in the glass wastes. Still, it is true that certain of his spellcraft continues to defy our best efforts to undo it. This, to return to the matter at hand, guarantees that you need not fear the bludgeons, which must now be brought into play."

The Thane drew himself up haughtily. "We shall indeed be immune to the giants' most strenuous violence, for what are they who follow

Simbilis, if not just men? I marvel that you report Simbilis as diminished and besieged, and acknowledge in the same breath that his will continues to bind and thwart your evil instruments."

Bogwad shrugged, and the bog-giants closed in on the travelers, brandishing the maces with their slippery, knotted arms. Cugel cried, "Surely you realize the fallacy of these proceedings. A man who is less than just need not necessarily be a child-trampler."

"The procedures are as they are," said Bogwad. The giants raised the jagged clubs.

Polderbag uttered a bleat of distress. "What is the penalty for child-trampling?" he asked.

"Imprisonment and confiscation of property," murmured Bogwad blandly.

"I can no longer deceive you," said Polderbag. "I am guilty!"

"Most emphatically," affirmed Cugel warmly. "My indignation at last overcomes my loyal reticence. With my own eyes I watched him exterminate the child, deaf to its imploring cries."

Polderbag nodded energetically. The indignant Thane was cut off by Bogwad. "Protest would be pointless. Guilt is established. As one is guilty, so are the other two guilty by association. The bailiffs will now conduct the three of you to your detention."

Sull, Cugel, and Polderbag were manacled at the neck and waist, in the manner of the procession Cugel had witnessed in the night at Millions' Gather. The squad of giants fell in beside them and marched them off.

They had gone only a few steps when, glancing back, they saw that the stretch of bog where they had been tried was already deserted, as if court, crowd, and jury had evaporated, mingling its substance with the unwholesome mists that wound sluggishly up from the endless steaming swamps.

CHAPTER VI

THE HOUSE ON THE RIVER

The three travelers, chained and weaponless, were escorted by the bog-giants for a short way only, and then brought to a halt. The she-zombie who had been their original guide appeared out of the shadows, accompanied by a second as ghastly as herself. Both creatures carried scourges, lashes whose tendrils were strings of live blue hornets.

She who had been the guide made them a gesture, which the bog-giants took as their dismissal. They turned back and their sinewy hulks vanished quickly in the bog's level murk. The she-zombies took up escort positions on either side of the chained three.

Mumber Sull burst into noisy remonstrations, but their erstwhile guide cut the Thane short. "You exert yourself to no purpose. I now act solely in a bailiff's capacity, and merely conduct you to your detention. Strict silence is required. The creatures on your shoulders will aid us in enforcing this silence by repeating aloud your slightest whisper."

And indeed, the glowing little reptiles harkened alertly. Thus compelled to silence, and urged into motion by the mere sight of the glittering whips which buzzed shrilly, the three captives trudged through the muck and the poisonous gloom of the bogs.

An unending trek ensued. The trio soon learned that the bogs were merely a phase in the geography of the subworlds. The first sign of change was that the marshy flats began to slope more radically downward, and at the same time became more and more thickly overgrown with a kind of luminous purple kelp. This grew in tentacled clumps of ever-increasing size, and from a distance appeared to the trio like static purple fire covering the dark slopes. And indeed, the growth provided them their only light, for the green-veined rock ceiling vanished from overhead as the jungle terrain sank more steeply down.

The steepness was made more dangerous by the fact that each clump of the luminous growth exuded a phosphorescent purple sweat which ran in a constant trickle from its base. The fluid had a rank smell like rotting sea life, and it slimed the rocks. The trio's chain caused the false step of any one of them to drag down the other two, and they toppled often, frantically embracing the handiest clump for support. They discovered that the tentacles contracted sluggishly but irascibly when thus clasped, and each concluded privately that rather than a plant growth, it was more like a coelenterate or mollusk.

Soon they were embracing these mollusks merely to move at all, so steep did the terrain become, and it was as if they were inching down a mountainside festooned with the slippery humid thickets of the rain forest. The purple fluid fell in thin luminous waterfalls splashing down to rock-ledge lagoons, and sluggish wraiths of violet fog haunted the face of the crags.

The mollusks' exudations had soon soaked every inch of the trio's skin, and for a long time they were too sickened by the smell to eat the coarse mash which the she-zombies gave them. Time prevailed, however, and in the end they ate ravenously.

For indeed, this phase of their trek lasted many days. Or rather, many sleeps — cramped, leaden sleeps in drizzly grottoes, sleeps from which they were awakened only to creep, slide, and grapple farther down through the oily medium — endlessly, like ants toiling across acres of sea anemones at low tide.

They saw the next phase of their trek below them a full two sleeps before they actually reached it. A network of blazing purple streams sprang out from the foot of the glowing jungle-slopes. Clearly the terrain leveled out, and the rivers were formed by the runoff from the mollusk realm whose vastness could only be guessed. For the panorama stretched beyond sight to either side.

On reaching the foot of the crags, the she-zombies set out along one of the stream-courses. It had been clear from above that the streams tended to coalesce into fewer and larger rivers, and the trio was not surprised to find that the stream they followed constantly intersected others, grew ever wider and deeper in its course. By the time the party had progressed three sleeps they were walking on the gravelly bank of a river a stone's throw wide which rumbled through a ravine so deep its top was not illuminated by the purple glare of the waters.

The three found this phase of the journey far more painful than the previous. The gravel and polished detritus of the riverbank, naturally treacherous as it was, was made more so by the oily river mist. And here there were no soft (if repulsive) mollusks to cushion falls, but only bruising stone.

There was an added agony. The region abounded in a species of land-crab whose upper shells imitated stones. The creatures were toughly resilient and when stepped on, which frequently happened, they wrenched themselves from underfoot with violent suddenness. This did not bother the she-zombies, whose feet were highly prehensile, but the trio was invariably cast down when any one of them stepped on one of the beasts.

But the landcrabs did not need to be stepped on to cause the trio woe. The little creatures were extremely irritable, and seemed to detest one another. Whence it often happened that flare-ups occurred, squab-bles between a pair of the animals which spread to their neighbors. Instantly a small storm of battling landcrabs would spring up, a whirl-wind tall as a man moving along the riverbank. When one of these little blizzards crossed the path of the party it engulfed the prisoners, baffled them with a hail of bites and blows, and threw them to the ground. Imperturbably the she-zombies set them on their feet after each fall, and hastened them along.

By the party's fourth march down the river, the frequency of these flurries had increased so alarmingly that the zombies simply tucked their prisoners under their arms and carried them, to save the time wasted by putting them back on their feet.

The she-zombies' strength was such that this labor did not seem to faze them. In any case they did not have to bear it long. After a few hours they reached a juncture of the river they followed with another, larger river. The angle of the juncture was acute, and thus the head-land it formed was narrow, little more than a high wall of natural rock, separating the two purple torrents. Yet a vast platform had been built with this knife-thin headland as its central support. This platform's great width overhung both rivers on either side, and was further supported at these sides by cyclopean pilings sunk deep in the beds of the respective rivers.

The party trudged to a point just under the platform, which loomed two hundred feet overhead. There was a gangway leading from the riverbank, across half the river's width, to the foot of one of the great pilings.

They crossed the narrow creaking gangway over the glaring foam, and the three were fascinated despite their predicament by the massive stonework over them. The platform's underside was dark, for it was too high to be lit by the river. But there was clearly a light source atop the platform, for its edge was sharply defined.

A glowing red stripe ran straight up the outer side of the piling. The guards pressed their captives against this bright band of cloudy substance. The manacled three, adhering instantly to it, were snatched aloft. Rocketing upward, they watched the river diminish dizzyingly beneath them. Then they were flung out, dazed, on top of the great platform. Immediately afterward, their guards appeared and took them again in charge.

What struck the awed trio first was the platform's light-source. High above its center point, huge and yet affixed to the overhead blackness without apparent support, was a form like a blossom. This giant single flower, this downward-turned cup of elaborate scrolled petals, emitted a soft orange light which shed on the platform's proceedings a wide if murky visibility.

What the prisoners saw was a vast cargo depot, swarming with activity. The shipments received here were delivered at various runways by great winged claws whose passage was like a scythe of shadow across the blossom's glow, and whose vast creakings were clearly audible. Their shipments were all encased in transparent globes which ranged from small to huge in size and which were trundled off to storage lots or sorting pens by great insectoid creatures. These arthropods showed as much variation in size as did the cargo-bubbles they handled. The largest of the bubbles might contain a full-grown tree in its hillock, or a house; the largest of the dockworkers were twenty feet high.

These cargo-globes seemed mostly destined downriver, for they were more or less continually being rolled off the edge of the platform which overlooked the rivers' junction. The prisoners saw little of this, though, for they were being led to the opposite side of the platform, toward a building over a hundred feet high. They could see derricks and cranes towering up from its vast flat roof. Evidently the building was some kind of inspection point, and there was a lesser cargo dock on top of it.

When they had drawn near this dark edifice, the three could see that an S-shaped rune was graven over its doorway. Mumber Sull grinned. "Behold," he gloated, "again the subworld's braggart folly is exposed. Bogwad boasted that Simbilis was diminished and defeated, yet everywhere we see his works. For there, unmistakable, is Simbilis' rune. One can see clearly this great depot is of Simbilis' fashioning."

"Indeed it is," answered their erstwhile guide, apparently indifferent now at journey's end to Sull's infraction of the silence. "You must realize, however, that the commerce now carried on here serves ends directly contrary to those of the moribund wizard. The extensive docking activity you observe is largely devoted to supplying our siege operations, to which Simbilis' last stronghold must inevitably fall. All the facilities that we have inherited from Simbilis have been converted to our own designs. A look within at your place of detention will furnish an excellent example." The captives were ushered through the great doorway.

What they entered was a large indefinite space with puddles of fierce yellow light scattered through it. Then a kind of miniature topography became evident in the gloom. The floor was of smooth paving, but it arched and dipped to form scores of hills, hollows, and grottoes. The light came from numerous lakes and ponds of bright yellow fluid collected at low points in the landscape. The she-zombie waved a gaunt arm.

"This was once the lounge and recreation facility for travelers. A system of transparent tubing distributed a discreet but more pervasive light through the artificial niches and glens — then amply provided with cushions and couches. We have punctured the tubing, causing the luminous fluid it contained to gather in pools, which we use for purposes of detention. And touching this matter —" the creature now turned to her fellow "— where is the dilatory Slog? Must we once again stand here interminably, awaiting our prisoners' pool assignments while the party responsible scants and dawdles at her duties?"

The other spat — a viscous orange fluid — and replied, "Slog's bulk and malevolence render it unlikely that you would express these sentiments in her vicinity."

The first creature snarled, causing the other to draw back, though not with undue haste. "Slog is aware of my ill-esteem. As for bulk and malevolence, I possess these qualities sufficiently to make you for one rue my anger. We will bestow the prisoners temporarily in the handiest pool and you will run to inform Slog of our arrival and obtain the pool assignments she is so lax in providing."

The trio was led down a dark dale of masonry at whose bottom was a yellow pool. A wide metal grate lay across the surface of the pool some six inches above it. The subordinate zombie unlocked this grate and, groaning, heaved it ponderously aloft. The first creature tumbled the chained three into the pool. The depth of the pool was somewhat less than a man's height, and they found themselves standing with their heads just clear of the pool's surface, and the iron grate a scant inch from their upturned faces. The subordinate zombie was sent to obtain detention-master Slog's assignments. The first remained brooding by the pool, shouting after her departing colleague:

"Such callous hedonists as Slog mock their office, neglecting both efficiency and correct procedure." The creature then muttered in a lower tone, "How gladly would I oil the wheels of office with the offal's blood."

Polderbag addressed the she-zombie urbanely. "You have our sympathy. It is always exasperating to see a fool wielding power of which he is unworthy. Do I err in supposing you to be unfortunate in your superior?"

"Say rather my inferior," the creature glowered, "for I excel Slog in all save gross witless might. Her insolence passes telling. It is specifically prescribed in the writs of procedure that all personnel should receive an equal share in the devitalization of prisoners. Yet Slog hoggishly appropriates all such prisoners for her private delectation. Of yourselves, for instance, myself and my co-worker are rightfully entitled to a share. We shall not receive it. Slog will be the one, and she alone, who extracts the vital essences from your flesh. It is such gluttony that sustains her vast foul bulk, allowing her to dominate her scantly nourished sisters."

"Is this then to be our end?" croaked Polderbag.

"Your fate continues," conceded the she-zombie, "but your active interest in it may be presumed to end with your devitalization. Thereafter your remains will be shipped via cargo-bubble down to the glass wastes, the cadavers being conceivably useful in experiments." At this point they heard the cry of the returning subordinate:

"The prisoners are assigned briefly to any three available pools, for Slog shall require them soon. First their amulet is to be brought to her, in payment of the childslaughter fine. They themselves — alive and untampered with — are to be brought up one at a time shortly thereafter."

"Then help me to separate the prisoners," growled the first creature.

The subordinate replied sullenly: "The first of them only. I am reassigned to patrol and must hasten to my duties."

The two she-zombies lifted the grate, separated Polderbag from the chain, and locked the grate once more on Polderbag alone. Then the second zombie hastened off to its patrol, leaving the erstwhile guide to jail the two remaining captives. The creature asked, "Is it not you of the deformed ear who holds the amulet? As per the terms of your contract, having been guilty of a felony you have forfeited this property. The periapt must now be surrendered. There will follow a short wait, after which your lives must also be surrendered."

Mumber Sull did not deign to reply. Cugel, however, said helpfully, "My lord bears the amulet you seek in the pouch at his belt." The Thane stared at this betrayal. The zombie extracted the amulet, grumbling, "This too Slog will appropriate. It is a maddening injustice."

"However that may be, please do not yourself don this dread periapt," quavered Cugel with manifest anxiety.

His manner evidently excited the zombie's curiosity, but at first she concealed this. Pocketing the charm, she tucked the captives under her arms and walked over a hill and down to another pool. Using one horribly prehensile foot to hold Cugel's wrists fast, she stood on the other foot and used both hands to raise the grate, shove the Thane under it, and lock it again. Now, confronting Cugel alone, the zombie drew out the amulet and asked musingly:

"Why did you so fervently discourage my donning of this charm?"

"Because I dread the awesome power you would assume should you do so. The periapt increases strength a thousandfold. I find you sufficiently awe-inspiring as you are."

The creature did not seem to find this answer implausible. But then, with an impulse of suspicion, she asked, "If such is its efficacy, why has your lord not employed it in preventing his capture?"

"The Thane," Cugel smoothly replied, "deems the honor and dignity of his exalted rank to be incapable of augmentation. He scorns the artificial additions of magic." This reply forestalled certain wrathful remarks the Thane was on the point of making, causing him, chin deep though he was, to nod with majestic agreement. It also seemed to convince the zombie.

"Indeed I have noted your master's priggish and supercilious air. More the fool he, then." She regarded the lucent bauble with a grin that displayed the complex tubes and suckers sheathed in her oral cavity. "Slog's hour has come," she cried exultingly. She hung the pendant around her neck.

Cugel felt the grip that crushed his wrists suddenly diminish. Whirling around he leaped on the slender, trembling, pale creature that stood amazed before him. He bound her and gagged her with the cords and straps of the zombie-garment that had been shed by her suddenly smaller form. He bound her stoutly, having in mind the creature that would be straining at the bonds once he removed the amulet from her neck.

This labor done, Cugel was at liberty to note that his naked captive was marvelously voluptuous, possessing fat insolent breasts and comely limbs. After a moment's thought, he proceeded to wrestle with his already powerless captive, heaving her from side to side with sounds of great struggle.

The Thane, neck-deep in the pool under the grate, cried: "Esquire! Why do you waste precious time? Free myself and Polderbag at once!"

"The creature is not yet subdued," panted Cugel. "She resists my most strenuous efforts to quell her." Still struggling mightily with the bound girl the Esquire moved up the slope, then out of the Thane's sight down the other side. There ensued a long interval during which muffled sounds of exertion and outrage reached the Thane from beyond the rise.

At length Cugel sprang into view, with the amulet in hand, and a second later a mighty but impotent roar rose from behind the ridge. The Esquire retrieved the keys from the zombie's fallen garments and released first Mumber Sull, and then Polderbag. The bound zombie, having apparently worked off her gag, was now bellowing hugely, and other zombies appeared in the building's main door.

Polderbag looked mournfully at his body, soaked with luminous yellow. He moaned: "The cleverness of their detention system is dismally evident. Saturated as we are, we are absolutely incapable of concealing ourselves in these dark surroundings."

"We must flee," said Cugel. "Even now new pursuers appear in the entrance." He snatched up the zombie's fallen hornet lash and the three, blatantly visible, fled across the miniature hills and dales of cold masonry. In the great room's far wall they made out a green light, and for this they headed, hoping to find a portal of some kind.

And this, indeed, the green light proved to be, a doorway filled with a shimmering verdant glow. There was a small orifice in the wall beside this doorway, and from the orifice a booming voice suddenly issued:

"Arkla! Arkla! Witless underling. Why do you delay in bringing me the amulet? I grow impatient!"

Cugel reasoned quickly. "Doubtless the voice of Slog. If she is unprepared, together we might overpower her. We might escape thence by the route designed for our cadavers."

The towering shapes of zombies, fitfully looming nearer among the distorted shadows, made action essential, and Cugel's plan had an attractiveness it would have lacked if viewed by calmer eyes.

A voice boomed from distressingly near in the shadows: "Cut them off from the door! Detention-master Slog is unattended. If these three surprise her, they might work her harm!" Hearing this, Sull and Cugel ceased to hesitate and made for the portal.

Polderbag, torn, cried after them, "Suppose it is a trap?"

The pair plunged through without regarding him, and Polderbag fled after them. He suffered a cushioned collision with a green medium that snatched him aloft. Gaining his balance he found himself in the flow of a conveyor-stripe similar to the one which had raised him and his friends to the platform from the riverbank, with the difference that this one streamed upward through a tunnel, a long glowing gullet ribbed with archways. Above and ahead of him Polderbag saw his companions, themselves still somewhat disarranged by their impact with the unexpected conveyor medium. Cugel regained his equilibrium, assuming a back-floating position, and was the first to speak.

"Let us take stock while we may. Our pursuer's remark about Slog's defenselessness may indeed have been treachery, but perhaps it was treachery aimed at Slog herself, a hint to ourselves that we will be left unhindered to slay her if we can. Note that we are still unpursued."

Looking down the steep-sloping green stream to the now tiny archway which had been their point of entry, they saw no dark spot in the climbing flow that might be a persecuting agency.

"Perhaps this means that they are even now ahead of us, laying an ambuscade across our path," Polderbag muttered.

"Pessimism ill becomes us," reproved Mumber Sull. "Our cause is a just one, and we may be sure to thrive. Behold — the end of the conveyor is nigh."

An archway loomed ahead. The three strove to reduce their forward speed, but vainly. They were pitched through the doorway and were flung out onto the great building's rooftop.

Most of the roof's considerable expanse was a scene of swarming activity — cargo operations such as went on, on the great platform below. Great insectoid laborers toiled among the transparent cargo-globes, rolling them into sorting pens or over to the roof's edge, where long curving ramps swooped down a hundred feet to the platform proper. Other cargo-bubbles hung from great derricks and cranes. Above, the incoming winged claws circled with their deliveries.

The entire rooftop, however, was not taken up by these doings. At the point where the trio had been flung out of the conveyor there stood a squat blockhouse fronted by a colonnade of equally squat arches. From one of these dark arches a large form now erupted, almost before the three fugitives were well on their feet.

This creature was like the other zombies the three had encountered, save that she quivered with a ghastly corpulence that the others had lacked. Her jowls, glossy black bulbs of fat, hung like wattles below the mouth. The latter orifice was hideously open with the obese she-creature's labor to breathe as she hurried. The complex tangle of tubes and suckers which served the zombies as tongues was in Slog's case especially large and colorful. As she lumbered toward the three, she rasped:

"Is Arkla bereft of her wits? Does she send you together and unfettered? Manifest treachery! Her death will follow your own."

Now close, the blubbery black creature lunged. The three scattered and easily evaded the clumsy swipes of her haggle-clawed hands. Clearly her torpor of movement was such that even Polderbag — thinned, it is true, by his late travails — stood in no danger of capture. Cugel turned sideways as he dodged and slashed the scourge of blue hornets across Slog's face.

The pain of this assault stimulated the gross creature to her only swiftness: she seized the whip and wrenched it from his grasp before Cugel could retract it. Transported then as she was with fury and pain, Slog clutched the tendrils of living wasps and, howling, crushed and wadded them together between her naked hands into an inert ball of blue pulp. Then she charged once more with juggernaut rage.

Still the three fled and dodged her with ease, glancing wildly around as they did so for some avenue of escape. The creature became doubly enraged by her impotence to catch her adversaries. She shouted for assistance from her guards, but none were in evidence. Glancing over the cargo deck, Slog thundered, "Dock slaves! Dock slaves! Apprehend these three. Seize them and put them in my hands!"

The great hinged, sticklike insects handling the cargo-bubbles froze in their work. Then they turned in a perfect unison, as if all moved with a single thought, and leaped forth toward Sull, Cugel, and Polderbag. Some of these creatures were twenty feet high, and moved with prodigious strides. Though all were rather distant when called, the embattled three saw they would be surrounded in moments.

Before danger so imminent, Polderbag ceased to think rationally. He cast about desperately. Not far away stood a great derrick, from whose boom a hundred feet above the rooftop a cargo-bubble hung. This bubble was large enough to contain a three-story house, and this in fact was what it contained. Polderbag, however, took no notice of these particulars. All his panicked gaze registered were the massive crossbars of the derrick, crossbars up which a man might climb to escape onrushing doom. Perception was as action. Polderbag fled to the great derrick and began to climb frenziedly.

Sull and Cugel, though dismayed, were not so distracted that they did not see the dangers of Polderbag's course, but they yielded to his example as the only available escape. They too rushed to the derrick and began to climb furiously.

The fugitives had enough of a lead to have climbed above — but only just above — the reach of the tallest of the dock slaves by the time these fleet machine-like beasts drew around the derrick. Here they milled anxiously, the thought of climbing the derrick in pursuit apparently not occurring to them, perhaps because it was a feat that they were never called upon to perform. The three profited by this delay by widening their lead, though the higher they scrambled the more strongly they felt their refuge to be a cul-de-sac.

Slog, incensed by this brief impasse, clenched her sting-swollen hands in fists of rage. The gesture cost her renewed agony. "Climb after them," she howled. Then, seeing the whole crew of dock slaves surge forth with uncanny unanimity, and sparing a rational thought for the stress which the derrick would bear, Slog shrieked an amendment:

"Halt! Desist! Kylops Seven! Kylops Seven alone will climb after them. Move! Bring them alive and conscious to my hands."

A single dock slave, clearly the largest of all, began a tentative, rickety ascent of the derrick. The fugitives, feeling a vast strain through the frame up which they clambered, glanced back and saw their huge pursuer. They addressed themselves to climbing with renewed zeal.

At a giddy hundred feet above the rooftop they reached the boom, a great horizontal arm from whose end the cargo-bubble dangled above the milling dock slaves. Looking in the opposite direction the three saw, much more yawningly far below them, the vaster decks of the main platform. Looking straight down, they saw Kylops Seven. The beast's horny barbs clattered on the metal, and it slipped and swayed frequently, but its ascent was steady. Its mass caused a sickening swaying that increased as it climbed higher.

"Our only course is out along the boom," said Polderbag.

"Hopeless," growled Cugel. "There we are cornered."

"Present action, though futile, is preferable to passive acceptance of such a fate as awaits us," the spell-monger retorted.

"This indeed seems our best course until a further expedient presents itself," said Mumber Sull. The three hastened out along the boom, whose frame was broad enough to permit them to run upright, leaping from bar to bar. Before them, depending from the boom's cargo hook by means of a leather harness encircling it, was the huge transparent sphere wherein, perfectly upright, uncannily suspended, and touching the clear shell at no point, was the three-story house.

The boom gave a heavy groan and shudder. Behind them the three saw Kylops Seven clamber up onto its great steel arm. They quickened their pace toward the boom's tip, a progress rendered perilous by the swaying which Kylops Seven's blundering mass created as the creature also advanced out along the boom.

From below, the beast's movements seemed slower than those of a beetle crawling along a branch, and Slog found the spectacle maddening. "Offal!" she cried. "Make haste! Bring them to bay and scoop them up!" Her fulminations goaded the obedient giant to greater exertion, but its stiltlike appendages and polished barbs slipped and wobbled across the treacherous iron grid work. And each time the creature faltered, the boom rocked and swayed over the void. The fugitives had reached its end, and felt the full whiplash terror of these vibrations. They crouched down and clung to the crossbars.

In the meantime, however, Slog, seeing that the bulk of Kylops Seven threatened disaster to both the derrick and the captives, had been inspired with an alternate plan much surer to deliver her prisoners to her in a state fit for punishment. She snarled to a dock slave standing near:

"Bring the bubble-opener."

The slave sprang locust-like off into the docking area, and returned with equal speed, bearing a small calibrated rod. Snatching this object with bloated hands whose pain she scarcely noticed now, Slog manipulated it, and a hundred feet above her the cargo-bubble hooked on the boom emitted a brief whirring sound. At the same time, a large, slot-shaped opening appeared in the globe's upper surface. Looking down, the three fugitives saw the house still uncannily suspended within the sphere, but discovered that now its lead-tiled rooftop was accessible to them through the wide slot.

"Behold," said Cugel. "By risking one drop of a few yards we might gain that rooftop and win within the house."

"But it is a manifest ploy to deliver us alive into Slog's hands," protested Polderbag.

"But our escape was not looked for, nor was the present situation guessed when this house was hung here. It may contain something to our purpose, perhaps weapons of which the fiend below knows nothing."

"My Esquire reasons well," said Mumber Sull. He clutched onto the steel bars under him even while he spoke, as did the other two, for just then one of the ever-nearing Kylops Seven's false steps shook the boom mightily.

"Agreed then," yielded Polderbag. Cugel went first, climbing carefully but quickly down around to the boom's underside, and catching hold of the cargo hook from which the bubble in its harness dangled. Clambering to the slot Cugel took hold of an edge and hung down within the sphere by his hands. He let go. There was a brief eerie fall through very cold air, and he was on the house's roof. His companions followed him.

Far below Slog watched them — indeed, seemed greedily to count them — as they dropped inside the sphere. When they were inside she touched the rod again. The slot in the globe whirred shut. "Crane foreman!" she bellowed. "Lower the cargo-bubble!"

But when she turned again to survey the execution of her order, her grin cracked into a howl of dismay. Kylops Seven, spurred by its mistress' harsh shouts and alarmed to see its prey disappearing into the globe, had made a frantic lunge. One of the huge insect's claws, however, snagged on a crossbar as it leaped, and its twenty-foot bulk was, with all the force of its spring behind it, flung sprawling onto the very end of the boom, directly above the cargo-bubble.

The creature's violent impact, witnessed with anguish by Slog, had two distinct consequences: when the flexible steel boom sagged under the sudden concussion, its hook was flipped neatly out from under the loop by which it held the sphere, causing the latter to fall; then, when the flexible steel boom snapped back from its flexion, it flipped Kylops Seven neatly out into the void.

Sull, Cugel, and Polderbag, oddly without any sense of falling, saw the crowded scene below loom terrifyingly toward them. They crouched and clung to the lead shingles of the house's roof. Somewhat above and to one side of them, they saw through the clear cargo-bubble the not ungracefully squirming body of Kylops Seven, who quite obviously *did* experience a sensation of falling.

Below them now the rooftop cargo deck exploded upward and then for one instant, and one only, it was blindingly full scale and then, in the next instant it was diminishing again below and the trio in the bubble were surging irresistibly up, while among the swarming and shrinking details of the rooftop they noted a big sprawl of broken limbs that must have been Kylops Seven.

Such was the cargo sphere's resilience, that it did not reach the apex of its first bound until it was off the roof and well out over the vast platform. Then, as the globe began its plunge, it faced a drop a hundred feet greater than its first fall from the derrick. With a fascination whose horror was only a little diminished by the memory of that first fall's non-fatality, the trio gaped at the upsurging panorama of globes and toiling dock slaves. A brief alarm disrupted an area which grew hugely, shockingly near, and then fled from beneath them, shrinking away and yet metamorphosed by the instantaneous contact into a wreckage of debris and scattered limbs.

Rising now in its highest bound, the globe hurtled within yards of the giant light-blossom that illuminated the platform. The trio, still without any sensation of momentum, saw the richly scrolled petals of amber light swell as if to swallow them and then, after a slowing and a pause, the blossom in its turn began to diminish above them.

Once more they hurried into an abyss deeper than the previous, for it was dizzyingly clear that their second bound would end in the lavender torrent that stampeded two hundred feet below the platform itself.

The turbulent area of confluence of the two rivers grew swiftly before their eyes and, though they were now twice taught their invulnerability, the three could not repress the awe and dread with which they beheld the uprushing soundless fury of purple light.

After a brief engulfment in the seething violet of the river, the cargo-bubble rose and settled in the swift foam, joining scores of other spheres in their race downstream to a destination none of the trio perched on the rooftop of the house could guess.

Alone of the three, Mumber Sull preserved an optimistic mien, for he considered the bare fact that they were headed toward Simbilis to be sufficient cause for cheerful confidence. He expressed these views while the three of them paused upon the roof, taking stock of their situation and shivering a little in the unnaturally cold air within the cargo-bubble. Polderbag showed little patience with the Thane's sunny attitude.

"Supposing that Simbilis is in fact capable of rendering aid to those who serve him," the spell-peddler said, "what hope have we of ever reaching him? The impacts we have survived show this bubble to be indestructible — how shall we break free of it before it arrives at the receiving station and we are recaptured? And assuming we could successfully escape the bubble, how could we hope to penetrate to Simbilis, whom we must suppose to be entirely hemmed in by the infernal legions which besiege him?"

The Thane dismissed these objections with a wave. "Do you so readily believe the patent fictions of Simbilis' enemies? Could the arch-sorcerer in fact be besieged and embattled if his spells still stand potent? As for how we shall escape this shell, let us enter this house, descend within. Perhaps we shall find implements which will aid us."

"This seems our most practical course," Cugel put in. "Whatever the actual condition of Simbilis may be, it is imperative that we effect an exit from this prison before it passes again into the hands of the sub-worlders who surely await it at the other end of its journey."

The three being agreed, they arose. Casting about, they spied a dormer window which jutted out from the roof's lead-tiled slope. To this Mumber Sull gingerly advanced, for the slope was steep. The window opened easily. Stooping, the Thane stepped inside, followed by his companions.

What they entered was a densely cluttered attic, whose furniture was piled in crazily tilting heaps and stacks. The purple glow from the river several stories below illuminated little, and served primarily to make the shadows of the attic more complex and misleading. Misjudging its distance from him, Mumber Sull pitched face first into one of the highest stacks. A spectacular series of percussions followed, and the darkness rained picture frames, boxes, and footstools for a moment. The din was all the more hideous in that the chilled air of the cargo-bubble proved unnaturally conductive of sound.

And then the trio — all three sprawled in the wreckage — froze to hear a sound which succeeded their own racket. It was a voice, coming it seemed from a floor or two below, and yet seeming to move upward even as it ranted and shrilly raged.

"What? Treacherous offal! You have contrived an overhead attack? Futile!" This last word was fairly shrieked. Now clearly accompanying the voice was a noise of feet pounding up a flight of stairs. The trio, unnerved for all that the voice's shrillness bespoke a small man, sought to rise, but in the dark tangle of rubbish made little progress. The voice was now coming from the bottom of a short flight of steps which emerged into the attic. "This clumsy ploy will be your doom, miserable ape! You are contained and thus undone!"

At this last cry the three struggling pilgrims were subjected to an uncanny onslaught. The purplish gloom around them was suddenly filled, packed tight, with a gelatinous green medium that muted all sound, numbed all sensation in their bodies — indeed, paralyzed them to the extent that they ceased to breathe. Then, completely embedded as they were in the green jelly, the immobilized trio felt it move with a great shudder and the entire blob of it, which a moment before had filled the attic, was sucked out of the attic and down the staircase. Here, like three fish frozen in odd poses in the quivering mass, the trio was faced — and regarded with amazement — by a small white-haired man wearing furred robes.

After a moment's astonished inspection, the man made a gesture and the green jelly melted instantly. The pilgrims fell with a splash to the floor, where the substance now lay in a pool, a circumstance the little man had apparently not foreseen, for he did a little dance of vexation to find his feet ankle-deep in the stuff. But his attention rapidly returned to the three now picking themselves up from the floor.

"Clearly you are not subworld minions come to seize us, nor do I recognize in you allies of the abominable Karf Klartbodd. Indeed, I know my barrier-spells to be still in effect, and the villain confined to the first floor. Who are you, then, and whence do you come?"

Mumber Sull was on the point of ceremonious self-introduction when Cugel, seeing the stranger's great tension and impatience of manner, forestalled the Thane with a succinct reply. "We are erstwhile prisoners of the demon myrmidons, but lately escaped, and come to our present position through a frantic series of accidents too complex to be briefly related."

"Your haggard and soiled aspect lends credence to your tale," said the stranger. "Deferring for the moment a more particular account of yourselves, I will act as the urgency of my situation dictates. I will offer you remuneration in return for your services — they will not be required long, but they must be entered in on the instant. Aid me and I will implement your desires, whatever they may be. Refuse me and I shall leave you here paralyzed in the substance from which I have just released you."

Mumber Sull showed some displeasure at the man's peremptory manner, but Cugel and Polderbag acceded readily to an arrangement for which such poor alternatives existed. The Thane remained silent, allowing himself to be carried along.

"We are agreed then," said the stranger. "I am Tor Anderbastor. Let us return now without delay to my wife. She may give birth at any moment, and likewise at any moment the dastardly Karf Klartbodd may unleash a new assault upon her lying-in room!"

With this cryptic exclamation, Tor Anderbastor bade the bewildered trio follow him, and turned on his heel. At a brisk stride that was nearly a run he led them down the hallways of what had clearly been a richly appointed residence. The carpets and carved wood moldings of the hall, the spacious chambers whose interiors the three glimpsed in passing, bespoke taste and affluent ease. But all this opulence had been blighted by what seemed a shocking, unearthly vandalism — and this quite recently.

The ceilings shed noxious fluids that pattered on the ruined carpets like the unwholesome drippings within caves. The walls were blistered and discolored by great burned patches which seemed still to smolder, and which indeed were still warm to the stealthy, exploratory touches of both Cugel and Polderbag.

Mumber Sull was less attentive to surroundings. His curiosity having been pricked by the mention of an impending birth, he was attempting to elicit further particulars from Tor Anderbastor who, wholly preoc-cupied, scurried ahead without replying. He led them down a stairway which was burned in places, with some of its steps broken out, to what had to be the house's second, or middle floor.

He ushered his companions quickly past the head of the stairwell which led down to the ground floor of the house. "Do not near the bar-ricade which confines Karf below — it is damaging to those who touch it from either side." Nothing was visible in the stairwell. Notwithstand-ing the pilgrims gave it a wide berth and hastened to a door whither Tor directed them.

The large room they entered was far better lighted than the attic or third floor had been, both because it was a story closer to the surface of the great phosphorescent river, and because it had an aperture through which the river's purple light could enter directly — a large window centered in the wall at one end of the chamber. Thus all the room con-tained was quickly seen: certain minor furnishings around the walls, a cold fireplace, and a large canopied bed, whereon lay a handsome, full-breasted woman whose belly proclaimed her to be very near her time.

Tor Anderbastor went to the woman's side, and administered to her sips of a liquid from a vial he took from his pocket. The liquor had a soporific effect, to judge by the woman's more relaxed demeanor after drinking. Tor then made a quick check of the room, and a rather closer check of the window, where apparently one of his barriers was in effect. Then he turned to the three travelers.

"I may now, gentlemen, describe the service I ask of you." Tor indi-cated seats near the empty fireplace. "Make yourselves comfortable, but please remain alert to anything — anything at all — of an untoward nature, which you may perceive to occur in the room. This indeed is the single service I require of you, for you must know that I am under attack. The infamous Karf Klartbodd, my former partner, even now skulks belowstairs, devising my ruin as best he may. Thus far we have battled to a standstill. In the first stages of our battle we engaged upstairs — you saw the ravages of our conflict — and he drove me down to this middle floor. Subsequently I was the one fortune favored, and I was able to contain him on the ground floor. But he is not one who gives up easily. He knows my wife's hour is near, when that which he most desires will appear, and he is bound to strike again. At the same time, even as she nears delivery I must devote ever more of my attention to her, lest that which she is to give birth to should escape. Thus I shall be less able to meet Karf's assaults with the necessary vigilance. It is for these reasons that I have, overhastily perhaps, seized the opportunity of taking the three of you into my employ. Be assured that if you aid me your reward will be munificent. But now, while circumstances permit, you must detail to me how you came here — something I am hard put to guess at."

Tor's suspicion, coupled with his demonstrated magical potency, moved the travelers to satisfy his curiosity before seeking to allay their own, which certain of Tor's remarks had greatly whetted. It fell to Cugel to sketch their tale which, though he did it with an eye to brevity, proved a lengthy task. He had scarcely finished, and had begun to answer some of Tor's skeptical queries, when their colloquy was broken by a gasp from Polderbag. "Look!" he cried, pointing at the window.

The three others turned as one. At first they noted nothing more than the view from the window of the seething river below and the black crags past which it foamed. Then their eyes focused on something much nearer, something suspended in the air inside the room, between them and the window.

This was not a single object, but a cluster of small ones — coins, jewelry, bric-a-brac — in short, all the oddments that had littered the bureaus and tables of the room. These things now spun in a tight, dizzy orbit in the middle of the room. Even as the four watched the cap was snatched from Tor's head, and a small vase of wilted flowers was whisked from a stand near them, leaping across the room to join the frantically spinning little galaxy of objects.

Tor Anderbastor jumped up, more exultant than agitated. "Can Karf be so desperate? Is he reduced to such elementary ploys? I am ready for him! I have long had a strategy prepared to meet something as simple as Poog's Vortex!"

And clearly, it was a vortex that they were confronted with. The trio now saw that the whirling objects, after spiraling at greater and greater speeds into an ever smaller orbit, sank at the center into invisibility, simply disappeared.

Tor Anderbastor rushed up to the vortex without hesitation. His gait was a halting, stumbling one due to the necessity of bracing himself against the vortex's attraction, for this attraction showed a steady increase — already the heavy quilt covering the woman in the bed had begun to rise and stir in its direction, and the trio could feel its tug against their own limbs. Tor, however, showed no emotion save jubilation. Flourishing his hands above his head, he thrust both of them at the little maelstrom.

From Tor's sleeves poured twin streams of scabrous green rats. For a full minute these foul rodents flowed by the thousands into the whirlpool aperture, vanishing from sight with a sound like tons of potatoes rolling down an endless scuttle. A great cry of dismay, muffled and yet vivid enough to make the skin crawl, rose from belowstairs.

Tor's triumph was slightly marred by an over-exuberant defense, for he seemed to fumble the spell that should have stopped the outpouring, and before he managed to perform it correctly the vortex filled to the top, clogged, and ceased to spin, and nearly a hundred of the repulsive green beasts poured onto the floor of the lying-in room. These creatures found hiding places quickly, but being of a very erratic and vehement temperament, they plagued the conversation which followed by their sudden scramblings across the carpet, and their equally sudden attacks on the feet of the four.

Despite this vexation Tor took his seat with a victorious air, and genially produced a decanter of brandy and some glasses, resuming the interrupted conversation in a manner markedly more expansive.

"So," he said with a courtly nod to Polderbag, "your services have already begun. Though the attack was by no means dire, your warning outcry is proof of your good faith, and is precisely the kind of aid I ask of you, until my wife has been delivered. Then your remuneration will be all you could wish."

"I speak, I think, for my companions in saying that we shall strive to deserve it," Polderbag returned. "Perhaps you now feel at leisure to explain the grim conflict on which we have unwittingly intruded?"

Tor smiled in a mystery-knowing way. "The explanation lies there," he answered, indicating the woman on the bed. Then he chuckled. "But I will speak darkly no longer. The conflict you witness scarcely deserves that name any longer. Call it rather the last futile effort of the defeated Karf to win from me the object that will very shortly be mine. Poog's Vortex! It is really too childishly simple a ploy!"

"And what precisely is the object which arouses so hot a contest, and which you hint your wife is about to deliver into your hands?" Mumber Sull asked.

"What is the object?" Tor echoed Sull's question with a wry smile. "The object, my dear sir, is the Imp of Ka. But what could that mean to you? Let me say then that it is possession of the Imp of Ka which will enable me to fulfill your slightest whims. Your reward for aiding me as lookouts — why should I not detail it now? — will be the granting of one wish for each of you. And let me stress that you must feel free to ask for anything — I shall have the power to satisfy you when I possess the Imp of Ka. Such is the object whose delivery I await, and expect momently."

The three pilgrims, glancing at the woman on the bed, saw that even though narcotized by Tor's ministrations, she was beginning to twist, and roll her head from side to side, and shiver in a manner wholly different from such labor-throes as any of the trio had ever witnessed.

"Your estimate of the imminence of parturition appears correct," observed Mumber Sull to Anderbastor. "Perhaps you could — speak in greater detail of the nature of the Imp of Ka, and the manner in which your wife came to..."

The Thane hesitated, and Tor smilingly indicated forthcoming explanations. It was evidently a topic which he, from his present position, reviewed with a certain relish. With a gesture he caused a blaze to spring up in the fireplace, for the cold air of the cargo-bubble bit them sharply now that they sat at their ease. Tor beckoned for their glasses, and liberally dispensed second portions of the excellent brandy in the decanter. Then he looked thoughtfully at the purple river churning past the craggy canyon walls outside the window.

"The Imp is extremely ancient. It is older than the most cyclopean of the demons which sleep in the cold honeycombed core of the earth. And since it is older than the demons, it is also older than sorcery. There is no spell which, once hurled at it, it cannot absorb unharmed and thenceforth wield as its own. In the uncounted ages of its existence, thousands of sorcerers have tried to capture the Imp, and have merely augmented its thaumaturgic power. It is only because of the Imp's rather whimsical and unpredictable nature that it has not used its power to rule the world. But it seems to care little for the idea. It spends its life in a different space and time, and only appears on earth, of late, when some magician has succeeded in conjuring it, though it never remains in the conjuror's power. Only on this occasion will it be different. For I have found the means of binding it."

"You have found some invincible containment?" asked Polderbag.

"I have found Voonbood's Thrice-fast Formula," Tor sonorously intoned. Polderbag nodded wisely. Tor went on. "Indeed it was the discovery of Voonbood's Formula that caused myself and my former partner, Klartbodd, to seek the Imp in the first place. We had long known of the Imp, but only the possession of the formula emboldened us to attempt its capture."

"You and your present adversary were partners? In what line of business?" Mumber Sull asked.

Tor waved the question aside. "A complex matter," he demurred. "Suffice it to say that, having the Thrice-fast Formula, we determined to seek the Imp, and at last succeeded, by pooling our efforts, in obtaining the Imp's seal."

"Its seal?"

"The amulet which invokes the Imp. It was upon our gaining possession of the seal that we felt the bonds of partnership begin to crack. The night after we obtained it I crept — entered the room where we had stored it, to check on its safety, and discovered that my partner had already — had stolen it. There ensued a lengthy comedy, and comedy it was, an infuriating farce wherein each of us in turn stole the seal from the other. You see, the seal is a very easy object to steal, and a very difficult object to retain once stolen. The conditions of its use require that it be possessed for some time before it can be activated, thus both of us were prevented from wielding it as soon as we captured it, but had perforce to store it for some time first. But the 'massiveness' of so potent an amulet, its magic ambience if you will, is quite strong. It is easily located, and easily purloined by magnetism. Thus no matter where one of us hid it, the other was able to locate it and win it back. Finally, Karf recovered possession of the seal, and secured it in such a manner that it seemed the battle was his, and the Imp would be his to conjure and command. He obtained a spell whereby he was able to merge the seal with his own body." Tor broke off here, chuckling quietly.

Cugel, on whose heel at that moment one of the irascible green rats gnawed, gave a jump, and then asked with irritation, "We may conclude, I take it, that you managed to outwit Karf, and extract the seal from his flesh?" Tor smiled and nodded. He opened his mouth. Mumber Sull cried out, "The walls! The ceiling! They are sprouting limbs!"

It was not merely human limbs which began to extrude everywhere with a rubbery sound, but tentacles, hooves, barbed claws, stingers, and mechanical tongs as well. Every species of grasper and pincer sprang out of the rich wallpaper and began seizing blindly in all directions.

Tor leaped up. "Insolent wretch! He tries a bolder tactic, does he? He finds me ready then!"

Flinging his arms wide, Tor cast — from what part of himself could not be determined — a largess of yellow spineballs which, by their hopping behavior once they hit the floor, proved themselves to be toads. These toads leaped to engage the limbs which the man downstairs had caused to sprout. When seized by the more fleshy appendages, these thorny creatures exuded a rank venom which caused the grasping member to swell and rot before the pilgrims' eyes. When clutched by the hornier claws, the little toads wrought destruction by exploding. Everywhere smoking or decaying stumps were being hastily retracted from the room, leaving the walls scarred and blistered.

As with the rats, however, Tor broadcast too many of these creatures. After the majority of them had been crushed or exploded, a substantial number remained to scamper under the furniture for cover. There they

encountered the rats, and throughout the time that followed, squab-
bling pairs of rats and toads would roll unpredictably across the floor,
hissing and squeaking in mortal combat. These struggles generally
ended in the explosion of the toad, an event which usually splattered
the accompanying rat all over the ankles of the pilgrims.

After one such explosion Cugel took the occasion of Tor's being
still across the room to mutter to Polderbag: "This sorcerer displays an
irritating ineptness I have not often observed in others of his calling."

Polderbag shook his head. "If you take this man for a wizard you
are greatly mistaken. To judge from the affluence of his house, he is a
spell-merchant who made his fortune trafficking with the subworlds
and is now attached by the sublords, who have laden him with chains
of debts. His ineptness is precisely what betrays him as a man who has
acquired his powers wholesale, rather than by dark and lifelong application. I have already mentioned to you the growing number of his
like in Millions' Gather. He suffers the fate inevitable to his kind and,
also like his kind, is so embroiled in a personal vendetta that he hardly
notices that he has been possessed."

Tor returned and seated himself, wearing a victorious smile and
ignoring the annoyance of the excess rats and toads. He made a third
dispensation of brandy and resumed his account even more compla-
cently than before.

"You may well marvel that I evolved a stratagem to frustrate so cun-
ning a scheme as Karf's of merging the Imp's seal with his own body.
Nonetheless, this I did. I obtained a charm used by witches to steal a victim's vital essences. Then I called my estimable wife to my chamber —"
Here all looked at Tor's wife, who lay in a cessation of movement, seeming to sleep, though her lips mumbled softly.

"I called her to my chamber," Tor continued. "I informed her as tact-
fully and gently as possible that it was paramount to my own interests,
and thus to hers as well, that she arrange an infidelity with Karf, my ex-
partner." A toad and rat exploded directly in front of the fireplace. The
green fragments sizzled and spat as they hit the flaming logs. The trio
jumped at the percussion, but Tor affected not to notice it.

"She was quite taken aback by my proposal, and hotly refused,"
he went on. "I studiously assured her that I not only condoned such

an adulterous interlude, but actively insisted on it as essential to our mutual well-being. Somewhat hesitantly she informed me that a liaison already existed between herself and Karf, whereby just such acts as I urged her to, she performed with him on an almost nightly basis." Tor's eyes sparkled. "This, gentlemen, was an unheard-of stroke of luck for myself. I had anticipated tears, demonstrations of outrage, not to mention the difficulties of lulling the suspicions of the wary Karf. Instead I found my strategy put, as it were, into operation for me. I was not slow to seize the opportunity. I raged at her infidelity, and brandished it as a mace to compel her obedience. Not only was she an adulteress, I ranted, but her paramour, as if specifically chosen to humiliate me, was a man who for several weeks past had been my bitterest foe. Justice sanctioned a grim punishment, but I forbore to mete out the full penalty her guilt had incurred. I would even allow her foul and illicit intercourse to run to one last night, but in return she must on that night, at the climactic moment for her partner, utter under her breath a conjuration I would teach her. The following night, Karf fell asleep after his amorous exertions, and my wife carried away the seal which, by the effect of the formula I had taught her, had now merged with her womb where it would germinate and, after a short time, bring to birth the Imp of Ka. Immediately on her return I barricaded my house, and applied all the spells in my power to hasten the parturition of the Imp. I staked all on gaining possession of it — I assumed the defensive and left the field to Karf to besiege me as best he could. I calculated that I would have my weapon before he could penetrate my barricades. It has taken weeks, despite my best efforts, and in that time Karf gained entry of the upper floor, whence at last I drove him to the ground floor and sealed him there. This is the reason he was taken with myself when the sublords attached my house. He has exerted himself mightily, but I have won. He cannot hope to penetrate before I have delivered my wife of the Imp and bound it with Voonbood's Formula into my service."

Mumber Sull regarded Tor somewhat incredulously. "You imply that you were aware that you were being taken by the sublords? Did you make no attempt to escape your house at this time?"

Tor shook his head slowly. "You still have not grasped the extent of the power I will shortly possess. What do I care if I be sunk to earth's coldest, blackest center? The Imp will provide me with wings. With the Imp as my chariot, the glass wastes are as a brief stroll for me to cross. With the Imp as my vessel, I could navigate the Sea of Earthquakes itself, and skim across the howling mountains of its waves. With the Imp as my sword, I alone am a mighty army. What fastness of all the subworlds can contain me? Who or what can stand against me?"

Tor's face shone with sweat, and his eyes with a hot light. His exalted gaze strayed vacantly to the bed and he started. "Her labor begins! I recognize her pattern of palpitations. Stand alert now. I shall deliver her — you must warn me of assaults from Karf."

The woman's movements were bizarre. Her whole frame was subject to a rapid, irregular vibration. Judging from her bewildered face, which was perfectly conscious now, her sensations were of amazement rather than pain. The three pilgrims stood around the bed. Tor knelt by his wife, uttering an endless stream of incantations in her ear, while her expression remained one of the greatest shock as if, in the incomprehensible tongue he was using, Tor were exhorting her to the most unspeakable acts. Things continued thus for long moments.

Suddenly the woman's body shook with a violent spasm and she shouted aloud, again more surprised than pained, and then Tor bent forward and plucked from the bedclothes an object blackish in color, and of the size of an ostrich egg. This he held aloft and crowed, "It is mine! The Imp is mine!"

Entirely ignoring his wife, who lay blinking in the bed, Tor rushed to a bureau and set the black ovoid on its top. Then he plucked a small scroll from his breast pocket and, losing no time, intoned a formula from it, gesturing at the black egg the while. He pronounced the syllables with verve and precision and, when finished, pocketed the scroll with a great sigh of accomplishment.

"I uttered it flawlessly. The Imp, when it wakes, will be bound to me by the unbreakable Thrice-fast Formula. It staggers me. I am now among the mightiest of the earth! I am the equal of Argove Thrumpp, yea even of Simbilis —"

"This is gross presumption," snapped Mumber Sull. "You are well advised to stifle such blasphemous comparisons when in the presence of three of Simbilis' staunchest retainers."

The other two of the vaunted three did not seem to share the Thane's outrage, but the sharply nettled Tor, thus jarred at the apogee of his fantasies, had eyes for Sull alone.

"Do you dare..." he growled, then cut himself off. "Hold," he hissed, "the Imp wakens. My first assignment to him will be the chastisement of your own impertinence."

The black egg-shape stirred — its shell seemed to loosen. They quickly saw that this impression was created by the first movements of a pair of leathery black wings which, up to that moment, had been tightly wrapped in a smooth sheath around the Imp. Now with an abrupt shrug they opened completely.

The Imp of Ka proved to be a creature of the simplest construction. It consisted solely of these large batwings, sprouting from either side of a fat furry egg of a body. At the moment its wings behaved like legs, and stood on the 'feet' of their padded tips while the fuzzy ellipsoid body hung between them. This otherwise featureless creature performed a brief, rickety dance, in the course of which its movements became firmer and more coordinated, in the manner of a colt gaining its legs. At last the creature executed a series of agile capers, which included a run up one wall, around the ceiling and back to the bureau top where it had hatched. This done, the Imp revealed its face.

A seam developed in the fur of its ovoid body, and then the fur opened in the manner of a large eyelid, revealing the chubby visage of a cherub. Performing a limber curtsey, the Imp smiled at each of the five persons in the room (for Tor's wife had sat up and was staring with the rest).

The spell of the Imp's strangeness was only broken when Polderbag leaped off his feet with a yelp and began a frantic dance of pain. The other three standing around the bed followed suit. The floor had begun to bubble, the very tiles seethed and slowly boiled, snapped and warped underfoot, and suffocating, sulfurous vapor began to fill the air.

"Imp! Imp of Ka!" cried the hotfooted Tor. "I command you to put an end to this assault, and hale up forthwith the felon who instigated it!"

The Imp's smile widened. Its fuzzy bulb of a body sank in a second curtsey, and instantly a fierce hail filled the room. The numbing barrage

of ice pellets issued from all four walls as well as the ceiling. The five
writhed blindly in the bruising storm, the floor hissed and steamed and
the uproar of hurtling ice nearly drowned Tor's enraged howl for the
Imp to end the blizzard.

The hail ceased, as had the floor's boiling. A fetid smoke now clogged
the air in sluggish wraiths rising from the ruined tiles. Before Tor could
voice his displeasure with the Imp's mode of service, however, he found
that the second part of his command was now being executed: the door
opened and through it a bald and richly dressed man drifted, his feet
some inches from the ground, his body rigid.

"Karf Klartbodd," gasped Tor, "delivered into my hands. O moment
of sweetness! You have done well," he said, turning to the Imp. "You
must in the future take greater care that in obeying my orders you do
not inconvenience my person, as your hailstorm did, but you are forgiven this first thoughtlessness. I now command Karf's evisceration,
and see to it that his consciousness is activated — I desire that he be
aware of my revenge."

The Imp performed a third obeisance, and the still rigid Karf was
seen to awaken, blink, and regard the scene about him with dismay.
But the next occurrence was not the evisceration which Tor had com-
manded — it was a movement on Tor's own part. He walked up to Karf,
bowed profoundly, took his enemy's hand in both his own and raised it
reverentially to his lips.

The astonished expression on Tor's face as he performed these acts
was ample proof that his own will was not involved. The respectful
ceremonies he had initiated were not interrupted for all that. Still staring amazedly, Tor bustled to get a chair and seat Karf Klartbodd upon
it. Then, graciously motioning the three pilgrims to be seated, and
bowing to his wife, Tor assumed a declamatory stance in the middle of
the room and commenced an oration:

"I, Tor Anderbastor, am a spindle-shanked fool and a greedy,
remorseless felon. I have committed repeated acts of homicide, always
through an agent. I am guilty of cheating Vamba Meeming out of her
inheritance and causing her and her kin to be sold into slavery. In my
younger days I committed several infamous rapes upon the daughters of the rich who were boarded in my house for instruction, and I

silenced them with threats and spells. Of late I am incapable of lechery, and am in the habit of eating fenleek soup for supper to befoul my breath and discourage the amorous demands of my wife's hot-blooded youth. At present my only lust is for power and limitless wealth. By way of summary permit me to remark that I am a scabrous cur, a ready bootlicker if it suits my safety, an incorrigible lick-spittle and infallible toad, and that my use of power would be to extort precisely the same shameless servility from all who surrounded me."

Having concluded, Tor Anderbastor bowed to all present, lastly to Karf. Karf Klartbodd applauded politely, and then rose from his seat and offered it to Tor. Tor accepted, and Karf in his turn took up a stance in the center of the room, bowed to all present, and began:

"I, Karf Klartbodd, am a sadistic monomaniac whose lusts are his law..."

The trio and Tor's wife, however, did not hear the body of Karf's speech. The Imp of Ka, while at first chuckling hugely at Tor's oration, had quickly lost interest. Now leaving Karf to have his say, the Imp crossed the ceiling and crawled out the window. Sull, Cugel, Polderbag, knowing that their fate now depended on its whims, rushed after it.

Craning their necks from the window they saw no sign of the Imp. Outside the bubble churned the river, littered with other cargo-spheres of different sizes, the whole ensemble passing through a swifter and narrower channel than previously.

Suddenly the cargo-bubble, by what agency they could only guess, began to rise from the river, which fell away. The canyon through which it ran was deep, and the house's ascent between its black walls — the river's light growing ever dimmer — was long. Then the bubble around the house dissolved and the building, having reached the top of the canyon, was set down gently upon its brink.

As one the four moved to seek the front door and embrace this miraculous opportunity, all of them suddenly mindful of the dire fate to which continuance in the house would have led. Their exit was blocked, however. Karf had concluded his address, and Tor had acknowledged it with well-bred applause, and the two now stood facing one another before the doorway.

Karf bowed, and Tor curtseyed. They joined as for a waltz and began, slowly, both smiling, to dance. Merrily, gracefully, chatting intimately, the pair revolved. They danced out of the room, and through the hall, and down the stairway.

The pilgrims, dumbfounded, followed them. On the ground floor, in the main room where the house's front door stood wide-open, Tor and Karf continued to dance. They circled the great hall thrice, and the light convivial air of their dancing made it almost possible to believe them surrounded by the fashionable throng of some great ball. Thrice around the room they danced, and then out the front door. The other four crowded thither, to watch the pair vanish from view. This they did rapidly, for the light was scant. Overhead, using its wings as wings for the first time, the Imp flapped, chuckling. He and the two puppets below him danced out of sight over the ragged black rock.

Chapter VII

THE STRONGHOLD OF SIMBILIS

Gunnruck, the wife of Tor Anderbastor, proved very helpful in guiding the trio on a foraging tour of the house. Her late parturition was wholly unattended by exhaustion or debility and, being a woman very much in her prime, she led the search for food and weapons with all the spry energy of her male companions.

And indeed she was as quick as they to strap on a short-sword and a poniard when her search for her husband's arms collection proved successful. The latter weapon looked especially dangerous when she allowed her hand to rest its grip on the hilt. Neither this gesture nor the look accompanying it was lost on Cugel or Polderbag. Both the Esquire and the spell-peddler, who had begun to favor Gunnruck with meaning glances, adopted now a markedly cooler manner toward her.

The house still swarmed with rats and toads, and while many of the pantry shelves were invaded by these ravenous creatures, the party found a shelf of preserved goods in glass jars that had survived unscathed. Then blankets, rope, and other miscellaneous gear were assembled and gathered in packs, and the pilgrims were ready to set forth.

However, though all were agreed that to remain longer in the house would be dangerous, no such accord existed concerning their direction thence. This Mumber Sull discovered when, setting confidently forth in the direction he knew to be downstream, he saw that the other three balked at the house's threshold.

"Why do you hesitate?" he asked. "Ahead lies Simbilis' stronghold — that much we may believe, while disregarding libels regarding his besiegement. Can any of you be slow to seek his aid while the dangers of this hellish region hem us around?"

"It is precisely these dangers which give me pause," replied Polderbag. "Having some slight acquaintance with the terrain we have just covered, and having as well the incentive of the spice-preserves which must also lie behind us, I turn thence more readily than follow you in a direction which holds dangers as yet unknown to me, and whither I have no incentive to travel."

"Are you mad?" gasped Mumber Sull. "What of the might of Simbilis the Sixteenth, might he will surely wield in your behalf, if you join your suit with ours? Is this no incentive?"

Polderbag shrugged. Mumber Sull turned his astonished gaze on his Esquire. Cugel spoke soothingly. "Consider, my lord. Polderbag has reason to some extent on his side. Can we be sure Simbilis' abode is downstream? Can we wholly trust the reports of subworld monstrosities, half whose testimony you yourself dismiss?"

The Thane shook his head impatiently. "The creatures admit what they must. The endurance of Simbilis' works is too manifest, even here, for them to conceal his presence. It is merely the lies with which they seek to obscure the true scope of his power which I disregard. Beyond doubt he lives and is to be found ahead, unbesieged and easily accessible to those who seek him."

Both Cugel and Polderbag remained silent. Gunnruck, who had been looking from them to the Thane, now addressed the latter. "I gather your mission is founded on some grounds of hope of which I myself am unaware. All I have heard of Simbilis is in the nature of legend, and places him in an era vastly remote from our own."

"On two occasions Simbilis' very foes have conceded his present survival," Sull replied. "Moreover, once the archwizard is found, I enjoy what amounts to a guarantee of his aid: I am his vassal." And here the Thane indicated his earlobe.

Gunnruck nodded, apparently understanding, and looked reflectively at Cugel and Polderbag. Then she turned again to Mumber Sull. "For myself, a woman and weak in body, my decision must be as much a choice of companion as a choice of direction. Lest I appear gullible, I must declare, Thane, that your quest seems a fool's errand to me. But lest I be found an even greater fool, to cast my lot in with wolves for my guards, I ask that you let me accompany you. I am sure that the perils of travel in either direction are in any case nearly equal."

Mumber Sull bowed. "Time will remove your skepticism, madam. In the meantime rely wholly on my unfailing service and protection."

Cugel still hesitated. His impulses were thoroughly mixed. Most realistic seemed a return to Millions' Gather, where a passable living might be won at any of a number of enterprises at which Cugel was adept.

Nonetheless, the months of his trek in Sull's company in search of Simbilis had had an habituating effect. He had come thus far in the hope of finding the archwizard, though sometimes it was less than half a hope that guided him. Somehow it damaged his self-esteem to consider that the whole quest had been foolish. Also, much more might be won by reaching the wizard, if a fraction of the reports concerning him were true, and it was undeniable that even his enemies affirmed that he still lived.

A consideration occurred to Cugel that proved decisive. Danger was as likely on a return as on a forward journey. In danger, Polderbag would be wholly untrustworthy as an ally. Sull, on the other hand, he knew to be stolidly moral in such matters, even to the risk of his own life, a trait the Esquire was not slow to appreciate in others. He joined the Thane and Gunnruck.

Polderbag, seeing that his way was a solitary one, yielded to necessity. Uttering a growled imprecation, he joined the trio which had already set out downstream.

The river itself was only distantly audible, for it rushed far below them in the chasm whence the imp had lifted them. The party did not walk at the very brink of the cliffs overlooking the river, for though the light was greatest along this margin, the rock was uneven, and slippery with the slowly rising purple mist given off by the torrent. They found it safest to choose their path some fifty yards in from the glowing brink.

Thus they never saw the river itself, but crept over the black crags in the liminal light of the chasm's peripheral ambience. All above them and all to one side was unbroken blackness. To the other side of them, twisting out of sight in the distance ahead, was the smoky purple scar of the chasm that grumbled and hissed with its deep torrent. The chasm lay in the darkness like a great frozen fork of purple lightning, and the four travelers toiled beside it, farther and farther into the subworld night.

Their laboring through this landscape endured some fifty days — or rather, fifty marches and fifty sleeps. For more than half this journey the pilgrims lacked even a hint that their surroundings would ever change. But on the thirtieth day, while his companions sat over their glum breakfast, Mumber Sull cried out that he saw a light ahead.

The others leaped up, expecting an approaching torch or lantern. What in fact they saw was quite distant — no more than a white glow visible just at the place where the chasm's great fork of light dwindled to a point — that is to say, at the edge of visibility.

As succeeding marches brought them closer, the pilgrims were convinced that the light marked a new region in the underworld topography, for the pale glow grew to a distinct zone of white, a low aurora that spread along an ever wider horizon as it was approached. By the wanderers' fiftieth march, the light resembled a wall of wavering white cliffs to whose feet the purple river and its chasm ran.

But the illusion presented by the light was the exact reverse of reality. When the pilgrims reached the river's end and the pale of the zone of light they were faced, not with the ascent of a cliff, but the descent of one, and an awesome cliff it was.

The black rock through which the river ran stopped short in a sheer wall two thousand feet high. The river, whose own bed was sunk a thousand feet in the rock, spewed out of the cliffs halfway down them. The purple falls thus formed, thick with cargo-bubbles, were received by a vast drain, and thus were lost immediately to sight in the new region below.

This was a region of glass. It had to be glass for it was clearer, more translucent than ice, and was surrounded by no such frosty zone as so unending a world of ice would have to be. It was an uneven, but otherwise featureless terrain. It could be seen to rise in knolls and fall in ravines, but the distance, combined with the restless underwater light suffused throughout the crystal continent, made judgments of its surface uncertain.

"These then are the glass wastes of which we have heard. An unpromising prospect," Cugel said.

"Perhaps when we have descended, a nearer vantage will make the prospect pleasanter," said Mumber Sull, a reproving note in his voice.

"And yet how may we effect our descent?" said Gunnruck. "Our ropes, combined, and augmented by leather straps from our other gear, would not reach even a quarter of the way down."

All assented to the justice of this estimate. A silence ensued, broken by Cugel, who had gone to inspect the waterfall more closely. "Listen," he said. "The river issues from a cleft shaped as a 'V', for the river chasm's walls lean back from the perpendicular at the point of the waters' egress from the cliffs. Thus a ridge is formed which might be descended without ropes. From the lip of the falls further descent may be devised, and the obstacle now facing us would be halved."

This plan was adopted. The wall of the river chasm, in turning out to become the face of the cliff, formed a kind of 'corner' — less than perpendicular because of the gentler angle of the chasm's walls described by Cugel. Hugging this ridge to their chests and inching down backward, the pilgrims descended in order.

The angle made the descent relatively secure, but it was a harrowing exercise. Each pilgrim on his left hand saw stretched out the unreal land of glass, an endless luminous waste of ecto-material, two thousand feet below.

Yet should he turn from this to look on his right side for relief, he saw down there the great river swelling climactically at the brink of its fall. Huge cargo-spheres bearing trees or houses were snatched past and down like chips of wood, to vanish another thousand feet below into the glass drain.

It was just beyond the lip of the falls that the ridge terminated. The seam of rock ended in a shoulder that had once marked the brink of the falls. The attrition of the water, however, had caused the brink to recede into the cliffs, and the shoulder on which the pilgrims huddled together now jutted some yards farther out. From here the party was afforded a direct view down into the throat of the maelstrom, where the purple waters clotted with cargo-spheres were received by the great funnel-like hole in the glass.

This observation platform was full of disadvantages that had not been obvious from afar. It was far from level, and the small part of it on which one could stand, sufficient perhaps for two, was inadequate for four. The pilgrims maintained themselves on it by keeping a nervous grip on one another. Moreover, the boiling purple mist had thoroughly slimed the rock, and only a wavering of balance or small slip on the part of any one of the four was immediately magnified to a perilous rocking of the whole party.

Cugel was quick to discover a further difficulty of the place. "I note an unforeseen disadvantage of our present position," he said. "This ledge juts out considerably, and overhangs all parts of the cliff within five hundred feet below. We cannot safely proceed from this point. I suggest we climb back up and follow the cliff seeking a better way down."

"A second expedient suggests itself," said Mumber Sull. "A man could be lowered. Those above could then cause the rope to swing. The man, aiding in gathering momentum for wider swings, could thus be swung in to the cliff-face. There he might catch hold and anchor the rope, down which those above might travel."

"An excellent notion!" applauded Polderbag. "Your Esquire, as the most agile among us, would be the man best fitted for the project."

"I assure you," said Cugel with some energy, "that I have no intention of being swung in the manner described above that vortex."

"This is indeed ungracious," said Mumber Sull to his Esquire. "It was yourself, after all, who counseled our descent hither."

"This element of overhang was not evident from atop the cliff," said Cugel. "Moreover my congenital —"

"You are all extremely fortunate," interrupted a voice from quite nearby. The four turned their heads with a suddenness that threatened their equilibrium. Once they saw who had spoken, their shock endangered their security on the slippery rock a second time.

The figure they confronted stood upon the air two yards out from the rock shoulder's edge. He was naked and all his body was of a solid shiny white, like enamel. His face was a white blank of the same material, save that it was featured with five black holes that possessed both the outline and all the movements of eyes, nostrils, and mouth — the shadows of features.

This figure, seeing he had the rapt attention of all the party, continued. "I do not normally patrol beyond the fringes of the besiegers' encampment. Had it not chanced that I was returning from a rare errand outside the wastes, I should never have discovered you here. You, then, in turn should not have been deterred from almost certain death. Is it not unsettling to consider the blind unlikelihoods that shape one's fate?"

"No such captious subtleties engross us at present," Mumber Sull replied. The white figure, suspended before the vast lucent wastes of glass below and beyond, was an unnerving and even dizzying shape to behold. As he spoke, the flexions of his shadow mouth formed the words with all the nuance of flesh, and a whiteness which intermittently obliterated his shadow eyes was uncannily like blinking. "More to the point is the matter of your allegiance," the Thane went on. "For what agency do you perform the patrols to which you allude? Who are the besiegers you mention?"

"My master is Simbilis the Sixteenth, and the besiegers are the demon hosts encamped outside his barrier."

"What!" said Sull. "Can you claim to be a vassal of Simbilis and yet spread the lie that the archwizard is besieged?"

The shadow eyes narrowed sternly. "I am Leemb, and no mere vassal of Simbilis, but one of his archangels. The role of interrogator is mine, sir, and not your own. I have so far ascertained your auras as to know that with a small exception you are devoid of thaumaturgic power. Your mode of travel is further evidence that you are not demon minions, for such would travel by bubble down the vortex and under glass to the encampments. Thus, gauging likelihoods, I saluted you as enemies of the subworlders. The possibility that you are spies on their behalf naturally remains. Thus it is I who now require certain explanations."

"Can these not be delayed until we have descended from this dismal crag?" Gunnruck snapped. Polderbag, to whom the straitness of their perch compelled her to cling, was taking ungallant advantage of her proximity.

Leemb nodded. "I must ask you then all to take hold of one of your ropes." The four pilgrims all took a double grip upon a length of rope, trusting Leemb because it was clear he could compel them if he chose.

The archangel floated forward and grasped one end of the rope. Then without warning he sprang out from the cliff.

His leap had irresistible power, snatching the other four from the rock like so much thistledown. The archangel did not plummet straight down, but sailed through a high gradual arc, trailing the pilgrims in the half-dangling manner of a kite's tail.

The great milky wastes of glass below were a nearly featureless plain, a shimmering not quite solid-seeming plain, the mere phantasm of matter and substance. It proved solid enough, however, when the pilgrims came to rest. Cugel, lowest on the rope, landed first, and the other three were dumped on him in succession, Polderbag last.

When the party had gained its feet Leemb joined it, and elicited from Mumber Sull the accounting he desired. The Thane sketched briefly the manner in which the four of them had become associated, and dwelt at length on the usurpations of Cil which had originally impelled Sull himself forth.

"You come, then, seeking vengeance," said Leemb.

"And restoration of my titular powers, as promulgated by Simbilis himself," the Thane added.

"It is well," said Leemb. "What will be Simbilis' answer to your suit, I do not presume to say. I will convey you safely through the siege and the barrier. Within, others will take you to the archwizard. To accomplish this, however, you will all have to undergo a temporary alteration. It is necessary that we adopt a disguise in order to pass through the besiegers' encampment. Moreover, it will greatly expedite matters if you adopt this disguise now, though we are leagues away from the barrier and the siege."

Leemb made a gesture. The four pilgrims found themselves joined by a chain, to which the neck of each was attached with an iron collar. But this was a circumstance that the four scarcely noted, for all were wholly distracted by a second metamorphosis. Each of them had had substituted for his own legs a prodigious pair of naked scaly limbs — backward-jointed, like a bird's or reptile's. Stiltlike, long-muscled, and each terminating in four squamous clawed digits, these appendages moved and fidgeted under their new (and astonished) owners with a springy power that promised great speed.

As one the four pilgrims raised an outraged cry. "What have you done?" cried Polderbag. "What malign prank is this? Return us our rightful legs!"

"Were I to do so it would mean your deaths. You shall have your own back once you are within Simbilis' barrier. Meanwhile, if you are to pass safely through the subworld encampment, you must appear to be a gaggle of the hybrids resulting from the demons' experiments with human captives, and I must appear to be your keeper. In addition, the alteration will enable us to travel more quickly to the encampment itself, for it is yet distant."

"But what folly is this?" asked Mumber Sull. "Surely you could transport us thither aerially, as from the cliff. For that matter, you could doubtless bring us through the siege without confronting the demons at all. Beyond question, the power of Simbilis is sufficient for such paltry feats."

"Indeed it is," answered Leemb. "Simbilis' power is sufficient to annihilate the armies that have for centuries now hemmed around him, let alone to transport his servants through his own barriers. But his great work demands all his vast energies for its realization, and he expends only grudgingly the bare minimum necessary for his defense. Consequently, we who serve him operate on a strict economy. You could be easily transported to Simbilis, but it is more cheaply done, in terms of thaumaturgic energy, to work a few metamorphoses and run you thither afoot."

"What project can this be," asked Mumber Sull, "that requires so complete an attention from the master, and so wholly involves his powers? It must be something of great moment if it can move Simbilis to allow his vassals, to suffer such an indignity as this." And the Thane surveyed with loathing the great springy legs restlessly flexing themselves beneath him, causing him to bob and rock as if he sat in a boat on choppy waters.

"What Simbilis' project is," Leemb replied, "is best deferred. Further talk seems pointless. Sooner started, sooner arrived."

But Cugel forestalled the white shadow-featured being's movement to be off. "This vague reply is unsatisfactory," the Esquire blazed. "To inflict so perverse a mutation upon our persons, and then to cavalierly postpone explanations, is too high-handed. Consider," Cugel appealed to Mumber Sull, "we have no reason to credit this interloper's claims to affiliation with Simbilis."

"What we believe or disbelieve," put in Gunnruck coolly, "is not to the point. Leemb's powers seem ample to override our objections."

Leemb acknowledged this with a bow. "This is of course true. And indeed we can waste no time in setting out, for I must return to my post. Still, a brief account of what that post is may calm your suspicions. My function is to patrol, with the aid of various guises, the camp of Simbilis' besiegers. Their encampment has two purposes, and the siege itself is now in fact only the lesser of these. More and more predominantly it serves as a developing grounds, a complex of laboratories in which the demons experiment with the property and persons brought down captive from the surface world."

"To what end are these experiments made?" put in Cugel. "What is their nature?"

"Their nature is entirely sinister — they concoct abortions, hideous distortions and hybrids of the life of the surface world. The results of their researches will be unleashed in the world above during an intensive invasion whose precise date is not known by us. Myself, with other of the archangels, believe it will not greatly precede the dying of the sun, whenever that occurs, but this is conjecture. What is certain is that the invasion, when launched, will be formidable."

"Your mission is the sabotage of the dire experiments which prepare that holocaust?" the Thane asked.

"Only incidentally. The earth is doomed, the invasion inevitable. Simbilis' concern, and the errand on which he sends all his archangels, is the rescue of such human captives of the demons as have not yet been perverted or grafted into obscene hybrids by the technicians. Our work is the incessant smuggling of such persons through the barrier, whence they are brought to Simbilis at his project. Thus I am quite practiced in the matter of bringing people through the siege. We need fear no detection thanks to your disguise, which you see will have to be borne with. And now we must be off."

The archangel gestured, and the chained four sprang up and raced forth, or rather, their legs did so. For the upper halves of the pilgrims, gesticulating with alarm, were merely dragged headlong by the great scaly limbs, which ran upon the glass with perfect traction and sure-footedness. Leemb appeared floating before them a yard above the glass. He stood musingly, and without apparent effort matched the great speed of the four pairs of legs.

This speed never flagged. The unending glass was molded in a choppy terrain of knolls, hollows, gullies, and hills, yet the clawed feet fled nimbly along without pause or the slightest uncertainty.

Leagues were crossed thus in what would have seemed moments to the pilgrims, had it not been that the legs, through some thaumaturgical oversight, drew more than half their strength from the travelers' relatively puny bodies. Their stertorous gasps and harsh cries finally succeeded in attracting the notice of the abstracted and speeding Leemb, who halted them for a rest.

Thereafter, the archangel had his party's weakness more in mind, but the pilgrims found it grueling work. The glass terrain became more spectacular in scale — hillocks became small mesas, gullies widened to ravines. And then when the travelers felt that they must soon die of their exertions, the archangel halted them before a somewhat higher bluff than any they had yet passed.

"I must now assume my own disguise," Leemb said. "If you proceed cautiously to the top of the rise, you will see where we must pass to reach Simbilis."

The four topped the rise, and from thence they beheld the encampment of Simbilis' enemies. The landscape fell away before them, sloping down to a immense crescent-shaped metropolis built at the base of a prodigious green wall. This wall was curved, but was so vast that the segment of its arc visible to the pilgrims seemed nearly straight, running beyond the limits of vision to either side.

The height of the green wall could be appreciated by considering the structures of the sublords' encampment, for these were dwarfed by the wall, and yet were themselves things of impressive stature. All were wrought by the blasting and melting of the native glass: great bulbs thirty stories high filled with liquid wherein swam creatures too distant to be made out; great open bowls of glass supported on tower-tall stems and containing what looked like villages; and ziggurats that would have seemed mountains of tiered ice had their terraces not been densely crowded with vegetation.

These more towering structures formed a thronging skyline etched against the green background of the overtopping wall. There was an additional stratum of buildings huddled around the bases of these more awesome works, where jagged igloos of glass crowded the encampment's ground level.

"We now enter the critical leg of our trek," said Leemb at their side. "Put aside fear, for I am placing you under a compulsion, and you will be incapable of giving yourself away by some wrong gesture or utterance. As you will remain sensible of alarm and curiosity, I will, when convenient, provide what explanations I may."

The archangel had donned chainmail and gauntlets, masked his face with a hood, and supplied himself with a lash. This he now flourished and the four sprang away down the slope to the great encampment. This time there was no disharmony of motion between the pilgrims' upper and lower portions, for each had become a powerless consciousness borne along in a body obedient to a foreign will.

They drew near the base of one of the great bulbs, where a squad of demons were being drilled by their lieutenant. Leemb saluted the lieutenant smartly. "Some batrachs for exercise in the aquacideum."

The officer, a bearish creature with a massive monocular head, bent his single orb skeptically upon the four. "These are harmless-looking creatures to be exercising as aquacides."

"Such is their guise. They are of extreme ferocity."

The demon grunted and made a gesture. A large disk dropped from the air and hovered near the ground. Leemb bowed and stepped up onto the disk. The pilgrims found their bodies doing likewise.

The disk soared straight up and hung over the open top of the thirty-story bulb. A vast bluish lake glittered in its crystal crater, the surface wrinkling with a myriad activity. The disk tipped and the five splashed down into the waters. During the brief fall the pilgrims felt the chain vanish from their necks.

Near the place where they fell a group of women — pale, lithe, naked — floated in a sportive school. Their breasts bobbed, lilies on the water. They laughed and splashed one another, beckoning to the pilgrims. Not far from them floated an empty sloop, one oar trailing over its gunwale. It seemed a comfortable little craft.

It was not Leemb's intention, however, to remain on the surface.

He dove and began to swim down, and the mighty legs of the four propelled them after. Just under the surface, they saw that each of the women was the puppet-like termination of a thick polypous stalk. The eerie bouquet thus formed merged, at some distance underwater, in a blobby coelenterate body whose central mouth was wreathed with cilia. As for the sloop, this proved to be the everted lips — whose act of camouflage was truly superb — of another fat, formless entity dangling beneath like some obscene spiny fruit.

Leemb and the entranced four swam deeper. The pilgrims were indefatigable, seeming to need no air. They swam through schools of tri-part hybrids. Powerfully propelled by sharks' tails, these creatures had the torso and arms of gladiators (each carried a net and trident) with the beaks and tentacles of squids for heads. They swam in tight formation, and moved with uncanny unison.

"Anglers," said Leemb's voice in the pilgrims' minds. The archangel spoke soundlessly to the consciousness of each. "Predatory marine troops. All in the aquacidia are predators. We seek the drainage system. Via this we can penetrate a half-league through the encampment before we must surface and again face demon scrutiny."

They reached the bottom of the great urn supporting the waters. Here they faced a battery of blue grotto mouths that breathed out a cold current. One of the orifices exerted a perceptible suction, and into this Leemb passed.

The swift transit through this blind vein was never truly dark. The glass conduit through which this drainage sped was permeated by the milky light that was suffused throughout all the crystal substance of the wastes, and thus the pilgrims were sucked through an endless pale blur, featureless and dazzling.

Suddenly the flow went into a sharp upward spiral. They whirled ever higher on a perpendicular path and then were spewed out in a fountain. They gained their feet and stood waist-deep in a pond on the top of some great eminence. The spectacle of the demon siegeworks stretched vastly to either side, and only its highest structures seemed of a level with the flat open space on which the party stood.

Leemb now addressed them with his voice: "We are atop one of the vegetation pyramids, having ascended via its irrigation system. From here the waters drain off and run down to the terraces on which grow the malign vegetable inventions of the sublords. We shall descend by the maintenance ramp, avoiding the dangers of that flora."

The chain was restored to the pilgrims' necks. Leemb led them to the edge of the ziggurat's crown, and leaped onto a steep glass ramp which ran down the side of the great pile. The pilgrims followed him, sliding down in a shackled cluster.

The wide ramp connected the tiers, and glimpses of jungle swept past the party. About halfway down the pyramid's flank the ramp was interrupted by a small cluster of glass outbuildings. Various personnel stood about here: long-limbed hairless entities with scissor-digits. Various pruning and digging tools were in evidence leaning against the walls. A gardener somewhat taller than his fellows lunged forward to confront Leemb.

"What is the meaning of this? Whither do you come and where are you bound?"

"These hybrids were intended as fodder for the aquacides," replied Leemb. "But they escaped the aquacideum via the drains and entered your irrigation system. I caught them at the upper level, and am returning them to detention."

"The aquacides dine on hybrids, then? An expensive diet. If the pyramids received as much bounty as the tanks, I am sure we could work marvels." The speaker's lanky compatriots murmured approvingly at this speech. Leemb made a deprecatory gesture.

"You cite an imaginary injustice. Your own project utilizes hybrids as provender." And Leemb indicated a gaggle of individuals who were even at that moment being led out of one of the glass buildings and onto the jungled terrace that was on a level with it. Some of this group were normal men and women, some were compounds involving non-human elements.

Leemb's interlocutor spat. "Such hybrids as are given us are all rejects, the spawn of abortive experiments."

"Even so are these that I lead back to the aquacideum."

"Indeed? They seem fit — they must be to have effected the escape you describe."

"They are agile enough. However, they were unsuccessful in their intended function. Their breed was designed to exercise the taran-tulurks, but they proved too slow. They were simply eaten, causing the lurks to grow bulky and sluggish with over-feeding and lack of exercise. These leftovers were consigned to the aquacidia."

While this exchange was going on, the four pilgrims watched the group of men and hybrids being marshaled by guards onto the terrace. The party of them, not clearly understanding their surroundings, began to disperse into the foliage. One of them, an individual whose sex was indeterminate due to the tortoise's carapace that sheathed its torso, bent over a blossom and idly plucked it.

Instantly on doing so the plucker howled and the flower began to grow at a prodigious rate. The plucker's visible members began to shrivel just as swiftly. Moments later the flower, swollen to a man's size with a bloated green body like a caterpillar's, waddled away leaving nothing but the tortoise's shell behind it. The flower's blossom had clearly become a carnivorous mouth. It caught sight of another of the party, an antlered female, and rushed in pursuit.

At about the same time a man, who instead of arms had a pair of scorpions' tails jointed to his shoulders, wandered under a tree and was crushed by a great anvil that plummeted down from overhead. The tree bore a veritable crop of such skull-crashing fruit. The scorpions' tails flailed briefly, breaking their stingers on the obdurate iron, and then were still.

These incidents quickly alerted the rest of the party to the nature of the place into which they had been herded. A panic took them and they fled out of sight into the vegetation, save for one whom a muscular cactus seized and proceeded to decorticate. From the dense growth into which the band fled, ominous rustlings, snaps, and muffled shrieks were heard.

"You say they were not swift enough?" growled the gardener in reply to Leemb. "They look like very marvels of fleetness."

"You underestimate the speed of a lurk," said Leemb solemnly. "Several breeds possessing intelligence are now being developed. These are nearly impossible for even the fleetest beings to escape."

The gardener looked with open fear at Leemb. "Pass, man. My sym-pathy goes with you, for you serve mad masters."

Leemb led his charges through the outbuildings and on down the ramp below them. Once more they slid past tiers of jungle. "The tale of the lurks was concocted," the archangel informed his charges telepathically. "Such rumors nourish the suspicions and internal rivalries that already plague the demon allies." After a pause, Leemb added in afterthought, "Of course, in strictest truth, we are not perfectly current on tarantulurk modifications. We sincerely hope, at least, that the tale we spread is only a fiction. Here. Our goal is nearly won."

The party reached ground level with a jolt. A jagged barrier ringed the perimeter's base, penetrable only through a guarded gate. This Leemb readily passed, using the story he had just employed.

Outside, they saw that the green wall delimiting Simbilis' domain towered much nearer. It could in fact now be seen to consist of a rank of immense trees, which seemed to wave and shudder softly, though the air of the glass wastes was dead still. Moreover, though this subterranean atmosphere was also dead black and lightless save for the glow of the glass itself, the great trees stood revealed in a light of their own, a rich light that brought out the green and silver of their leaves, and which accounted for the barrier's vivid color even when seen from a great distance.

Leemb indicated the dense region of glass igloos, and huts — broken here and there by taller structures — which lay between themselves and the trees. "Safety is at hand. This last phase should not be at all harrowing. We will pass through a zone of subterrene workshops, and may cover much of the distance in the corridors, without passing through the hellish rooms themselves." The party arrived at a rude portal from which a ramp descended under the surface of the glass.

Entering here, they came to an antechamber from which several corridors diverged. Leemb led the entranced four into one of these corridors. The passage's course was erratic and took many turns. The all-surrounding submarine light of the glass went past the runners in a warm blur. There were frequent intersections with other corridors, and at some of these crossings gusts of sound burst on the pilgrims — aborted moans, nonsensical outcries, and the far rattle of unguessable machinery. They passed many doorways too, some open, but the haste of their spellbound bodies denied the pilgrims' eyes more than a glance of the chamber interiors.

A series of particularly shrill outcries, terminating in a slam, echoed from a passage they crossed, and Leemb's thought came in explanation.

"The development laboratories among which we pass are the scene of many experiments. Rapacious entities which perfectly resemble furniture, and which possess both sexually perverse and anthropophagous traits, are engineered in one area. In another paintings are being made — idyllic landscapes and such — which have the property of freezing and then shattering the eyes of beholders. In yet another area musical instruments and compositions are made which at first delight the ear and then eviscerate it — barbed music, it is called. These numberless atrocities account for the sounds you hear, for each project requires test subjects. But happily we have nearly traversed the zone, and the barrier is near."

A damp rampaging form erupted into the corridor ahead, and bore down on the group. The ample light showed the creature to be a pack-animal of a species common in the surface world and known to all of the party — a semi-intelligent quadruped, hairy and possessing a massive squarish skull. However, this particular animal did not move with the agility usual among its ilk. It lurched forward on a top-heavy scramble, and pitched repeatedly off its feet into a struggling heap.

The cause of this ungainliness was a second body attached to the pack-beast's. The upper half of a man sprouted at an angle from the beast's flank, fused at the waist to its hirsute musculature. The man cried out and flailed his arms, and this caused the beast to stagger. Its face wore an evil leer uncharacteristic of its dull-witted kind, and it ran with frantic energy.

It plowed directly into Leemb and his party. The pilgrims collapsed under the onslaught and the beast, like a tempest of flailing limbs, trampled across them and rushed on down the way they had just come.

In the next instant a second figure bore down on them, clearly in pursuit of the first. This individual was anthropoid save for his long arms and flat-topped skull. He checked his rush on spying Leemb and noting Leemb's charges.

"Quickly!" he panted to the archangel. "Driver! You must set your charges after my beast." The pack-beast was now some way down the corridor. It could be seen to run with an ever-steadier gait, while the attached torso flailed its arms more weakly, and moreover seemed to have sunk farther into the pack-beast. It was now joined at the armpits to the creature's back. "Look," cried the technician. "As its rider is more completely assimilated, it will grow stronger and flee with greater speed."

It seemed true. As the beast neared a turning, only the man's forearms and head from the neck up still protruded. The sinking head wailed feebly, and then the ensemble rounded the turning and was gone from view.

"Your charges are clearly designed for speed. Hurry or I shall lose a valuable model. Its only flaw is its hyperactivity upon the consumption of a rider. I did not foresee this excess of energy, and the animal burst its tether. It is too valuable to be lost for so slight an error!"

Leemb gazed frigidly at the technician. "Is your creation as valuable as a wurn? These are slaves of the wurn battalions, and serve more vital ends than yours. They must fetch back a component for an experimental wurn now under construction. They are not available for petty errands."

The technician swelled with anger. "Petty errands? You are an arrogant fool. What component are they charged to fetch? Can it not wait?"

"The component is a reproductive organ. As for waiting, this my masters will not abide."

"What? Are wurns being given generative powers? This is a blatant violation of alliance terms."

"Superior factions of the alliance, such as the wurn battalions, may with perfect justice ignore the repressive restrictions to which you allude."

The technician had for a moment forgotten his own concerns, and looked at Leemb aghast. "Can your engineers have been so ambitious and foolhardy? Wurn mutations are wholly unpredictable even in the first generation. The creatures' great size renders all uncontrolled reproduction doubly dangerous. This recklessness is typical of the wurn sector. But do not think all other sectors naive, or unprepared to deal with treachery, should it be attempted." The technician, again mindful of his creation, spat a curse and rushed on in pursuit of it.

Leemb's will animated the four, and they too fled on their way, while the archangel's thoughts addressed them. "My efforts to sow discord are hardly needed. Factionalism is rife throughout the encampment. On the eve of the invasion of the surface world, tensions here will be at their peak. Surface dwellers may hope that internecine struggles will greatly weaken the invasion's impact…But here. Our passage is nearly completed."

The corridor took a last turn and ended in an empty chamber. It seemed a defunct laboratory, judging from the loom-like frames, the vats, and tanks it contained.

"Carnivorous clothing was made here," Leemb informed them, speaking now. "The vats held the voracious threadlike organisms, which were woven to form rich and modish garments. These could have proved a ghastly success as hazards to humankind. But the organisms are both irascible and cannibalistic. The clothing tended to devour itself when deprived of wearers for long periods. But our present business is with the vast yonder."

Leemb approached a glass grating in the wall, and removed it with a practiced air. The four were once more magically disembarrassed of their chain. At Leemb's impulsion they pushed themselves one at a time into the narrow vent the grate had sealed. The relentless propulsion of the great backward-jointed legs drove the pilgrims with a worming motion through a white opacity.

One by one they emerged, and found Leemb already before them, stripped of his disguise. To one side of them sprawled the encampments, a vista of fractured, hewn, and blasted glass. Even the nearest of the vegetation pyramids and towering aquae were distant.

On the other side of them, huge and near, were the trees of Simbilis' barrier. The party had to climb to approach the trees, for they stood rooted atop a chain of small hills. The hills were of fragrant black soil and bore a lush growth of deep grass. Both hills and trees alike occupied a zone of their own private daylight.

The pilgrims climbed into this anomaly with an amazed and solemn tread. Over all the demon encampments arched a null and windless black, but when the four looked up between the long shuddering drapes of silver-green leaves, they saw sky of a rich blue. The green of the grass blazed as if in the noon of a sun younger and more ardent than any the pilgrims had known. Each of the four experienced a shock of falling, due to Leemb's restoring to them their natural legs. They took scant notice of the change, and continued climbing.

"These trees, though enormously larger, are such as I have seen before above," said Gunnruck. "But I have never known such light as this. Is all within Simbilis' stronghold like this? Is his realm indeed a great garden, as has been rumored?"

Leemb smiled a shadow smile. "What you will find within will strike you as more desolate than all you have yet seen."

"What?" said Polderbag. "Does not the archwizard's power suffice to procure him pleasanter surroundings?"

"You are impertinent, friend Polderbag," snapped Mumber Sull. "Certainly his power suffices."

"Simbilis has not retired to these regions to indulge an idle taste for bucolic scenery," Leemb said. "The inconveniences you have lately suffered, necessitated by the strict economy he has imposed on all expenditures of energy, should convince you of Simbilis' dedication to his project in hand."

The party came to the crown of the ridge and stood among the giant trunks. Before them, under another endless black ceiling, a region of white dunes stretched out of view. The travelers found it strange to see this pale silent desert before them, and yet to be standing in sunlight with the windy leaves rattling about their ears.

"This is the wizard's domain?" asked Cugel.

"Yes," said Leemb.

"And is the barrier then so easily crossed?"

"It is easy to us, but not to Simbilis' enemies. The besiegers have long renounced barrage as useless, but there was a time when they assailed these trees with corrosive sprays, and gouts of leprous fire, and juggernauts twice as high as a vegetation pyramid — all without bending or scorching a leaf."

Gunnruck cried out shrilly. "The dunes. They are upheaved!" The earth stirred beneath the party's feet. Far across the dunes an immense crest rolled through the sands, lifting the pallid hills and hollows into a steep remorseless wall. The mountainous wave ran athwart the ridge where the party stood. It swooped by with a vast splintering noise, as of the shattering of acres of glass, and broke on the barrier some hundreds of yards down. Then all was as before, for the wave had left new dunes in its wake.

The four stared aghast at the archangel. "These disturbances have a cause you will learn," Leemb said. "They are infrequent, and you will be in the care of skilled navigators. These must now be summoned, that I may return to duty."

The archangel led the four down the slope to the brink of the dunes. Polderbag bent over to poke the sand experimentally, and pulled back bleeding fingers with a curse. "Glass!" he exclaimed. "The dunes are of broken glass!"

"Even so," said Leemb. He produced a whistle, on which he blew. A hissing, as of a sleigh over ice, was heard to approach. A small craft topped the crest of a dune and glided toward the barrier.

It was a boat-shaped vessel propelled by two paddle-wheels. Seated in the stern between the wheels was a squat figure manning the tiller. The craft hissed to a stop before the group. Its paddlewheels — while in motion were blurs — proved when stationary each to be a cage containing a creature whose frantic exertions were its source of propulsion.

Leemb addressed the steersman peremptorily. "These four are to be conducted to Simbilis." The pilgrims boarded, and seated themselves in the prow. "I now bid you farewell," said Leemb. "Do not ask about where you are going, for you shall see for yourself soon enough. May your audience with Simbilis bring what you desire."

Mumber Sull nodded. "We thank you for your aid, discommoding though it has been in some respects. We look for our speedy restoration to the surface world, and the chastisement of those who have wronged us."

Leemb shook his head. "Have you not learned here how dangerous a place the surface world will one day become? Surely you would not regret it if you found Simbilis unwilling to return you thence?"

All four found these words ominous. They would have risen, but Leemb signaled to the steersman. The creature — a legless hulk with powerful arms — barked an order, and the paddlewheelers leaped into scrambling motion. The craft shot away from the bank.

The creature at the tiller was a skillful husbandman of the boat's momentum. Avoiding the peaks of the dunes, he utilized the downslopes wisely to build his speed for the upslopes. The course seemed to wander as a result of this technique, yet it sped unflaggingly, kicking out behind it high twin arcs of sparkling glass whenever it topped a crest and shot down into a hollow.

The vessel's crew were on poor terms. A short time after getting under way the steersman said to the starboard paddleman, "Why do you run so sluggishly? You are an inveterate slacker and malingerer. When Simbilis leaves and we are free I shall relish throttling you."

The paddleman replied — or rather, his panting voice issued from the wheel's blur: "You never will. Lort and I. Have made a pact. To join against you."

"Bah!" said the steersman. "An alliance of the impotent. After the master's bond is dissolved, I shall easily kill you, while you remain still encaged by your wheels."

The paddleman muttered at this without retorting. Gunnruck and Polderbag simultaneously cried out. A vast wave had surged up on the starboard horizon, and swelled crackling toward the craft.

"Hard port paddle," snapped the steersman. "Cut starboard power." The legless creature leaned on the tiller, and the port paddleman scrambled frantically, causing his wheel to blur with speed and spew behind it a shower of pulverized glass. The starboard paddle stood still, and the craft sharply turned its prow to run athwart the wave. "Full power both paddles!"

The boat drove up the seventy-foot face of the giant. It soared amid the shattering din. It crested and hung, heavy and still for an instant on the wave's peak, and then swooped down the behemoth's back onto once more motionless dunes.

Before the wave's passage had diminished below a soft roar in the darkness, the ferry slaves renewed their bickering.

"Indolent churl!" hissed the tillerman at the starboard paddle-wheeler. "Your sloth nearly lost us critical momentum. Have you forgotten the time we were dashed against the barrier by a wave we failed to overtop? You had the wheel to protect you and only I was injured by the impact. Your criminal laziness will not go unpunished.

When Simbilis departs I will strangle you both in your prisons, and feast on you there at my leisure."

"Never," gasped the paddlewheeler with rage. "While the wheels move. You cannot touch us. And we shall run. Until we have caused. An identical wreck. While you are senseless. We shall escape. You will be slain. Before you can move to. Defend yourself."

"Futile fantasy," said the steersman. "I control the tiller, and shall cause us to capsize. I can leap free and suffer only minor damage, but without Simbilis' protective charm, the glass which would fill your wheels in that event would cut you to pieces if you sought to stir an inch. You would be at my mercy."

At this point Mumber Sull addressed the steersman. "You have spoken of a time when Simbilis will leave. What occasion will this be? Is Simbilis to rise and reassume dominion over the surface world?"

"We are enslaved to be Simbilis' ferrymen," hissed the creature in reply. "We are not compelled to satisfy our charges' idle curiosity."

"If you wish. Information you must. Pay for it," put in the creature in the starboard paddlewheel.

"The form of payment. We accept," added the creature in the port wheel. "Is your flesh. One of your fingers. To each of us. Will buy an answer. To one question."

"This is a repulsive proposal," answered the Thane indignantly. "It is not even justly conceived. One of you alone might give the answer. Why should three be paid?"

The steersman shrugged. "None of us would consent to see either of the others the sole recipient of flesh, each being willing to answer a passenger's question gratis to prevent it. Thus we have agreed to join in silence till a triple fee is rendered."

"Bah! I scorn this loathsome extortion." The Thane returned to the bow.

Gunnruck addressed him as he took his seat. "It seems we must wait to learn what Simbilis' situation is. Meanwhile, whatever the nature of his stronghold, we face the possibility of being detained there indefinitely. Did that not seem to be the implication of Leemb's last words, Thane?"

"They bear that interpretation, madam, but that cannot have been

the archangel's meaning. Simbilis will surely dispose of us as we petition him, in consideration of my faithful service."

"And my own service as well, honored Thane," put in Cugel.

"Just so."

"And yet," said Gunnruck, "might not a great lord have his own ends
to serve, and might not he deem his servants' ends less important than
these?"

Mumber Sull disagreed at length. Polderbag recalled his services
to the Thane, expressing his hope that the wizard would indeed prove
generous and compliant. Gunnruck repeated her doubts.

These matters engrossed them as the boat dived and crested over
the dunes. They encountered further tidal waves — several score of
them, in fact. The intervals separating these disturbances were so long,
it was some time before the four realized they were regular.

Of course, familiarity with these waves made the overtopping of
them little less harrowing to the pilgrims. But from the peak of one of
them the travelers made a discovery that distracted them somewhat.

"See there," cried Cugel in the perilous instant at the apex. "A great
mantle lies on the dunes ahead." The craft was already plunging down
the rushing slope, but all had seen — very distant — what appeared an
immense drape of jet-black lying sprawled upon the lucent pallor of
the dunes.

Their course in fact seemed bent for this object, and from atop succeeding waves they inspected it, each time more nearly, until at last it
was visible without the added elevation of a wave.

From this nearer distance it was clear that the vast mantle, if such it
was, was draped over an object of awesome proportions. From farther
away the solid blackness of the sky had left visible only those portions
of the mantle that lay spread on the white of the dunes. Now the pilgrims could make out the bulk which the mantle shrouded rearing up
thousands of feet into the dark…

Murmuring amazed conjectures, the four waited through the long
approach of the craft to the skirts of the mighty fabric. They determined that the mass covered by that sable drape was roughly ellipsoid
in shape, and the size of a small mountain.

Drawing nearer yet, they perceived that the mantle was not a woven material, but was composed of loose parallel strands. The craft nudged its prow among these fibers, and docked.

"It is like hair!" said Polderbag, lifting a double handful of the cable-thick strands, and then looking aloft again at the rounded bulk down from which they hung.

The other three followed his gaze, and thus all beheld a small brightness leap into view overhead, like a star catapulting off the top of the shrouded mountain.

The dazzling particle plunged toward them, growing as it fell into a vast-winged wasp that slowed and came hovering down on the dune-boat.

The insect was of a crystalline substance. The glassy membranes of its wings were threaded with filaments of color, but the wasp was otherwise transparent. Expertly it plucked the four pilgrims up from the boat. Each, though startled, hung securely and comfortably in the grip of one of the creature's claws. Then it rose straight up.

"I must say," Polderbag cried peevishly as they rose past the glossy slopes of the great black mantle, "that Simbilis takes small thought for the dignity and convenience of those who seek him."

"It is not for us to question the methods of one who sees so much farther than ourselves," Mumber Sull reproved.

They quickly neared the top of the shrouded bulk. Its edge was visible against the blackness due to a faint light somewhere on top of it whose glow demarcated the brink. The wasp's wings whirred invisibly fast, and in another instant it had shot up past the edge, and arched high over a pale plateau.

This plateau was of a pale substance, slightly and uniformly pitted and seamed. The plateau ended some distance ahead at a tall hedgerow of black material. The hedgerow had a gap in the center of its length, and through the gap could be seen a pale peak of the same substance that composed the plateau. The right side of this peak was lit up, and indeed it was this light — its source sunk from view beyond the black hedgerow — which made the mountaintop's topography visible at all, for the glow of the dunes lay now some thousands of feet below.

"My god!" cried Gunnruck. "It is a face!" This realization paralyzed the other three almost before Gunnruck had voiced it. They hung in the wasp's grip, momentarily numb as the acres of forehead passed beneath them.

When, shortly, they crossed the dark fence of the brows, they came directly over the sunken light-source: the right eyesocket. This was filled by a black lake on which floated an illuminated platform. The left eyesocket was a gulf of darkness, but the saliencies of the rest of the face were lit by the overflow light. Beyond the distant pale hill of the chin, nothing was visible, even though the four had several moments to strain their eyes, as the wasp hesitated above the platform on which it apparently intended to land.

"A titan!" said Mumber Sull. "Can Simbilis inhabit the body of this giant?"

"Perhaps he overcame the creature in combat," said Cugel, "and, securing its vitality, has made it his home."

"For what conceivable purpose?" said Gunnruck.

"Only the head is visible," clarified Polderbag. "Therefore it is possible that Simbilis inhabits only the *head* of a titan."

"Either hypothesis leads to apprehension regarding the wizard's soundness of mind," Gunnruck insisted.

The wasp began its descent. As they neared the circular platform floating on the dark lake, the pilgrims perceived a figure seated near the center of it. They also noted that the light surrounding the platform was supplied by several powerful globes suspended in the air above it.

The wasp set them down some yards from the seated figure, rose into the dark, and vanished above them. The pilgrims moved cautiously forward.

The figure they approached was an old man, and he sat upon air in an attitude suggesting that of a draftsman perched on a high stool. Indeed, an array of charts was spread before him at a tilt like that of a drafting board, though the charts were likewise unsupported by anything visible. The pilgrims, having drawn near, waited some time in silence before the old man turned from his charts.

When he did they saw his stature was only slightly taller, and his legs only slightly less bowed, than those of a dwarf. His head was large and utterly, brilliantly bald on top. A profusion of white hair, beginning at about the latitude of his ears, fell down to his shoulders in the manner of the neckguard to a helmet.

But he possessed one feature more striking than the rest. His large eyes had rainbow irises, such that to look him in the eye was to gaze on a constantly changing sequence of rich colors. To make the effect the more hypnotic, the eyes were not in phase, and presented contrasting patterns. They seemed as well to be perfectly unblinking.

"All of you," began the dwarf in a piping, penetrating voice, "come to me seeking power."

"What? Are you Simbilis?" broke in Mumber Sull.

"I am."

The Thane found himself embarrassed by his own incredulity. He bowed. "Forgive me, my liege. We have traveled far and come to doubt we would ever meet you."

The wizard nodded dryly, and resumed. "I have said that you all come seeking power. Three of you seek revenge as well. Only two of you could be described as honest, and one of these, as often is the case, is a fool. Nonetheless, I welcome you and invite your petitions. Let me assure you, however, at the outset that I serve purposes of my own, and will consult my own will first when it comes to the disposing of you."

All save Sull found something sinister in this last statement. The Thane advanced solemnly. "Unequaled lord, whichever the fool may be, please accept my earnest testimony on his behalf. I may say of all three who accompany me that I personally vouch for their generally good intentions, whatever their occasional deficiencies of insight. In myself, my lord, I do not doubt you recognize one of your own vassals of the village of Icthyll."

"Indeed," said Simbilis with an enlightened air. He now assumed the attitude of one who reclines at leisure in a comfortable chair. "That explains the queer deformation of your left earlobe. I do recall the matter now. Is not yours a coastal town on the Imlac Sea?"

"Upon the Sea of Cutz, my lord."

"Just so, following that first war…"

"The wars of the eighteenth aeon, my lord. And it is my express mission to tell your worship that one of your allies in that war — or his descendant at least — has grossly violated the bounds of jurisdiction laid down at that distant time."

"A distant time indeed. It would be the line of Pandu Slaye that is guilty of the trespass of which you speak."

"Just so, my lord. The ruler of Cil has been newly restored after an absence from power. He has been so over-exuberant in its exercise as to usurp your vassal's governing rights in the village of Icthyll."

Simbilis smiled just perceptibly. "Naturally you wish to be returned thence with sufficient power to chastise the interloper."

Before Sull could reply, Simbilis detained his speech and turned to Gunnruck. "And you, madam? Kindly come forward and state your desires."

Gunnruck advanced. "I wish transport to some center of humanity where security of life and limb prevails. I also wish sufficient wealth to purchase me an untroubled life. You have said we all desired power, but for my part all I wish is what I have named."

"You speak without considering, madam," Simbilis answered. "In these times the vast majority of the earth live meagerly by toil in the shadow of violent death. In asking for wealth and security, you are asking for the power to live — rare and difficult to come by."

"Mere sophistry," snapped Gunnruck. "All that can be reasonably asked of one is that he seek his own necessities."

Simbilis nodded. "Of course. And it is according to my own necessities, the necessities of my art, that I will dispose of yourself and your companions."

"To what art does my lord refer?" asked Mumber Sull.

Simbilis smiled more broadly now, and the ceaselessly changing meld of colors in his irises went through much speedier mutations, apparently an accompaniment of mirth in the archwizard. He looked up toward the ragged barrier of the titan's eyebrow — a looming wall of tangled shadow at the shore of the dark lake.

"The art I practice, and my only purpose in the world, estimable Thane, is what surrounds us now. We are floating on the lake of visual ichor which fills the socket of its as yet unconstructed right eye. Its eyes, by the way, will be lidless, for it is to know no sleep."

"This titan is of your making?" gasped Sull.

"Ages and ages of making." Simbilis nodded. "Of all things on earth, flesh and blood is the most difficult to make. Yet at last it nears completion. Its great wings lie buried under the glass — they also act as sails propelled by starshine. Its heart beats only slowly, awaiting its awakening — otherwise you would have been plagued by a great many more tidal waves in the dunes."

Fascinating though the topic of the titan was, Cugel could not help being distracted by matters which seemed to him more urgent.

"Peerless highness," he began, "surely you are impatient to learn my own humble requirements. They may be briefly —"

"They need not be stated at all," Simbilis said. "Both you and your plump companion seek return to the surface world and revenge upon a wizard. The wizard you yourself would punish is a fellow of indifferent worth, while your companion would harm a far worthier man. Beyond this slight difference in your objectives, however, you and your companion are remarkably similar in all that regards aims and ethics. I will grant both your suits in part, for you have been instrumental in bringing to me two valuable additions to my titan. I will return you to the surface world at the spot you designate. The Thane and the lady, however, will remain in the titan."

The four pilgrims stood speechless. Simbilis smiled. "Please do not be alarmed. My intentions are wholly benevolent. For the moment some refreshment is in order. Your trek has been taxing, I am sure." With a gesture the archwizard caused the four to be lifted from their feet, and set upon the air a few feet above the platform. The air supported them in whatever attitude they adopted. Though at first their uneasiness caused them to assume various grotesque positions, the four quickly adapted, and eased their limbs as if on luxurious couches. Servants materialized with panniers of loaves both white and brown. Cupbearing imps dispensed chilled nectars, while a four-armed steward went around with platters of cold fowl and cheeses studded with nutmeats. The pilgrims ate with great single-mindedness, while Simbilis looked on.

At length they were sated, and then it was Gunnruck who spoke first. "Lord Simbilis. There is no place in the surface world I should be very sorry never to see again. I could accept confinement here if I knew the kind of existence offered me here."

"A reasonable demand," said Simbilis, "and what of you, good Thane? Do you share the lady's open-mindedness and equanimity?"

Mumber Sull had been brooding for some minutes. Now he replied with feeling. "It is hard, my lord, for a man to leave his home behind him forever. You must yourself recall the charm of Icthyll, the magnificence of its prospect."

"Is it so lovely that you would accept the dominion of Slaye for the sake of living there?"

"I would never accede to that indignity."

"Then do not consider that by keeping you here I compel you to an unsavory fate. I offer you an alternative to an insupportable one. And after all, you do profess to be my vassal."

Sull bowed. "I do not contest your will, my lord. But I cannot help thinking how easy it would be for you to quench the impudent imperialism of this upstart Slaye. Have you no regard remaining for your dominions on earth, my lord?"

"None. I have told you that the titan is my sole regard. I begrudge all expenditures not lavished on its perfection. I have even restricted rescue operations in the siegeworks to exiguous rations of power. I only spare what I do so that among those rescued we might find new material for the titan's soul. It is highly finished in its present state, but one can never regard that aspect of the titan as being completed."

"And how is it," asked Mumber Sull in wonder, "that those rescued from the siegeworks can add to the titan's soul?"

"The titan is a treasure-house of human experience," Simbilis answered. "At the time of the rescued person's natural death, his mind is amalgamated to the titan's. His whole life, as it is recorded in his memory, becomes one of the titan's memories. Then in the random course of the titan's thoughts, each such person will be resurrected, will live again, on countless occasions through countless ages. It is a kind of immortality that I impose upon you, my dear Thane. As for the life you would lead while a worker on the titan, it is pleasant. Three hours a day of unstrenuous work is rewarded by free access to the titan's memory."

"Its memory?" asked Gunnruck. "What sort of place is this?"

"Quite various. Enormously various, in fact, for I am not so sure that its mind has not begun producing its own dreams, which naturally would add to its memory. In any case I have given it an abundance scarcely conceivable. It is a treasure-house of the ages. To wander in its memory is to pass weightlessly through a thousand lives, speaking and responding in tongues unheard-of, and moving about under a different sun, whose light was a lavish gold. Naturally, all who enter the memory are secured by psychic filaments so that they may be drawn out at the close of the period of immersion. For all but the most expert 'divers' become absorbed by whatever experience into which they first wander."

Simbilis fell silent, regarding Mumber Sull. The Thane did not speak. His eyes were lowered but the set of his jaw was unreconciled. Simbilis spoke again. "I am not unaware, Thane, of the attachment one can form to even the most preposterous surroundings, merely by virtue of their being for a time one's home. I have myself known many homes, and also known the leaving of each of them. You must face realities. You cannot live in Icthyll under Slaye, and I will not free it of him. I have no interest in dominions over which the implacable snows will fall, and the glaciers come grinding, when the sun is dead. It is for that moment the titan is made. When the sun has died it will rise, and force its passage out to the freezing air. It will burst from the dead egg of this planet and travel the universe in search of a new world. So you see my efforts are bent wholly on the abandonment of the realms you wish to save."

"But why must the world be abandoned?" asked Sull. "Has she not served us well? Could you not devote your powers to the feeding of the sun, or some such labor?"

Simbilis shook his head. "All things die. The earth is exceedingly old and has come to her rightful time. She has been the stage of enormous crimes, and has earned her icy quiet."

"You speak of the mortality of all things," put in Gunnruck. "Do you not mean to exempt the titan and yourself from that dictum? Is not the titan your means of perpetuating yourself? Will you not in fact act as its will and intelligence?"

Simbilis shook his head. "The titan, though made to live through many aeons, will die. It is a hermaphrodite, and will not perish without issue, but its own personality and memories will die, and myself among them. For to answer your second charge I shall, at the moment of the sun's death, graft my own mind onto the titan's memory. From that moment on I will exist in precisely the same occasional manner as will yourself and the excellent Thane. The titan will remember and understand me as its creator. But you must realize that in the making of its soul I have brought about new combinations. The titan will have perceptions and intelligence vastly exceeding my own. Its mind will be totally excogitated from its superior impulses in interaction with its memory, and the only compulsion I have laid upon it is that of escaping into space and seeking another world."

Simbilis turned again to regard Mumber Sull, and the Thane felt a reply expected. "I may not question your demands, my lord. Insofar as I have exercised power in your name, I have acknowledged your authority."

"Excellent. The position I have in mind for you involves the supervising of a small number of underlings. I hope this does not meet with your distaste?"

Only now did Sull's jaw lose its unreconciled set. "I am your lordship's to command." He bowed.

Simbilis now turned to Cugel and Polderbag. "What remains is to learn where you two gentlemen require to be transported. I will equip you comfortably and provide you with funds sufficient to live a year in any large town. Where would you be sent? I am now impatient to return to my charts."

"Ineffable majesty," said Cugel, "the terms in which you have referred to the surface world are most unsettling. Do you look for the sun's death in the near future?"

"I do not read this aspect of the future. Such calculations as I have made do not lead me to expect it sooner than your own demise of other causes may be expected, for as life on the surface world goes, it offers many ways to die, and those who surround my stronghold are busy devising new ones."

"You paint the prospect of returning there in ever glummer tones," said Polderbag. "I am a man of imaginative mind. The delights of memory-diving in the titan seem most appealing to me. Please consider my formal application for membership in your work force."

"I am sorry. The Thane and the lady possess relatively unique moral patterns, and represent a meaningful addition to the titan's soul. As regards yourselves, I fear that the titan already has been given a sufficient supply of what are your own unique qualities. You will spare us both embarrassment by not pursuing the question. Kindly state your desired destination."

Cugel and Polderbag looked at one another. Polderbag said, "Esquire. I have long felt a likeness in our minds which has made me think that a partnership between us could prove quite fruitful."

"I have long felt the same, worthy Polderbag. Since it seems I must give up hope of punishing the scurrilous Iucounu, I feel free to indulge my spirits of enterprise. Where would be the most promising place to begin operations?"

"I know no center more thriving than Millions' Gather. Does your native locale have equal commerce?"

"Almery thrives, but not so intensely, if I am to trust my brief experience of your city." Cugel turned to Simbilis. "We would be sent to Millions' Gather, my lord. May we not beg some small increase of the stipend you have mentioned?"

"It shall be as I described. But now I must be brusque, for my work calls. Do you wish to exchange valedictory remarks?"

Cugel smiled and approached Mumber Sull. "Our ways part, admirable Thane."

Sull nodded. "Our association has on the whole been an amicable one. I shall remember it with pleasure."

"As will I. But, Thane, put it in my power to recall you the more vividly. Give me some keepsake of our adventures — the amulet, for instance, of which, you will recall, I first came into possession."

The Thane nodded stiffly. "Quite right. I have no use for it now." He handed Cugel the amulet, which he had demanded from his Esquire during their march from the house on the river.

Cugel pocketed it, and nodded a frosty adieu to Gunnruck, who he thought regarded his taking-off with all too good a humor. Polderbag was meanwhile murmuring in her ear, and she shoved him off with a jovial push. Then the Esquire and spell-peddler, at Simbilis' direction, walked to the edge of the platform. The archwizard gestured upward. Cugel and Polderbag looked overhead. The blackness above suddenly became a blinding green which snatched them up into itself. They experienced a harrowing acceleration upward through dazzling unending greenness, and then they found themselves standing in the plaza before Steep's Jaw.

Before them the city fell away down the slopes, stained purple by dusk. Near the subworld portal's black triangle were the arches of the customs house portico. Figures moved among them with the bustle of business just before closing for the night.

A pair of she-zombies sauntered across the plaza toward the customs house. They regarded Cugel and Polderbag suspiciously as they passed, and left an acrid odor hanging on the air in their wake.

The pair stood still gazing until the woods of the valley floor lost their remaining vestige of green, and the color had drained from the town's motley rooftops, leaving all the hue of bone and charcoal.

Cugel came first to full possession of his wits. He looked down, and discovered he was richly clad. He wore a tunic of purple wool, breeches of leather and a jerkin of fur, an ample cloak and a plumed hat. Dangling at his belt, beside a costly sword, was a fat pouch of coins. He discovered with a curse, however, that the pouch of skubbage counters and the pouch of gold which he had taken from Verdulga were gone. He must perforce make do with what Simbilis had provided.

Turning, he found that Polderbag had been similarly accoutered by the archwizard. "The first question facing us," Cugel said to Polderbag as they started down a crooked byway in search of an inn, "the first question that must detain us, most excellent Polderbag, is how we are to invest our funds."

Colophon

This book was printed using 11,5 pt Adobe Arno Pro as the primary text font, with NeutraFace used for titles.

Special thanks to Linda Shea and Steve Sherman.

Book composition & Typesetting: Joel Anderson
Typographic design: Howard Kistler
Jacket blurb: Zeno ter Brughe
Management: John Vance, Koen Vyverman

Made in the USA
Middletown, DE
09 February 2020